WITCH'S SOUL

THE HEMLOCK CHRONICLES BOOK 2

EMMA L. ADAMS

This book was written, produced and edited in the UK, where some spelling, grammar and word usage will vary from US English.

Copyright © 2018 Emma L. Adams
All rights reserved.

To be notified when Emma L. Adams's next novel is released, sign up to her author newsletter.

Extracting poltergeists from public places required a delicate touch.

When that place happened to be a house belonging to a mage, however, the fate of the universe might well depend on us removing the wandering spirit before it broke Lord Bentley's collection of hundred-year-old antique china. Why couldn't poltergeists pick deserted fields to haunt instead of places worth more than my life's savings a hundred times over?

Unfortunately, poltergeists' one goal in life—well, death—was to wreak as much havoc as possible, which left it up to Lloyd and I to get the little bastard out of the mage's expensive cabinet. The poltergeist hovered on the other side of the glass with a grin stretching its ghostly face.

"Please don't," I said. I didn't usually stoop to begging, but there was more than my neck on the line this time. If we ticked off the mages, we'd be hauled in for questioning, and I had very good reasons to want to stay from the supernatural council for the foreseeable future.

A plate wobbled. Lloyd made a whimpering noise in the background, while I moved imperceptibly forward.

"You don't want to be here," I said to the poltergeist. "There's nothing much to do. You can't walk anywhere or talk to anyone, you can't read a book, you can't eat…"

"I can't do that in the afterlife either," said the poltergeist. "This is much more fun."

The plate wobbled a little more. Ack. I reached out both hands, wishing fervently that my necromantic powers extended to being able to rescue falling china. We couldn't even set up a banishing circle around the cabinet without risking the banishment causing even more damage. Magic didn't come with control settings, and neither did pissed-off spirits who'd abruptly departed the land of the living.

Lloyd crept in, folding his tall, lanky frame out of sight behind another cabinet. He was tall and dark-skinned with locs, and wore as many witch spells on his wrists as I did, rainbow-coloured bands hidden under the long sleeves of the black coat that we had to wear as our uniform. With the help of my friend and mentor Isabel, I'd amassed quite a collection, but spells generally didn't work on the dead. Only necromancy did, and it didn't stop them from destroying crockery beforehand.

"If you stay there too long," I continued, "you'll get stuck in there. Forever."

The poltergeist snorted. "That's bollocks. This isn't a magical cabinet. Maybe I want to break Lord Bentley's toys."

Oh, yay. A poltergeist with a grudge against the

person he was haunting. Generally, poltergeists were fuelled by rage and angst, and had the maturity level of a five-year-old regardless of their actual age when they died. The worse his rage got, the more damage he'd be able to do.

"Lovely sentiment," I said. "Unfortunately, my job is kind of on the line, so if you don't mind, there's a table for one in the afterlife with your name on it."

I held my hands out, delicately, and pushed. While the spirit wasn't solid, his instinctive reaction to being touched caused him to move backwards. Unfortunately, so did the cabinet. I lunged to steady it, and Lloyd threw one of the band-shaped spells. The trapping spell's red lines appeared over the cabinet, fixing it in place. The poltergeist yelped and flew up into the air, panicking automatically at the sight of the glowing spell even though it only worked on solid objects.

Next step: lure our wayward spirit into the candle trap. We'd opted to set up the candles in the doorway, hidden beneath an illusion. This ghost had no magic save for his poltergeist abilities, so we should, in theory, be able to avoid any more unpleasant surprises.

A cushion rose from the sofa. Maybe not.

"Don't," I warned, grabbing for the cushion. Another threw itself at the bookcase, making it rattle. We didn't have enough trapping spells to cover every piece of furniture in the house. Even senior necromancers had trouble trapping poltergeists without trashing the place in the process, but Lord Bentley had given us an extensive list of instructions as to what not to break (anything) and what level of noise to make (as little as possible). Considering he'd decided to live in a house right in the middle of a spirit line, it was a miracle he'd lasted this long before the dead paid a visit.

The whole sofa lifted into the air. "Oh, come on."

Poltergeists' strength levels ranged from rattling spoons to knocking walls down, based on the circumstances of their deaths, how powerful a magic user they'd been while alive, and whether they were close to a spirit line or not. This guy was definitely some form of supernatural, but hadn't decided to share his name yet, and neither had Lord Bentley. I'd figured they'd argued before the spirit bit the dust, which I wouldn't normally care about, except he'd picked out the room most likely to annoy our host and refused to leave.

I grabbed the edge of the sofa, tugging it towards the floor. "Put it down. Easy."

The sofa dropped, onto my toes. I muffled my yelp of pain with the back of my hand, eyes watering. Lloyd swore and stepped towards me, and the wine cupboard flew open. Oh, bugger.

I'd spent my teenage years with the upper-class magical elite thanks to being adopted by a former Mage Lord, and yet it never ceased to amaze me what they wasted their immense wealth on. Since I'd moved away, my living standards had gone down a bit. I lived in jeans and a T-shirt underneath the necromancers' standard plain black cloak, and while I had a special badge to mark me as Lady Montgomery's assistant, my dyed black hair and lip piercing worked against me. If I got hauled in for questioning, nobody would take my side over the distinguished Mage Lord's.

A wine bottle flew from the cabinet, right at Lloyd's head.

My hand snapped up, kinetic power knocking the wine bottle off course, where it hit the trapping spell on the cabinet. Lloyd lunged and caught it before it broke open—and the poltergeist vanished.

"Give me a simple zombie banishment any day of the week." I massaged my toes. "Hey. Spirit. Get back here. Unless you've gone over the veil and done us all a favour?"

"No." The poltergeist appeared, hovering above the bookcase. It wobbled, the books rattling within it. "I think not."

A book threw itself at my head. I caught it on reflex, wishing I'd risked setting the candles up within this room after all. The poltergeist cackled, several books rising into the air and juggling themselves. I glimpsed gold-plated spines and velvet coverings. *Oh, come on.* "Really mature," I said. "What was this guy to you when you were alive?"

He paused his juggling and said in a mock whisper, "He poisoned me."

A book smashed into the side of my face. *Ow.* I should have ducked, but the word *poison* brought up some unpleasant memories. Also, *the guy we're helping is a murderer?* The ghost might be lying... or he might have given me an opening to get through to him.

"That so?" I said. "Someone tried to poison me once, too. It wasn't nice. But you know, neither is being in jail. Which is where I'll be going if you wreck the place and my friend and I get blamed for it."

"That's a nice argument." The poltergeist rose into the air before us, still juggling the remaining books. "Pity I don't care."

I danced backwards to catch another book, causing the

ghost to erupt into howls of laughter. I heard Lloyd sniggering, too, and gave him the finger.

"Yeah, hilarious," I said to the spirit. "Is this really what you want the last memory you leave on earth to be? You have a family, right? Would you want them to find out you came back to have petty revenge on an old man?"

Another book threw itself at me in answer, and I caught it by my fingertips. Lloyd yelped a warning as the cabinet began to rattle again. The ghost's hands glowed with kinetic power. We'd reached stage three—the 'oh hey, I can levitate things on the other side of the house!' stage of poltergeist fun.

"What is going on?" bellowed the old mage from the room below.

"We've got it under control!" I said, in a failed attempt at a breezy tone. An alarming crash came from downstairs, and the old man swore loudly. Having the ability to shoot lightning from one's hands yet being unable to do anything about an invading poltergeist must be fairly demoralising. Where was a telekinetic when you needed one?

"Whee!" The poltergeist zipped through the room, rattling the furniture.

Dammit, Lord Bentley. Why didn't you ward your house properly? I guessed being able to make lightning strike intruders had seemed like it would be sufficient enough on its own. Mages tended to overestimate their own prowess.

I pulled a spare candle out of my pocket, waving farewell to caution. It'd boost the poltergeist's power as well as mine, but I was out of options.

The candle light grew brighter, and the ghost appeared

in front of me. "Pretty light." He reached out a hand, and a cold breeze kicked up.

I tapped on my spirit sight. Grey light filtered in, showing me the ghost pulsing brightly in front of me. This time, his features became more distinctive, more human. Hoping I wasn't as rusty as I thought, I reached out my hands towards him. "Go beyond the gates of Death."

The banishing words rose to my tongue, well-practised, but pulling this off without a candle circle was almost certain to go wrong. With no other props, though, it was a last resort.

Lloyd's voice rose to join mine, and the poltergeist burst into hysterical laughter. "That barely tickles, little necromancer."

"Get out of here," I growled, continuing to grip the candle tightly. Blue light burned my hands, pulsing through the spirit realm, but my hands passed straight through the ghost. *Damn. It was worth a try.*

The spirit realm disappeared as the poltergeist threw itself at the bookcase. Lloyd and I both jumped in to steady it, and the kinetic blast knocked both of us off our feet. Books rained down around us. One struck me in the forehead and stars blinked before my eyes. "Ow. Bastard. It's way too strong."

"Can't you borrow a boost from you-know-who?" Lloyd said, groaning.

"You know why I can't." If I revealed my Hemlock witch magic in front of anyone remotely connected to the mage council, I could say farewell to more than my apprenticeship. More to the point, I couldn't invite Evelyn

Hemlock to give the poltergeist a fright, because she was out of commission.

The ghost reappeared, the ceiling lights flickering above his head. Oh, no. Now he'd figured out he could screw with electricity as well as throwing shit around.

As the room was plunged into darkness, blasts of kinetic energy struck the walls and the wine cabinet rose an inch or two off the ground.

"Please, no," I said.

The cabinet moved higher, tilting forwards. Meanwhile, the crisscrossing red lines of the spell trapping the other cabinet flickered and died.

"No!"

Lloyd grabbed one cabinet, I lunged for the other, and a spell went off like a firecracker. A second later, a foam-like substance filled the room, smothering everything in thick fluffiness.

"Ow," said Lloyd, pressed against the wall. "Didn't know what that one did."

"Isabel's, by any chance?" The foamy fluffiness had shoved me right up against the cabinet, but at least it'd stopped anything from falling over.

"Yep," he said, his voice muffled. "Now we need to squeeze the bugger into the candles."

"Uh, Lloyd, I can't even move." The squishy substance filled the entire room, and moving between bubbles was like wading through thick toffee. The spirit wasn't affected by the spell, but with everything encased in foaminess, he could no longer destroy any of the mage's possessions, either. But the moment the spell wore off, the ghost would unleash all its rage, and we'd be looking at a bill that would take a lifetime to pay off.

I squeezed my way around the cabinet, found a gap in the foam, and eased a spell off my wrist into my hand. Taking careful aim, I raised my palm.

Power hummed in my hand beneath the spell, briefly. Even with Evelyn gone, I could still feel the echo of her presence whenever I held a witch spell in my hand or went near a ward. White light sparked at my fingertips, and I drew in a quick breath before letting the spark grow. *I can control this,* I told myself, and threw the spell into the air.

Flames tore through the foam, and a body appeared below. I'd got only a glimpse of the ghost's real face, but it was enough.

The poltergeist appeared, looking down at his own dead body, and screamed.

When all else fails: force the ghost to come face to face with their own mortality. With a wail of anguish, the poltergeist flew out of the room—right into the candles.

Lights snapped on at my command, trapping the ghost between them.

"Is it gone?" said the mage's demanding voice from below.

I looked down at the illusion of the dead man. *Yeah. Your friend is.* Getting a mage locked up for murder wasn't exactly avoiding attention, and yet...

"Tell me the truth," I whispered to the trapped poltergeist. "Did he really poison you? Can you prove it?"

The man floated in the circle, his eyes luminous, his mouth stretched wide in horror. "The wine cabinet... the poison... my body is in the basement..."

Footsteps sounded on the stairs. Lloyd squeezed out of

the room and grabbed my arm. "The foam. Jas, turn off the foam."

"On it." I raised my hands, let the merest trickle of magic flow through, and the foam disappeared, leaving the room bare. Lloyd scrambled to shove books back onto the shelves, while I walked up to the wine cabinet and employed a quick unlocking spell on it. I didn't like holding the magic in my hands for too long, even knowing Evelyn couldn't touch me. I'd been forced to imprison her in the spirit realm to stop her from hijacking my body and going on a rampage, and I sincerely hoped she'd stay that way.

"Don't break the expensive furniture, don't smash the windows, and don't get us blacklisted," said Lloyd. "I think that went pretty well."

"Don't hold your breath," I said in a low voice. "Someone's going to get an unwelcome visit from the mages' enforcement squad."

Mages were rich snobs, but even they couldn't escape justice when it came to the murder of their own people. I was surprised at the dude's audacity if nothing else, but maybe he hadn't figured his friend would stick around and haunt him.

When we'd shoved the last book back into place and checked there weren't any scratches on the cabinets, Lloyd and I returned to the candles. As we did so, Lord Bentley appeared on the stairs, giving our dishevelled appearances a look of disdain. "You definitely didn't break anything?"

"Nope," I said cheerily. "One spirit, signed and delivered."

The mage sniffed. "Good enough, I suppose."

"Just need to banish him," I said, though there was fat chance of that happening, not when the ghost was the only person who could testify against his killer. Still, I could put on a good show.

I faced the candles, which looked oddly pale. Grey light filtered through, showing me the spirit realm. Being on a spirit line, ghosts were brighter than they usually were and kinetic power hit harder, which gave us less time than usual to get him out of the circle.

The only problem was, the ghost wasn't there.

"Did you banish it?" said the mage expectantly. Mages couldn't detect changes in the spirit realm the way necromancers could, and they didn't get the same boost other supernaturals did from being close to spirit lines. It was the one area they weren't leagues ahead of the rest of us in.

"Er. I think he went over the veil by himself." So much for a confession. "He's definitely not in the house, and he can't have got out of the circle."

"You know the ghost was a 'he'?"

Oh, great, quiz time with a murderer. "Yes, since we're able to see the form they used when they were still alive," I said. "Generally, they haunt someone they know, or a place they lived in. Maybe someone they argued with before dying..." I trailed off, letting him chew on that for a while. The old mage remained silent as I retrieved the candles and packed them into my coat's fathomless pockets.

"Your profile said you know the mages," Lord Bentley said to me.

He'd looked me up. Figures. "Have you ever met Lady Harper?"

"Her? Awful woman. Terrible manners, dreadful attitude."

I couldn't say I disagreed. "Yeah. She was kind of my..." Ack. I couldn't say 'mentor' without having to admit I'd lived with the mages. "Er, guardian. We're very distantly related."

"Yes, I can see that. We don't usually mingle with necromancers."

And there was the hierarchical bullshit I'd been happy to leave behind. If Lady Harper had one redeeming quality, it was that she didn't value one type of magic over the others. As a mage serving the Hemlock Coven and who'd had been part of the original Council of Twelve across all supernaturals, she had to be unbiased. But many of the other mages had got it into their heads that they'd come across their mage powers though superiority over other supernaturals. They particularly looked down on shifters, though witches and necromancers got the short end of the stick, too.

I had no patience for his attitude whatsoever. "Yes, my family is a mixture of mages, witches and necromancers," I said. "We're pretty involved in the council, actually, and we cooperate with other supernaturals. Thank you for your time."

As soon as his house vanished from sight, I pulled out my phone and composed a message telling the boss to check if any mages had met a sudden end lately and advising them to run a thorough search of the wine cabinet and basement in Lord Bentley's house.

"What was that about?" said Lloyd.

"I just praised Lady Harper," I said. "Give me some water. I need to wash the bad taste out of my mouth."

"I want to meet her," said Lloyd. "She sounds like a riot."

"That's like saying necromancers throw amazing parties."

He snorted. "Did that ghost seriously just vanish without us having to lift a finger?"

"Apparently. A voluntary banishment. Can't say I blame him, considering his so-called friend poisoned him."

"He said that?" Lloyd stared at me.

"You were fighting off foam at the time, but yeah, it sounds like another mage rivalry ended badly. I hope they arrest him before he figures out who my family is. There aren't many witch-mage-necromancer families around, let alone people who've had a positive experience with Lady Harper." I kept my tone light, a product of years of being a part of the necromancer guild. Having a sense of humour was the only way to handle spending twenty-four hours a day around death.

Lloyd didn't laugh. "Do you think the boss might know why the ghost vanished?"

"Maybe." I pulled up my hood against the bitter December air. "It's not like she can blame us for it. We did our jobs."

He pulled his own hood back up and dug his hands in his pockets. "What was that spell you used to make him freak out?"

"Illusion," I said. "My own variation. It's lucky it worked."

Lloyd rolled his eyes. "And you made him see his own floating dead body?"

"It was that or turn the floor into snakes, and I thought you'd be more scared than him."

"You're not wrong."

We walked down the cobbled street past the route to the house belonging to the vampires' king. He was currently under guild investigation for letting his fellow vampires get away with flaunting the rules, and as far as I'd heard, the vampires were none too thrilled at that development. Serve him right for looking the other way while his fellow vampires kidnapped a psychic and forced her to obey the orders of my depraved distant relative.

Did I mention my family life was a little complicated? The Hemlocks needed an heir, and I was the only surviving member of the coven who still had their magic. Without it, the world would be devoured by giant gods, so you know, it wasn't something I could turn my back on, however much I'd been trying to do exactly that over the last few weeks.

Lloyd's gaze darted the same way as mine. "No fanged friends spying on us? Or do they hibernate in winter?"

"I have no idea *what* they're doing," I admitted. "Again... not our problem."

That included Keir, the vampire who'd helped us in the battle, and who I'd become... I hesitate to say *intimate* with, considering he'd had to feed on my soul to avoid death when a rogue vampire had attacked us. Rather than blood, vampires fed on human life essence and needed it to survive. Keir had invited me to join him and become a rogue and I'd turned him down, but I hadn't expected him to ignore my messages after the thoroughly non-verbal goodbye we'd said the night of the battle. With the spirit realm so close, there was no reason Keir couldn't get in touch with me if he wanted to, despite the fact that we didn't typically travel in the same circles. After all, he knew that since I'd accidentally used blood magic while Evelyn had been in control of my body, I was one mistake away from becoming an outlaw myself.

Would Keir know about the malfunction in the spirit realm? Maybe. Vampires were capable of projecting outside their bodies to control the dead and communicating over a distance no other necromancers could reach. Maybe one of them had yanked the spirit out of the circle before I could banish it.

One thing was for certain: I sincerely hoped that this time, the trouble wasn't related to my coven.

2

"Do you *want* to get possessed by an evil faerie ghost?" Morgan Lynn, the guild's resident psychic, said to his apprentice.

Mackie Chen, the guild's newest recruit, stepped out of the way of the door to the weapons room as I pushed it open.

"There's no such thing as faerie ghosts," she said to him. "They can't possess people."

"They can, too, and they nearly killed me," said Morgan. "Put the bloody iron on or the next thing you know, you'll be taking a swim in the Firth of Forth."

"That sounds fun." Mackie shrugged and picked up a spirit sensor from the nearest shelf. "What does this do?"

"Spits ectoplasm everywhere," said Morgan, grabbing the spirit sensor and holding it out of reach. "Can't you pretend to take this seriously so the boss doesn't put us on cleaning duty?"

Mackie folded her arms. "That's rich, coming from you."

She wasn't wrong. Not only was Morgan barely qualified as a necromancer himself, he'd also been the guild's least-consistent rule-follower before Mackie showed up.

He scowled. "All right, leave the iron, then, and leave your mind wide open. Don't blame me when another psychic tries to fuck with you."

"They never will," she declared, her hands fisting at her sides. "Never." Her ringing tone carried a hint of her most deadly power—the ability to scream loud enough to shake the entire spirit realm. None of us had the faintest idea where she'd come across that power. The most we'd managed to drag from her about her background was that her parents were from Hong Kong and had died when she was a baby. Given her age—maybe eighteen, twenty at most—we could only guess at how she'd ended up living on the streets. An awful lot of people had disappeared in the years following the faerie invasion, and she'd have been a target the instant her psychic power manifested. While her slight build didn't look like she was capable of knocking out a full-grown man, she'd done exactly that when Morgan tried to teach her self-defence. She might be a little behind on basic necromancy, but she was a lethal force of destruction and didn't intend to give us an easy time of it.

"Training's going well, then?" I pulled two candles out of my pockets and returned them to the nearest shelf. Iron weapons and other necromancer props filled each wall in the room, a testament to the guild's history as a stronghold in the time of the faerie invasion twenty-two years ago. "Did either of you feel a blip in the spirit realm about half an hour ago?"

"A what?" said Mackie.

"Lloyd and I were in the middle of banishing a poltergeist when it disappeared over the veil by itself," I explained. "We didn't even use the banishing words."

"Huh." Morgan returned the spirit sensor to the highest shelf, which Mackie wouldn't be able to reach. "You sure?"

"Yep," said Lloyd, coming into the room behind me. "Jas checked the spirit realm. We didn't have time to banish it. The candles switched off, too."

"Are you sure you didn't use the fake candles?" asked Morgan.

"What fake candles?" I asked.

"Someone—" he jerked his head at his reluctant apprentice—"thought it would be funny to switch out some of the candles with scented ones from the market."

Lloyd snickered with laughter. "That is pretty funny. Nice one, Mackie." He high-fived her.

"I think the old mage would have noticed if his house smelled of begonias. The candles are real, look." I held one of them up for inspection. "So was the ghost. Stage four poltergeists don't politely hop over the veil without a fuss." Not in my experience, anyway.

Mackie took the candle from me, where it promptly lit up in her hands. "Maybe it's trapped in the candle."

"That's not how it works." Morgan snatched the candle from her and put it back on the shelf. "I dunno, maybe there was a glitch. The spirit realm gets them sometimes."

"Only when someone's screwing around with necromancy," I said. "Lloyd and I were the only necromancers there. Has anyone at the guild seen anything weird?"

"I don't know," said Mackie. "I've been stuck in here with *him,* learning to banish ghosts like an amateur."

"You kinda need to be able to banish ghosts to do the job," Morgan said to her. "You're a self-taught psychic, not a trained necromancer."

"I don't need to learn," said Mackie. "Because I never said I'd be staying here."

"Whoa," said Lloyd. "Calm down—"

Mackie spun around, and a gust of kinetic energy buffeted all of us. My back hit the shelf, causing several candles to topple to the floor. The door slammed behind her with another blast of air.

"Ow." I rubbed the back of my head. "I see her self-defence training is ahead of schedule."

"Everyone else needs protecting from *her*." Morgan climbed to his feet. Apparently, his ego hadn't quite recovered from her drop-kicking him out cold the other day.

"Who needs poltergeists when you have a pissed-off psychic?" said Lloyd.

"This is a bad idea." Morgan shot a disgruntled look in the direction of the door—and by extension, Lady Montgomery's office. "She knows Mackie doesn't give a crap about training. This is as much a waste of time for me as it is for her."

"You'd just spend that time hanging out at the pub," said Ilsa Lynn, entering the room through the partly open door. "Mackie didn't leave the building, by the way. She went upstairs."

"Good, because I'm not chasing her." Morgan scowled at his sister. "What are you doing here?"

Ilsa left the door half open behind her. "Just came to see how you were all getting along. Lady Montgomery's orders." She walked to pick up the knives that had fallen to the floor when Mackie's kinetic blast had hit the room.

Ilsa was the more sensible of the Lynn siblings, intelligent with a rather frightening side when pushed. Tangled dark hair swept past her shoulders, and she shared the same dark brown eyes as her brother. That was about where the similarities ended. Ilsa was tall and solid and very much alive, while Morgan had spent so much time in the land of the dead that he'd started to look like one of them, thin and pale. To be fair, he was a powerful psychic, and despite his abrasive and sarcastic attitude, he wouldn't have made a terrible teacher. If not for Mackie's refusal to take on any training, that is.

"The boss can take over herself," he said to Ilsa. "See how she likes dealing with bratty teenagers."

Ilsa rolled her eyes. "Now you know how the rest of us felt when we had to bring you up to speed on necromancy."

Morgan crossed his arms over his chest. "I never stormed out of the place when I signed up here."

"Yes, you did. Twice."

I cleared my throat and addressed Ilsa. "Did *you* feel anything weird in the spirit realm?"

Ilsa turned to me. "What do you mean?"

"A ghost vanished without prompting. Stage four poltergeist."

"Oh, the one you went to banish from that mage's house?" asked Ilsa. "The guild's not on the same spirit line as you were on, so nobody here will have felt it. If something big happened, like on the Ley Line, we would, but I didn't sense anything weird."

"Oh, right. Of course." The guild only rested on one

spirit line, but it happened to be the same line that linked with the forest most of my coven lived in. When Leila Hemlock, a former Hemlock Coven witch, had forced Mackie to unleash her psychic scream, it'd rippled down the spirit line and knocked half the guild unconscious. That alone was reason enough to keep an eye on her. Since she was old enough to be jailed for life for that crime despite the fact that it'd been committed against her will, she had no choice but to accept Lady Montgomery's offer to work for the guild.

"Have you told the boss?" Ilsa asked.

"I was on my way, after Lloyd and I return these props," I answered. "I got distracted watching today's entertainment."

I moved the remaining candles from my pocket to the shelf, while Lloyd picked up the ones that'd fallen to the floor when Mackie had knocked them over. "You should let her pick what she wants to learn," he said to Morgan. "Forcing her to follow the guild's novice curriculum is gonna piss her off even more."

"What do you know?" Morgan said, walking towards the door.

"I have a younger sister," Lloyd said. "Also, Mackie's strong enough to blow your brains out, so if I were you, I'd face her on her own level rather than treating her like a kid."

"She *is* a kid," said Morgan. "Besides, she can pick up everything I teach her in five minutes just by watching another necromancer, the same way I did. She doesn't need a tutor."

"Then let her tag along on missions," Lloyd suggested.

"Uh, that might not be the best idea," Ilsa said. "At least, not until you can get her to wear the iron."

"Rather you than me," said Lloyd. "I'm glad I'm just a garden variety necromancer."

I'd have agreed, but that would have been a lie. I was as far from a typical necromancer as it was possible to be. And while the vanishing poltergeist had solved one problem, ghosts didn't usually disappear with no prompting. No other necromancers had been in the house, otherwise I'd have sensed them. So who—or what—had sent the ghost packing?

Keir's face briefly flashed before my eyes. I'd read up everything the guild had on vampires and they certainly *could* banish ghosts over a distance the same way powerful necromancers could, but again, I'd have sensed if he was there. Whatever the reason, he was outright ignoring me at the moment.

I shoved the vampire firmly out of mind and went down the corridor to report to the boss. Before I had the chance to knock, she called from behind the door, "Come in, Jas."

"I'm taking that as an invitation to stay here," said Lloyd quietly, as I grabbed the door handle. "Are you gonna tell her about the murderous mage?"

"She already knows. I texted the information to the guild's main number." Hopefully, since I'd been involved in such a minimal way, the former Mage Lord would never know who'd 'accidentally' left his wine cabinet unlocked. It wasn't like he could prove the ghost had given the game away.

I entered Lady Montgomery's office, finding her standing behind her desk expectantly. Tall and strong, with her dark grey hair tied into a bun, she looked more like a stern headmistress than a woman who'd taken on the Sidhe of Faerie face to face and had the scars to prove it.

"Ah, Jas," said Lady Montgomery. "How was the mission?"

"Great. Except for the end." I explained the ghost's disappearance. "The candles seem to work fine. It seemed like a minor glitch. Ilsa said nobody felt it here, because we're on a different spirit line."

"Yes, that is unusual," she said. "Did you use necromancy on the spirit line after the incident?"

"Er, no. I didn't need to, considering the ghost was gone. I assumed nobody else was around. I guess the poltergeist just went over the veil."

"That may be the case," she said. "But given the level of strength he possessed, it might be an idea to check if something else occurred on the same spirit line that caused the veil to shift and the poltergeist to vanish. Ilsa, come in."

The door opened, and Ilsa entered the room. I'd find it creepy that the boss always knew who was outside her office, if I didn't know she constantly used her spirit sight to check whoever was around her at any given time. I could technically do the same thing, but I wasn't proficient enough to slip in and out of this realm without it being glaringly obvious to anyone looking at me that I wasn't mentally present.

"Ilsa," said Lady Montgomery. "Won't you and Jas go and have a look to see if anything is happening on the spirit line where she completed her last mission?"

"Sure," said Ilsa. "I was actually going to ask if you had

any more instructions for Mackie. She's refusing to listen to my brother."

The boss turned her sternest stare onto her. "Your brother is going to have to learn to handle the responsibility himself. Jas, Ilsa, take a patrol to the spirit line."

"Sure thing," I said. "Do you want the report on today's mission when we get back?"

"Yes," she said. "As for the mages, don't worry. The guild sent a team to his house to scope out the... source of the trouble."

"Good," I said over my shoulder as we left the office. At Ilsa's puzzled look, I added, "We accidentally solved a murder again."

"As you do," said Ilsa. "She said take a patrol..."

"Meaning me," Lloyd said, where he'd been waiting outside. "I take it back, maybe I do want special powers. What am I, the third wheel?"

"Isn't being a necromancer special enough?" I said. "Come on, you know she only put me in charge because I'm her assistant. Whatever happened on the spirit line had nothing to do with... psychics, witchy ghosts, vampires, whatever."

"Did you see anything weird, except the vanishing ghost?" asked Ilsa.

"Nope," said Lloyd.

"That's what I don't get," I said. "Usually, there are signs if there's someone messing around nearby in the spirit realm."

"'It *was* on a spirit line, right?" she asked. "Where's the nearest key point?"

"I'd need to look at a map," I said. "But they move around a lot anyway."

"Okay. I can check while we're there." Ilsa took the lead as we headed back to the weapons room.

Once we were armed and ready, we made our way downstairs. While the damage from the attack a few weeks ago had been cleared up, there were a lot more guards by the doors than there'd been before. Necromancer deaths weren't uncommon and dealing with the dead didn't come without significant risk, even for the experienced. But attacks on that scale were a rarity, and despite our attempts to make Mackie feel welcome at the guild, she still didn't seem at ease enough to confide in anyone about how she'd ended up the captive of a rogue witch.

The three of us walked Edinburgh's cobbled street, thick dark clouds gathering over the stone buildings. December had brought no snow but a lot of freezing rain, and most of us had deliberately sped up our patrols to cover twice as much ground so we wouldn't freeze to death. I wished the necromancer candles carried actual warmth, but if anything, they were like freezing weights in my pockets. Our coats were durable and made for movement, not keeping us warm.

"Let's get this done fast," I said through chattering teeth.

"Agreed." Lloyd yanked his hood up. "Would you judge me if I admitted I'm wearing fluffy pyjamas under this coat?"

"No, I wish I'd done the same."

"Which way is the mage's house?" asked Ilsa.

"Best not go back there, considering he's probably being arrested as we speak," I said. "The spirit line goes through this road at the far end, we can check there."

Ilsa nodded. "Yeah. I'll need to actually be on the line to have a proper look around."

Ilsa was the Gatekeeper of Death, which meant she had the ability to project further out of her body than almost anyone at the guild. If something was up on the spirit line or in any nearby key points, she'd know pretty quickly. She was also perceptive enough she'd figured out there was something different about my magic, but even she didn't know I was bound to a shade or that my coven had broken supernatural laws in doing so.

Ilsa paced to the middle of the road. "Here."

"I'll take your word for it," said Lloyd, huddling closer to me for warmth.

At key points, where two spirit lines intersected, liminal spaces sometimes formed, gaps between dimensions which tended to be a little lax with the laws of reality. Humans generally had no idea they were there, even supernaturals. But nothing appeared to be here except a road riddled with pot holes and crooked houses that'd seen better days.

Ilsa's gaze zoned out as she tapped into the spirit realm. She hadn't yet mastered tapping into her spirit sight while doing other tasks like Lady Montgomery did. It was kind of bolstering to know that despite her off-the-charts talent, she was still learning.

Ilsa stepped back and shook her head. "No. I can't see anything odd. Want to check?"

"I believe you," I said. "Do you want candles? I know you can leave your body without them, but you know, procedure. Plus we don't know what's out there."

"Yeah, I vote in favour of not breaking the rules," said Lloyd.

Ilsa nodded. "It'll be easier with two of us."

"Oh." It wasn't as though I hadn't seen this coming. I couldn't avoid going deep into the spirit realm forever, especially as it was a major part of my job. "Sure."

I set up the candles in a circle of twelve on the cracked tarmac, my hands shaking a little.

"It's okay." Ilsa crouched down behind me. "There aren't any liminal spaces here. It's totally clear."

Oh. She thinks I'm traumatised by the battle. Well, I kind of was, but even she didn't know that I'd been trapped in a summoning circle with Evelyn Hemlock and left to die. I'd had to use necromancy on my own body to escape, and that was *before* Evelyn had taken control and nearly killed my friends.

Relax, Jas. Evelyn Hemlock was locked away. She couldn't take control of me from her prison, even if I left my body wide open to possession.

"Yeah," I said, straightening upright. "I can just have a look around from here. It's fine."

In a single blink, the grey fog of the spirit realm rose to surround me. The moment the shift happened was swift and easy, because technically, my spirit existed in this realm all the time, visible only to other necromancers. I raised ghostly hands in front of my face, part of me expecting to see two pairs of hands as I had before.

I shook my head fiercely to dispel the thought and searched for Ilsa instead. She wasn't hard to find, her spirit blazing brighter than mine and outlined in shimmering blue light. Below our feet was a faint grey line. The spirit line. It extended as far as the eye could see in each direction. I'd never seen anyone actually travel on the lines before, but it was possible for higher necromancers to learn how to do it. But if you went too far, you risked leaving your body behind for good.

Ilsa floated forwards a few steps, apparently unconcerned about the risk. "Hmm. No signs here. The nearest key point is there." She pointed up ahead to our north.

"How in the world can you tell?"

"Reach out," she said. "It's like… a vibration along the line. When it gets intense, that's a key point."

By 'reach out', she didn't mean in a physical sense. I'd used my spirit senses to track down Lloyd when he'd been captured, so I knew what she meant, but it still took several moments before I managed to 'feel' outwards from where I was standing. It was easy to extend my consciousness towards Ilsa and Lloyd because they were close by and I knew how to recognise them, but not something that wasn't human.

Maybe locking Evelyn up had made me into a normal necromancer, after all.

Dammit. I can do this.

I searched for Ilsa's presence again, shining in the middle of the line. She had some serious necromantic strength, enough to make the spirit line itself hum with magic. I extended my consciousness outwards from her presence, and moved north, towards—ah, *now* I felt it. The line vibrated with power, and the echo of Evelyn's magic hummed so suddenly, I broke the connection and slipped off the line.

"You okay?" Ilsa looked down at me where I'd sprawled in the air. If you fell over in the spirit realm, you either floated on the spot or just kept falling until you landed back in your body.

"Yep. Nobody saw that."

She smiled, and then a jolt along the line snapped my attention back to the key point. The faint hum of magic faded in and out—and disappeared. Then the trembling stopped, and I blinked awake in my body in confusion. The candle lights had gone out.

Ilsa's bewildered eyes met mine. "I think someone just switched *off* the key point."

3

I lsa and I stared at one another for a moment. "Are you sure?" I asked.

"I can't think what else might have caused the line to turn off," she answered. "Let me look..." She paused, her gaze going out of focus. "Nope. Nothing. It's gone."

I switched on my spirit sight to check, but nothing remained but the thin line under our feet. It was as though the pulsing point of energy to our north had disappeared altogether.

I'd witnessed more than a few flare-ups on a spirit line, where a key point would suddenly get a power boost. Usually it meant some intelligent person had decided to summon a poltergeist or raised a horde of zombies. I'd never seen a key point switch *off* before. Hadn't thought it was possible. Though it was clear that the necromancers' rulebook wasn't nearly as transparent as it seemed, and there were certain things kept to the higher levels only. Like the existence of vampires and shades, for instance.

"Please tell me if you decide to wander off the line," Lloyd said. "Don't forget it's me who'll take the heat if one of you dies. Been there, done that."

Ilsa shot me a curious look. I felt bad for constantly dodging her questions, but the geas my coven had put on me prevented me from letting slip even the most minor piece of information about the Hemlocks, including the time I'd nearly died from being poisoned a few weeks ago. I was a terrible liar, and I wouldn't have minded telling Ilsa about my family, since she kept her own set of secrets. But while Ilsa wasn't breaking the law by being Gatekeeper, being bound to another spirit was another thing entirely.

"I think the same thing might have happened to the poltergeist," I said, changing the subject. "The ghost vanished. So did the candles' light, as though all the spiritual energy got turned off."

"That's definitely not normal," said Ilsa. "Not here, certainly. This isn't a major spirit line, but I can't tell if it affected the whole line or just this part."

Ah, crap. Knock-on effects were generally a given, and if you summoned a zombie on a spirit line, it was likely to cause several others to rise as well. By that logic, another necromancer must be responsible. Maybe there'd been a zombie attack elsewhere on the line and the banishing had gone too far.

But it'd have to be a powerful necromancer... and not a guild one.

"Did you see if any patrols went that way?" asked Ilsa, pointing north where the key point had been.

"Two will have been there earlier." I was the one in charge of the rota, but I'd more or less left it the same for weeks now. "We can check back with the guild. Or maybe just look ourselves."

"Why am I not surprised," said Lloyd, scooping up candles and handing them to me. "You know the key point might be in the middle of someone's house, right?"

"Yes." I took the candles and slipped them into my pockets. "We'll get to that part later. I'm pretty sure I'd want to know if someone had switched off a key point in the middle of my house, besides."

"How did I guess you'd say that?" said Lloyd, with an eye-roll.

I took the lead, though I didn't have much more of a clue about the way than Ilsa did. I might know the patrol routes by heart, but I'd mostly avoided the areas of the city where the mages hung out. As for Ilsa, she'd lived with humans for most of the time she'd been in Edinburgh as far as I knew, since she and her brother had only discovered their necromantic talents in adulthood.

"How can you even see the spirit lines?" asked Lloyd, when we paused at a side street to get our bearings. "For that matter, why do they even exist?"

"They're like… paths," said Ilsa. "Places where the boundaries between the worlds are thin. We don't notice it as necromancers because we can see the spirit realm everywhere, but the spirit lines divide this realm from the afterlife. If things go really wrong on a spirit line, ghosts become visible to everyone, even humans."

"Lovely," I said. "I guess that's in one of the advanced training books?"

"Yep." Ilsa's curiosity knew no bounds, and it wasn't surprising that she'd read her way through half the archives by now. She'd also sought out a bunch of books on vampires I wanted to get my hands on, as unlikely as it was that I'd find anything useful about shades in there.

We turned the side street into an unfamiliar neighbourhood—a human one, judging by the iron wards on all the doors and the sprinkling of salt on doorsteps to deter the wandering dead. Standard precautions. As we walked, the houses grew sparser, and some were fenced off and under repair. In places like this, you could imagine tourists exploring the underground catacombs as they did before the dead had risen for real and the places where ghosts lurked turned into death traps. A sign in one of the windows said, "Zombies can suck my cock."

"Nice decor," I commented.

Lloyd snorted. "I could tell some stories that would give the most badass mercenary nightmares."

Mercenary district. That explained it. Mercs lived anywhere rent was cheap, since people desperate enough to hunt monsters for cash couldn't afford to be picky. But almost all mercs were humans. Supernaturals generally had more sense than to poke the dead, the guild being the obvious exception.

A small twig-like humanoid figure danced onto the road, light sparking between its palms. "Fire imp." Ilsa dug a hand in her pocket.

"Un-glamoured," I added. Ilsa had the Sight, being related to a faerie family, but the rest of us were oblivious to any faeries unless they chose to reveal themselves.

"They're attention seekers," she said, grasping a handful of iron filings. "Little bastards."

Ilsa threw the iron in the little faerie's general direction, and it danced gleefully away, giving us the finger.

Lloyd scowled. "Lovely neighbourhood. Are you sure we want to be here?"

"We're almost at the key point." Ilsa pointed ahead to a house set slightly apart from its neighbours. Despite the iron bars on its gate, it looked abandoned. The roof was half caved in, and the front door lay wide open.

"That's the key point," muttered Ilsa. "But it's still faint."

I tapped into the spirit realm to have a look around and saw nothing but fog. I tentatively pushed my consciousness towards the house, sensing for anyone living. A flicker of blue light stirred, and my heart sank.

The spirit realm didn't lie. Someone was in there. A vampire.

Keir?

No. Not Keir. The shadow was too faint. Like the dead. My throat went dry.

"I think there's a vampire in there," I whispered to Ilsa. "They can control any number of undead from a distance, and considering it's on a key point..."

"It might be a trap." She nodded, her hand dropping to her pocket. "Are you two ready?"

"Yes," I said, with a glance at Lloyd. "You don't have to—"

"I'm coming," he said. "Go in there with you or wait out here with the fire-slinging faerie? My money's on you two."

"I'm flattered," I said. "Stay close to me."

After the battle, I couldn't help feeling like I'd been at least partially responsible for his being taken captive and nearly killed. But Lloyd was a stubborn arse as well as being my best friend, and I wouldn't leave him behind if he didn't want me to.

Ilsa pushed the house's door open and walked ahead into the hall. A faint blue glow enfolded her, making her look taller, more intimidating. Lloyd and I walked close behind, leaving the door open.

A body lay sprawled on the floor of the hallway. Dead, from the awkward sprawl of his limbs and the utter silence in the spirit realm. I checked for the traces of a necromancer or vampire, and found none.

"Uh," said Lloyd. "Does that say, 'blood sacrifice' to you?"

"No," I said. "There's no blood, for a start."

Or chalk symbols or creepy glyphs. But a shiver traced down my spine as I looked down at the man's body. The problem with dealing with the dead on a daily basis was that it was too easy to remember that death wasn't the end, far from it, and a corpse might hide a trap.

"Weird." Ilsa crouched beside the dead man, carefully moving him into a sitting position. "Not that I'm a medical expert, but I can't tell how he died at all. Can either of you?"

"Fell downstairs?" Lloyd suggested, indicating the dusty, bare wooden steps a few feet away.

I shook my head. "You can't get upstairs. The roof's caved in."

"Didn't you sense a vampire?" Lloyd asked.

"I thought I did," I said. "Maybe this dude got drained. It explains why there's no visible injuries."

Ilsa nodded slowly, rising to her feet. "Nothing in the spirit realm as far as I can see."

I turned on my spirit sight again. A person didn't just drop dead on top of a key point. Not without prompting.

Wait. Shouldn't the key point be pulsing with life? Or death? It seemed entirely too quiet. I turned to Ilsa. "The whole key point is still off, isn't it?"

She gave a tight nod. "Yes. I think the person who did it is still here."

I switched on my spirit sight, and outside the hall, blue lights flickered on and off, too faint to be ghosts.

"Undead," I warned. "I think."

"Gotta be zombies," said Lloyd, frowning. "Where the bloody hell are they, then?" The half-open door to a sitting room on the right revealed nothing, and my spirit sight was too fogged from the spirit line's proximity to pinpoint the flickering lights.

"What did you say vampires looked like, shadows?" asked Ilsa, turning on the spot with her head tilted slightly upwards.

"Ah, crap." I tilted my head upwards and sensed an unmistakable flicker of blue light. "They must be hiding under the caved-in roof. And—I think the vampire controlling them is already dead."

Vampires, like powerful necromancers, didn't always disappear when they died, and it stood to reason that their link with their zombies might last beyond death.

"Creepy," Lloyd muttered. "Show me where to throw the salt."

Ilsa took a step backwards towards the door. "We need to break the vampire's connection with the vessels, right?"

"Yep." The creaking grew louder. "Break the connection, blast him into the afterlife."

Shuffling came from above, and the first zombie

lumbered downstairs. Despite its lack of coordination, it was clearly recently dead, judging by the lack of the usual decaying smell. No wonder they'd hidden so easily.

Lloyd gripped a salt shaker in one hand, while I took aim with Isabel's spells. The zombie's legs collapsed as my trapping spell hit, blocking the stairs. Ilsa hissed out a warning as the dead man in the hallway abruptly rose to his feet, but Lloyd got there first. Salt flew from the shaker, and as its face dissolved, I plunged into the spirit realm and grabbed the blue thread of light controlling it. It came away in my hands so fast, the others exclaimed when the zombie rose under my own control.

"Uh. Oops. Didn't mean to do that." The zombie turned its half-dissolved face away, and I sensed another pulse from... under my feet. "Crap. Guys, there's a basement—"

A trapdoor flew upwards beside the stairs and several more zombie heads popped up.

"Oh, bloody wonderful," said Lloyd, throwing salt at the zombies pawing at the spell barrier I'd tossed at the stairs.

Ilsa had backed up to the door, a knife in her hand and an expression of concentration on her face. A line of salt surrounded her, and her vacant gaze showed me she was hunting down the vampire through the spirit realm.

Trusting Lloyd had enough salt to keep the dead away, I joined her. Grey light filtered in, showing me Ilsa floating outside her body before the undead. From this angle, they were empty spaces piloted by threads of blue light, connecting them to a single person in the spirit realm—a shadowy shape too far back to see. *Clever.* The vampire had left the bodies here as bait, but was hiding out of reach. I was sure the guy was dead—living vampires had a stronger presence—but maybe he was way off. Like outside the city.

Luckily, in the spirit realm, there was nothing I couldn't reach, given the incentive.

I grabbed two of the undead by the threads of light and turned them on one another, causing them to punch and strike every other zombie that came near them. "That'll keep them busy." I floated onto Ilsa's level.

Ilsa raised an eyebrow. "Wow. I didn't know you were that proficient with undead."

"Everyone has their talents," I said. "Mine is creating zombie warfare."

Ilsa's own hands glowed with faint blue light. I had the distinct impression that she was holding herself back—I'd seen her use far more impressive magic—but with the key point underneath our feet, if any of us used too much necromancy, we might well create a disaster of our own.

I reached past the zombies, for the connecting threads, and followed them to their source, the shadowy figure beyond the lights. Now I was definitely out of my body, but without the key point, I couldn't tell whereabouts I was. Ah, crap. I hadn't used candles. So much for playing by the rules.

"Hey!" I yelled, in the general direction of the vampire's shadowy presence. "Get over here and face me, you coward."

I grabbed the nearest blue thread, yanking hard. My hands glowed blue-white, and a sudden shiver racked my spine, along with the certainty that I wasn't alone.

I spun on the spot, expecting to see Evelyn Hemlock

floating there. Instead, I saw Ilsa, her brow furrowed in confusion. "Uh, Jas, did you catch the guy?"

Nope. I'm losing my mind. I tightened my grip on the threads of light. "Yeah, but he's out of reach. I'm going to have to go off the line."

"I'll back you up."

I nodded thanks, and felt the threads of light threaten to slip away. My ghostly hands clenched tighter as the vampire grew closer. Looked like he was within the city after all. His shadowy form became larger, more present —a cut-out shadow of a man, floating in Death.

"Use your magic, Gatekeeper," he taunted.

"Not happening," Ilsa muttered, and spoke the banishing words instead.

I did the same, our voices joining in chorus. The vampire struggled but couldn't fight the call of Death, and he disappeared in a scream of light.

The blueness dissipated, and I rotated on my heel, looking around for my body. Instead, I found Ilsa. "Jas, relax. Just focus and you'll go back. Spirit lines are anchors—you won't go floating off into space from here."

I'd long suspected Ilsa knew some tricks for navigating the spirit realm without candles, so her advice came as no surprise.

"Thanks." I closed my eyes, concentrating hard. A moment later, I was back in my body, with Lloyd shaking my shoulder.

"Oi. I killed the zombies. Don't die."

"We banished the vampire." I nodded to Ilsa. "He was already dead. I guess one of these bodies was his." That, or his body was lying in a gutter elsewhere.

"Glad to hear it." Lloyd backed out onto the doorstep. "Want to destroy this lot?"

"Only when we find out who they are," I said. "That's a *lot* of recent dead." Their half-dissolved zombie forms concealed how they'd died, but I was positive the guy we'd first found in the hall had had no visible injuries whatsoever.

I walked into the hall, kicking a zombie off the corpse that we'd first found here. Something told me that he *was* the vampire I'd just banished. While the shadow had hardly resembled the man, necromancers possessed a sixth sense that let us see the essence of a person. "I think I know how he died," I said. "He went too far away from his body and the connection broke."

Ilsa frowned. "Are you sure?"

I shook my head. "Nope. But he was miles away. I know vampires *can* travel further than normal people, but his body was on top of the key point when it switched off."

Ilsa's eyes rounded. "Oh. You think… I guess if there was a big enough surge of magic on the key point, it might have broken the connection…"

"Or his death turned off the key point?" I suggested. "I don't know. It's all guesswork."

Had some invisible force had yanked him out of his body and switched off the spirit line at the same moment? Nothing else in the house registered with my spirit sight, and yet…

"Who knows," said Ilsa. "If it's any consolation, a key point can't permanently be switched off. The spirit realm has healed from worse."

"You talk like it's alive," Lloyd said. "Tell me it isn't. This is wacky enough as it is."

"It's not *living*, but there's a balance between the realms that has to be maintained," said Ilsa. "The mortal realm, the spirit realm, and the faerie realm. If something goes wrong in one of those realms, it affects the others. The key points are part of that."

"We can at least figure out who he is," I said, reaching for the vampire's body. I pulled him upright, grimacing when his cold, dead hands brushed against mine. Though there wasn't a spark of life inside him, we'd still need to destroy the body to prevent him from rising again, as per the rulebook. He wore a simple jacket and jeans, not a necromancer's coat or anything else to indicate his identity. I dug in his pockets but didn't find a wallet or ID. Nothing, except a piece of screwed up paper, torn across the bottom. It contained only a handful of words. "The Society of Ley Hunters."

"What does it say?" asked Lloyd.

"The Society of Ley Hunters," I said. "That rings a bell."

"Not to me," said Ilsa. "Ley as in Ley Line?"

"Probably." But I knew that name...

"People who hunt Ley Lines?" Lloyd said sceptically. "Uh, isn't there only one of them, and most people can't sense it anyway?"

"There is," Ilsa said. "It's on the other side of the city, but... what's that, a flyer?"

"Looks more like an invitation." I read the words again, as though to parse out a double meaning. "An event... an exclusive event, by the looks of things."

"And these were the other invitees?" Ilsa poked an

undead with her foot. "Hmm. Maybe. Not sure if they were supernaturals or humans, though."

"Search their pockets," I said. "Watch they don't rise again."

"They won't with the key point switched off," Ilsa commented, digging into another dead man's jacket pocket. "Same invite. He got invited to a secret meeting, and the prize was to end up being ripped from his body?"

"That's just creepy," said Lloyd.

If we were doing things by the book, we'd search until we found someone who carried ID, take it back to the guild, and they'd use their channels to hunt down the person in the real world. Usually when we found an undead in the more well-known parts of town, someone eventually figured out who that person had been. But not always.

"This one has an ID card," said Lloyd, dropping a zombie's limp hand. "But no photo ID."

"This is just weird," I said. "Were they specifically told not to bring any identification to this top-secret meeting?"

"Because they were going to be used as sacrifices and the person running the show didn't want anyone to be identified?" suggested Lloyd.

Ilsa stiffened at the word *sacrifice,* and I gave him a look.

He bowed his head and went back to searching the pockets of the dead. "This one has a business card," he said. "Except—it's the same. Ley Hunters."

"That's not a business card," said Ilsa. "It doesn't have contact details on it."

"Or anything else," Lloyd added. "Just the name."

"I don't get it," I said. "Humans looking for the Ley Line? I've seen the name before." There was such a thing as a coincidence, but the Ley Line was the largest spirit line, and as I'd found out recently from Ilsa herself, the boundary between this realm and Faerie. Humans couldn't cross that way unless accompanied by one of the Sidhe, and it was a one-way street even then. Necromancers didn't contact the spirit realm on the Ley Line if they could help it. It was too volatile. So the mere presence of the word cemented my certainty that this foul play went beyond a few undead.

"You've heard the name before?" asked Ilsa. "When?"

I hesitated, then figured it couldn't hurt to ask. "There was this shop in the witch district of south Birmingham… it looked like it was under construction or abandoned, though. But it had the same name."

"Really?" she asked. "When was this?"

"Uh. I went back to visit a few weeks ago… I have family there." Even now, the geas my family had put on me was in full effect. I couldn't tell anyone about the Hemlocks' forest, which existed outside of space-time and could jump to Edinburgh from England in a heartbeat. "Anyway, I ran into the shop when I got lost in witch district. But it was empty, as I said. Probably means nothing."

"Considering all these people died, it's worth mentioning to the boss," said Ilsa. "A death—several deaths—at a key point, when it seems to be switching on and off randomly… it's a bad sign."

"You're telling me," said Lloyd. "I don't think I want to know why humans would be stupid enough to go hunting for Ley Lines. What would happen if they found one?"

"There's only one," said Ilsa. "And nothing. They've been walking on top of the Ley Line for their whole lives without knowing. The Line only opened in the invasion, and I don't think they want a repeat performance."

Damn. It was the Ley Line that had brought the Sidhe into this realm, twenty-two years ago.

"I can tell the boss, but there's nothing I can do about it," I said. "Like I said… the place was abandoned."

And the only way to get home was to do something I'd been dreading for weeks—talk to my fellow Hemlock witches again.

"So, Jas," said Lady Montgomery. "Am I correct in hearing that you've encountered this 'Ley Hunters' group before?"

"Nope," I said. "I just saw the name. Might belong to anyone. Do you think it's weird that all we found in the house were undead? I mean, it's pretty obvious someone used necromancy there, aside from the vampire. But they left no props behind."

"If they were foolhardy enough to use magic on the spirit line at a surge, they might not have needed to," she said.

"Surge?" I echoed.

"The amount of magic in a spirit line is never constant," she said. "It ebbs and flows. Sometimes you can use necromancy on a spirit line and have no more effect than using it anywhere else. Other times, you might cause a dozen spirits to come back from the veil. It's entirely random, and very dangerous."

"So, the vampire decided to hop over the veil without a

candle and got ripped out of his body?" I suggested. "And… the others did the same? I'm sure they must have been human."

"It seems so," said Lady Montgomery. "But don't forget: most humans have the *potential* to use magic. It's not all related to ancestry, however much the mages would like to have you believe that. Not all magic users come from magical families. If the vampire lured those humans to the key point during a surge, even non-supernaturals might have been caught in the spell."

I doubted it. A surge that powerful, Lloyd and I would have felt when we'd been at the old mage's house exorcising his spirit. Rather, the opposite of a surge had happened, and the key point's power had all but disappeared. But if even the boss didn't know what was going on, I was lost.

"I guess," I said to her. "Maybe they were dormant necromancers or people with distant ancestry." I was an eighth necromancer, technically. My great-grandfather had been one, according to Lady Harper, and the slightest hint of the spirit sight could be harnessed and used to teach magic, the same way the tiniest proficiency for magical remedies could develop into skill at witchcraft. Lady Montgomery had put me through a few basic tests to make sure I developed the ability to see ghosts, then put me into novice training. Very luckily, I'd been good enough to scrape by until I was fully qualified.

"And do you have plans this weekend?" she enquired.

I stared for a moment. Lady Montgomery did not, as a rule, ask questions about my personal life. "Uh, volunteering in the archives, if there isn't anyone else on duty?"

I'd been sneakily reading every book the guild had on

vampires, shades, and dark magic… which wasn't many, because the good ones were in the boss's office where nobody could access them. Her on-point spirit sight would catch me in an instant if I sneaked into her office without permission, and besides, it wasn't worth it. The Hemlocks had used magic that nobody had on record at all, and unless they chose to volunteer the information, I'd remain in the dark.

Lady Montgomery gave me a sweeping look. "Jas, don't mistake this for permission to shirk your duties, but I've hardly seen you leave the guild's premises except on missions for weeks."

My mouth hung open for a moment before I closed it. "I've been, uh, short on cash." Not really a lie. I'd spent most of my savings at the witch market to build my own stock of spell ingredients. Just because I kept my use of Evelyn's magic to a minimum didn't mean I'd given up using witchcraft altogether.

"Do you have hobbies?" she asked.

"I… took drawing lessons." Okay, the last class I'd taken was two years ago. The guild's unpredictable shift schedule made it impossible to regularly keep up with any kind of hobby, so I'd switched to spending my evenings marathoning zombie movies with Lloyd. Besides, Lady Montgomery could hardly talk. She lived and breathed her job. If *she* was concerned that I had no social life, ice-skating ghosts would come to bear me into hell at any moment.

"And when was the last time you saw your family? You said they live in England?"

"Er, adoptive family. But yes, they do. I guess I haven't seen them for a while." Mostly because I hadn't exactly told everyone I planned to run away to Scotland seven years ago.

"No," she said. "We do allow family visits at the weekend, you know, and I believe this Ley Hunter shop you saw might be important in getting to the bottom of this case."

Of course. The guild's shift rota covered seven days a week so I never got a full weekend off, and she wouldn't let me go on a weekend away during our busiest season if it didn't have a purpose. Not that she knew about the forest, which would at least be easier than an overnight coach trip. There was just the slight issue that I was not on speaking terms with the owners of said forest, and I wouldn't put it past Cordelia Hemlock to use it as an excuse to force me to resume my position as coven heir. On the other hand, I couldn't avoid my coven forever, and I had a few questions I wanted to ask Isabel about my witch training. If I swallowed my pride and faced the Hemlocks. Who knew, they might even apologise this time. Okay, let's face it, that was probably less likely than Lady Montgomery giving me a free holiday. But I could dream.

"All right," I said. "I'll get the bus tomorrow morning. I'll let you know if I find anything out."

"Do that, Jas. You're dismissed."

I left her office, closing the door behind me.

"Verdict?" asked Lloyd.

I pulled a face. "I'm being forcibly sent on a holiday."

"What?" He looked at me like I'd announced I planned to relocate to the North Pole. "Where on holiday?"

"To the Hemlocks' forest, for a start. Then all the way

over the Midlands until I find out if this 'Ley Hunters' society is an actual thing."

"You saw a sign in a window and she's giving you a free holiday for it?" he said incredulously. "Okay, I know what to do next time."

"It's not free unless I go into the forest," I pointed out. "Also, I don't have anywhere to stay overnight, so it'll be a quick day trip. That's all."

Lloyd made a sceptical noise. "If I didn't know better, I'd say she's concerned about you. Maybe she's guessed you're pining over a certain fang-free vamp—" He cut off in a yelp as I grabbed the scruff of his neck. "Jesus, your hands are ice blocks."

"That's Death for you. And for the record, no, I wasn't thinking about Keir at all. He made his intentions clear when he blew me off. Anyway, you'll have to stay here and cover for me. She thinks I'm getting an overnight coach. And if the Hemlocks kick me out of the forest, I might have to do exactly that."

"They're really mad at you? The witches?"

"No, they're obnoxiously smug and not at all remorseful about the fact that I nearly died," I said. "I'm still mad at *them.* They value Evelyn's life more than mine. And then there's Lady Harper. You know, the last time we spoke, I sort of yelled down the phone at her for manipulating me. I'll ask Isabel to warn me if she's going to be there."

Was it too much to ask that I was allowed to avoid my former coven for the rest of my existence? Yes, apparently. And Lady Harper might be worse than the lot of them. Willingly walking back into the home of the mages was a headache I did *not* want to deal with.

But the Ley Hunters... breaking a key point was a violation of the supernatural law, not to mention highly dangerous. For that reason alone, it was worth checking out.

———

Early the next morning, I slipped out of the guild's headquarters before the sun had fully risen. It'd been another restless night plagued with dreams of cages and nets, which I assumed were either echoes of Evelyn's emotions reaching me from her captivity, or my subconscious's idea of a joke. I'd never actually heard Evelyn's thoughts—other than the occasional flash of emotion from her—but whatever the dreams had come from, they made me tired and crabby and even less inclined to deal with the Hemlock witches.

Apprehension stirred as the ruins of the train station came within sight from Waverley Bridge. It'd been three weeks since I'd last set foot in the station—three weeks since I'd nearly lost my life at the hands of Leila and Evelyn Hemlock. The train station looked even more dismal under the thunderous grey sky, and there was no telling what might be lurking inside it. I adjusted my rucksack on my shoulders, took in a calming breath, and felt for the world beyond this one.

The bridge became a cave with snaking tree roots covering the floor, walls and ceiling. A small furred creature sat on a rock, and hissed at me. The half-fae servant of the Hemlocks didn't seem to like me much. But that paled in comparison to their leader.

The stone sculpture dominating the cave moved,

shadows dappling its surface, lit in the pale green glow of the glyphs on the walls. A pair of eyes stared from the rock, condemning.

"Jacinda Hemlock," said Cordelia. "Have you come to resume your training?"

"Nope." I sidestepped the half-fae, who swiped at me with a claw as though to repudiate me for rudeness. As far as I was concerned, I treated Cordelia with the same level of respect she showed me, which wasn't a lot. "I'd like to travel home for a temporary trip. You owe me at least one favour for saving your necks."

They owed me more than that. If I'd died or Evelyn had driven my body into an early grave, the coven would have died along with me. I wasn't sure what actual relation Cordelia was to me, because the coven's tangled history meant that everyone of the 'pure' bloodline was stuck in the forest. The Hemlocks, as far as I knew, were the only coven who passed on leadership through blood and not by electing a leader based on merit. It was just plain bad luck that I'd been the only surviving member when Evelyn had been close to death, forcing the coven to bind our souls together so that I'd be able to use her magic.

"If you wish to use the forest for your travels," said the old witch, "then you have the ability to do so, should you choose to use it."

The cave vanished, leaving nothing but trees and a murky path. No argument? That was a first. Lady Harper would doubtless be more difficult, but I'd do my best to avoid her. For now, I had to figure out *how* to use my magic to make the forest let me cross the country.

Hemlock power was ever-present here, humming in the

trees, in every shadow, and inside me. Like when I was concentrating on my spirit sight, I kept an image of the road outside the forest in my mind's eye and stepped forwards, my eyes closed. My feet caught on a tree root and I tripped, my knees smarting as they hit the ground. Ow.

A whisper of laughter sounded in my ears, and my eyes flew open. "Uh. Evelyn?"

Silence. I detached my legs from the tree roots, mourned my dignity and my new jeans for a moment, then focused on her magic again.

Had I imagined her faint laughter? I'd go with *nope...* but it wasn't like she could escape her prison. Maybe using her magic brought me closer to her. Despite my vow not to let her take over my body, her power still rose to my hands whenever I tapped into my witchy nature. It was as much mine as hers, after all.

"Come on, dammit," I muttered.

My hands glowed with light. *That's more like it.* The forest turned transparent, the path folding in on itself, and abruptly ended at a road almost flooded with rainwater, with a snow-capped hedge on the right-hand side. Looked like the half-faeries had decorated their territory for winter. A self-contained blizzard covered the area to my right, blocking out the rain, and over the hedge, I glimpsed faeries skiing down artificial slopes and skating on a giant pond. I wished witchcraft could do cool things like that, but you couldn't have it all.

Beside the hedge, Isabel stood under a large umbrella, her hood pulled up over her curly hair and faintly smudged chalk marks on her warm brown skin. I'd asked her to meet me for moral support in case the Hemlocks kicked up a fuss, but Lady Harper wouldn't be outside in this weather.

"Hey, Jas," she said. "They didn't give you trouble?"

"Nope," I said. "I'm a little suspicious, to be honest, but I'm not complaining at this point. I guess that's the closest to remorse I'll get from them. Is Lady Harper not around?"

"Haven't a clue. She hasn't spoken to me since the day I came back."

"I seriously pissed her off," I said. "And you set Ivy on her. That couldn't have helped."

"She's in the wrong and she knows it." Isabel glanced behind me at the forest. "So… what's this Ley Society?"

"Haven't a clue, but my boss sent me to investigate it," I said, walking to her side. "We found a bunch of dead bodies carrying flyers with the words 'Society of Ley Hunters' written on them. Since I saw a shop with the same name the last time I was here, I'm supposed to see if it's the same people."

"Fun," said Isabel, adjusting her umbrella so I could stand underneath it too. I'd gone without my cloak, so I didn't have a hood. "New spells?" Isabel eyed the bands on my wrists.

"Hope you don't mind I copied your recipe. I'm not planning on selling them."

"Don't worry about it," she said. "You added your own touch, I'll bet."

"I toned it down." Or tried to. When left unchecked, my Hemlock power amplified spells far beyond what they'd otherwise be capable of. Not only would it be unethical of me to sell spells made using someone else's recipe on the market, it'd be downright dangerous to hand-make my own and sell them for spare cash.

In the supernatural world, there were two strands of spells: the type which were mass-produced and sold at eye-watering prices to anyone who could afford to fork out the cash, and the type hand-made by witches trying to scrape together a living. The latter sold cheaper but carried more risk depending on who you bought them from. Isabel had told me she'd progressed to selling her own spells direct to the mages because they were better than the market variety, but everybody knew someone who'd bought a healing spell from a hedge witch and grown an extra limb or something instead. Besides, in order to sell magic, you needed a licence straight from the Mage Lords. I'd have to expose my coven to make a living off my magic. It definitely wouldn't be worth it.

"Trapping spell," Isabel said, identifying the red band on my wrist. "Healing, shield… heating spell?"

"Trust me, they're a lifesaver after two-hour patrols in the cold," I answered. "But I went overboard with the first few and turned them into fire spells instead." I'd caused a few minor explosions in my flat during my experimenta-tion, but I'd sooner swallow a fire spell than confess to Lady Harper that I actually enjoyed doing it. I understood why Isabel spent half her time playing Mad Scientist.

Isabel grinned. "I can tell you have a few stories."

I recounted a few of my wilder experiments on the walk to witch territory, skirting the faerie market which must be a new addition to town. My former home had changed in the years since I'd left, but the memories of begging on the corner of this very street, and sleeping on hard wooden floorboards at an overcrowded orphanage packed with witches whose parents had died in the invasion—every single one was as clear as though it'd happened yesterday.

"So where's Ivy?" I asked, raising my voice over the raucous sounds of the market.

"At the Mage Lord's," she said. "Normally she'd be hunting fae, but there's a major council meeting coming up soon with the Council of Twelve and she's left everything until the last minute as usual."

"Did you say the Mage Lord's?" I said, frowning in confusion. "She's not a mage, right?"

"Oh, right, you won't know," she said. "Ivy and the Mage Lord are engaged."

I cast my mind around to figure out who the Mage Lord even was. "I'm assuming the last guy retired, because when I lived here, the Mage Lord was like... sixty or something."

"I think he died," said Isabel. "The current leading Mage Lord is Vance Colton. Do you know him? You grew up with the mages..."

"Yes. I did." Oh, wonderful. The leader of the local mages was Lady Harper's other former apprentice. So much for avoiding a run-in with her. I wasn't surprised Vance had been elected, considering he'd had two Mage Lords as parents, but I'd hoped I'd be lucky enough to avoid another collision with my past.

"You grew up together?" she asked.

"Not exactly," I said. "I mean, he was already an adult when we met. And an insufferable snob... don't tell him I said that. I take it you're both part of the same council?"

"Yes, the Council of Twelve. We meet a few times a year to discuss the current situation in the supernatural community, new developments in this realm and Faerie, that kind of thing. Lady Harper used to be a member of the original council."

I nodded. Like everything else, I'd only found that particular piece of information out second-hand, after the Council of Twelve had gathered in Edinburgh a couple of months ago. Suspicion reared its head. "Er, would that include the Hemlocks? Does everyone on the council know they exist? I know Ivy does."

"Nope," she said. "It's up to Cordelia herself if she wants to volunteer information or not. When I asked, she insisted the council not know of their existence. Half of us know already, though, because you can't hide a forest like that easily. Ivy and Vance are the ones who put the council together."

"I've missed a lot," I said. Until recently, I hadn't known anyone aside from Lady Harper knew about the Hemlocks at all. If Vance did, I'd have to pay a visit, while hoping that none of the mages knew about my slight *extra soul* problem.

We reached the plain cheerful brick house that I'd woken up in last time I'd been here.

"Do you live in that house, then?" I asked Isabel.

"No, it's the property of my coven, inherited from our last leader," she said. "My flat isn't far from here, though. Ivy and I mostly run our business from there, but I do most of my experimenting at the coven's place. Did you say you ran into this... Ley Hunter Society somewhere here?"

"It was a boarded-up shop with a sign in the window." Rainwater dripped down my back as I ducked from underneath the umbrella to peer across the road. "Closed down. I think that's it."

We crossed the road to find the shop in the same condition as last time I'd seen it. It was far from the only empty shop on the street and its whitewashed walls were identical to its neighbours'. The sign was still there, on the other side of the boarded-up window: *The Society of Ley Hunters.*

"Fancy a little breaking and entering?" I switched on my spirit sight. No signs of life showed within, but there was at least one person in the shop next door. It looked like a junk shop, filled with bits of furniture and other miscellaneous objects. "Nobody's home."

"Not yet," said Isabel, approaching the neighbouring shop. "Let's see what the neighbours say. They might have seen who owns the place."

"Perhaps."

Inside the small, cramped shop next door, every item looked used, dusty and half broken. The paunchy man behind the counter eyed both of us suspiciously. Being human, he'd probably recognise us as supernaturals right off. The bright bands on our wrists were enough of a clue.

"Hey there," said Isabel, in a cheerful tone. "I wondered if I could ask you a question."

"Can't tempt you with a fresh and shiny piece of silverware?" he asked, smiling a gap-toothed smile. "Or a genuine oak wood cabinet?"

I followed his gaze. This stuff was way under-priced for what it was. I knew what he must be: a raider.

When the faeries had attacked over two decades ago, huge proportions of the city had been left uninhabitable. Raiders made a living by breaking into those abandoned properties, pilfering whatever they could, and selling it at discounted rates. That was the theory, anyway, but most raiders were human and didn't want to carry the risk of breaking into a home that might be infested with wild fae. Instead, they had a nasty habit of raiding properties with people still living in them, terrorising them into leaving, then pretending they'd found everything fair and square. They were crooks through and through, even more than mercenaries were.

"No thank you," said Isabel. "I wanted to ask if anyone had moved into the property next door. I couldn't help noticing that it used to be abandoned until a few weeks ago, but now there's a sign in the window."

"Is there?" grunted the man. "Supernatural business. Not ours. Are you supernaturals? Witches? Want to trade me a spell for this silverware?"

"No thanks," said Isabel. "Are you sure you've never seen anyone break in?"

"I'll trade you this one," I said, easing a spell off my wrist.

Isabel shot me a sideways look, but I knew how people like him worked. When it came to spells, humans didn't like anything too complex, but what they valued most was protection. Specifically, against people like us.

He looked at the spell. "What's it do?"

"Iron ward," I told him. "Keeps the nasty faeries out."

"I like the way you think. Give me two and I'll tell you who you saw."

My eye twitched. I knew exactly how much those spells were actually worth, and most people would flat-out refuse. But I was soaking wet and fed up with the whole business already.

"Two," I said, though gritted teeth.

"All right," said the raider. "I thought I saw a man walk in there the other day. He was wearing a coat with a hood."

"That's not descriptive," Isabel protested. "Two spells aren't worth—"

He rose to his feet. "Give me an illusion spell to conjure up a beautiful woman and I'll give you all the info you need. Alternatively, one of you two could step in."

I grabbed Isabel's arm warningly, but she was on it.

"Touch me and this spell will blow your nose off," Isabel said, in calm tones, twisting a band on her wrist. "And this one will rid you of any hope of ever gaining any pleasure from any illusion charms again."

He sank backwards, fear filtering into his expression, and I grabbed her arm and pulled her out of there.

"That," I said, "was amazing. But I'm not sure we should have ticked him off."

"I wouldn't have done it if I didn't leave a spell on his doorstep that'll turn him into a mouse if he tries to follow us."

"That's if he gets his hand out of the biting spell I put on his desk."

Isabel grinned. "See, you did learn something from me."

"If we have to report the Ley Hunters to the police, can we 'accidentally' report that guy too?" I said, pacing back to the neighbouring shop. "I know, I know, the human police can't prove he stole that stuff from living humans, but come on. It's unethical to say the least, without getting into the 'creep' factor."

"Yeah." Isabel's face pinched. "Can't hurt to drop a line

with the mages. But this place… it's weird. The name is too distinctive to be an accident."

"Someone owns it," I said. "A supernatural. Who else has heard of the Ley Line?"

"I'd say it's time to try your breaking and entering idea, then." She walked to the door, raising her hands. "Damn. It's warded on the inside."

"Seriously?" I joined her, my hands flat against the wooden door. The hum of a spell reached my fingertips, but too faint to grasp. Evelyn's magic whispered through my palms, but I hadn't yet mastered the art of moderation, and we'd need a warrant to actually break inside. "Damn. I don't think I can turn off the ward without blasting the door to bits. And we can't prove these people are breaking the law from a simple sign."

Isabel swore under her breath. "I don't have the tools with me to get the spell off the door without drawing attention."

I stepped backwards, my foot catching on a scrap of paper, plastered to the pavement with rainwater. Crouching down, I picked it up. *The Society of Ley Hunters* titled the page, and below, a date and time, smudged. "Today… I'm sure that says today's date. Seven p.m."

"It does," said Isabel, reading over my shoulder. "Does it mean it's happening here?"

"I would guess so." I tilted my head, trying to see through the upstairs window, but the curtains were drawn. "Weird. The ward suggests a supernatural is running the show, but they might have done a better job fixing up the place."

"Warding the door on the *inside* seems a little paranoid," said Isabel. "Unless there's something in there that shouldn't be."

"Precisely my thinking," I said, turning over the scrap of paper again. "I'd say it can't hurt to come here to their meeting as a human. But I'll pay a visit to the mages before then."

"In case we need backup." Isabel nodded. "Have you ever been to Oak Drive before?"

"Yes, I have," I said. "You're going back to the witches' place? I'll meet you there after I speak to the Mage Lord." If nothing else, I could try to get a warrant to sneak around the Ley Hunters' place and see what they wanted to hide so badly.

I knew the mages' headquarters, since I'd spent a fair bit of time there as a child when Lady Harper had put me in home-schooling with the other mage apprentices. I didn't know how Vance would take my sudden return, but I was reasonably confident he wouldn't execute me on the spot.

As long as none of the mages found out about Evelyn Hemlock.

5

I knocked on the door of number 15 Oak Drive, trying in vain to shake the raindrops from my drenched hair. The heavens had opened again on the way, and while Isabel had lent me her umbrella, the wind had blown the damned thing inside out. The manor-sized house which served as the headquarters of the local mages had whitewashed walls covered in protective glyphs, balconies on the upper windows, and a large front garden filled with carved hedges and a well-tended lawn. As the only member of the Colton family who'd survived the faerie invasion, Vance had inherited the house early, and continued to use it as the mages' main headquarters. While the mages hadn't exactly been cruel to me when I'd been a kid, Lady Harper's continuous insistence that I shouldn't act like an ungrateful brat hadn't erased the memories of starving in an orphanage without a smidgeon of magical talent to buy my way out of poverty.

Please don't let Lady Harper be here. If nothing else, she'd blow our chances of sneaking into the Ley Hunters' place undetected. Subtlety was not the mages' way. They had power, they wielded it, and they got their way through intimidation and skill in conjunction. Lady Harper had only served two years on the council the second time before retiring, but had presided over training new novices for a while. I figured it was because she got some morbid entertainment from yelling discouragement at people.

The door opened. "Er, hey, Vance," I said.

Surprised widened his grey eyes. He looked exactly as I remembered—tall, broad-shouldered, his dark hair neatly combed and his expensive clothes tailored to fit his six-foot-two frame. He didn't wear one of the Mage Lords' infamous knee-length coats that sometimes got them confused with necromancers until they blasted people with lightning or set things on fire, but his intimidating stature and the shimmer of magic at the back of his eyes reminded me he wasn't someone I wanted to cross. Maybe this wasn't a good idea after all.

"Jas?" he said. "I wasn't expecting a social call, so I assume you're here to see Ivy. I didn't know you were back in town."

"Not for long," I said. "Er, can I come in?"

"Of course." There was a faint breeze from inside, and a band-shaped spell appeared in his hand, drying the rainwater from me the instant I crossed the threshold.

"You didn't need to do that. I have my own spells."

"I wasn't aware you were proficient in witchcraft." He gave me a brief once-over as though determining whether I was going to drip any dirty rainwater on the overpriced carpet. "I also wasn't aware you could travel from Scotland to the middle of England in the space of a few hours, either. It took Ivy and me two days to drive up there last time."

"So you two are a thing?" I asked, in the clumsiest attempt at a diversion ever. "This is the same Ivy who carries a sword and often skewers faerie corpses into the wall we're talking about, isn't it?"

"We're engaged, yes." He stepped aside to let me enter. The interior of the house looked the same as I remembered. A long hall extended before us, carpeted in red and wallpapered in white. At least the carpet would hide bloodstains.

"Watch out for the piskie," he said, over his shoulder.

"Bad faerie!" shrieked a high-pitched voice. A winged creature flew out of the door on my right, emitting a shrieking noise, its twig-like fingers jabbing me in the cheekbone.

I jumped backwards, swatting at the creature as his sharp little teeth came down on my ear. "Ow! I'm not a faerie."

"Bad faerie!" The piskie pursued me down the corridor and after Vance, buzzing like an oversized wasp. He opened the door into a living room, which served as an informal meeting place if none of the other rooms were free, and also appeared much the same as the last time I'd seen it. The expensive mahogany bookshelves looked as though they'd never been moved in seven years.

Ivy sat in an armchair by the fireplace with a stack of papers balanced on her lap. "Erwin, cut it out," she said. "Jas, you look like you swam here."

"Cheers." I swatted the piskie away again and activated another quick-drying spell on my coat. "Why do you have a faerie living in here?"

A faint current of air gusted past, sending the piskie flying to the other side of the room. "Erwin, don't bother our guest," said Vance. "He's Ivy's pet."

"More of a pest than a pet," said Ivy, though she said this in affectionate tones. "He moved into my old flat and never left, so he had to pick me or Isabel when we moved out. He spends all his time trying to break Vance's antique china."

I'd bet that drove the Mage Lord out of his mind. From the look of the place, Vance's neat-freak tendencies hadn't changed an inch. He must care for Ivy a lot to put up with an unwanted housemate.

"Is there something you wanted to ask us?" the Mage Lord enquired, lifting a stack of papers from the table. In a gust of air, they disappeared. Vance's displacing talents hadn't changed, either. His mage ability involved moving things around without touching them... including people.

I weighed the odds, then said, "Have either of you heard of the Society of Ley Hunters?"

A furrow appeared in his brow. "No. You mean the Ley Line?"

"There's a shop near Isabel's coven's place with a sign in the window that says it belongs to the Society of Ley Hunters," I explained. "It only appeared in the last few weeks, but Isabel said the place is magically warded on the inside. Then I found this outside." I held up the piece of damp, crumpled paper. "There's a meeting there tonight. It doesn't look like something on the legal side, let's put it that way."

"Huh," said Ivy. "I might have walked past it once or twice, but I can't say I was paying too much attention."

Vance tilted his head. "Did you see anybody inside?"

"The window was boarded up. The sign was on the outside." I took in a breath. "I'm actually here on behalf of Edinburgh's necromancer guild. I was on a guild mission yesterday and we found a bunch of dead bodies at a key point, carrying fliers with the same name on them. The Society of Ley Hunters. They died due to some sort of disturbance on the key point, so naturally, my boss wants to get to the bottom of it."

"You're saying someone killed them by switching off the key point?" Ivy frowned. "That's… weird. And probably not possible."

"No, it isn't," Vance said, taking the note from me to examine it. "I certainly haven't heard the name before. It sounds like a human endeavour."

"The guy running the show was a supernatural," I said. "But he was dead, too. I don't know how, but a bunch of people dropped dead right on top of a key point which switched off with no warning. Even my boss is stumped. And I know activity on the spirit lines can cause knock-on effects in other places."

"Maybe that's why the necromancers were having trouble contacting their ancestors at the summit the other day," Ivy said. "I just figured they were having their usual trouble with giving a crap."

"Are the local necromancers that bad?" I asked.

"More incompetent," said Ivy. "Their leader died nearly two years ago and they've still kept his ghost around instead of nominating a decent replacement. Mostly because there isn't one."

"So if there was a mass zombie attack…"

"There has been," she said. "Somehow, we dealt with it. But they avoid all responsibility if they can help it, and we've pretty much left them off the list for the council altogether. It looks like your guild has its shit together, though."

"Yeah, that's mostly down to Lady Montgomery," I said. "She sent me here to look for these Ley Hunters, but there's nobody in the house. The neighbour refused to give us any useful information, either."

"Is that so?" Vance said. "I'll send someone to look into it, and the Ley Hunters' place, too. If they're breaking the law, we have licence to inspect the premises."

"Wouldn't sending a witch work better?" I asked. "There's a ward on the door even Isabel couldn't undo."

Ivy gave a wry smile. "Asking for permission before breaking and entering? This has Isabel written all over it."

Actually, I'm just trying to avoid getting on the wrong side of the law. The mages could kick the door in and storm the place on the word of a rumour if so inclined, but that wouldn't do much good if the person responsible fled without us ever finding out if they were the same Ley Hunters as whoever had killed those people in Edinburgh.

"There's nobody in there," I said. "I checked, using the spirit sight, but last time, the person responsible had hidden way deep in the spirit realm. Nobody who isn't one of us would be able to find them."

The Mage Lord nodded slowly. "If that's the case, take Isabel with you to search the place. I'll alert the mages."

"I don't think that'll be necessary," I said. Unless they'd hidden themselves, I hadn't even seen the flicker of a vampire's presence. The owner might have activated the ward from the outside, but that didn't make the setup any less weird. Still, I had permission to kick the door down. One problem solved.

"I'd come, but I don't want us to blow your cover," Ivy said. "Yes, that goes for you, too, Vance. Use your official channels to find out more about these Ley Hunters. See if the name has been mentioned anywhere."

"That's what I'm intending to do," Vance said. "If it turns out this is a matter for the council, however, I'm required to tell them."

Oh, damn. I'd momentarily forgotten I was in the same room as someone partly responsible for setting the mage council's laws... including executing people who broke them.

I shook off the thought. Vance and I had known each other when I was a kid, for god's sake, *and* he'd actually met the Hemlocks. Not to mention Lady Harper. That alone would be reason enough to spare me, if the truth came out. Besides, I didn't need to drag the entire mage council into this investigation. These Ley Hunters were probably human amateurs who needed a wake-up call.

Didn't make them any less dangerous, though. And just where had they got hold of a powerful witch ward?

"Wish I could come along," Ivy said, looking despondently at the small mountain of papers on the floor in front of her. "I swear Lady Harper's punishing me by making me fill out twice as much crap as usual."

Ah, damn. "She's not here, is she?"

"Not at the moment," Vance said.

Relief swept through me. "Good, because I'd rather she didn't know I dropped by. We had a major argument." I didn't need to give details. Lady Harper was capable of starting a feud against a garden gnome if she was in one of her moods.

"Yeah, thanks for making Isabel tell me to annoy her,"

Ivy added, moving some of the papers aside. "Joking. Kind of. It was my fault anyway."

"What did you do?" I asked.

"Isabel told me that you wanted her distracted at any cost, so I set Erwin loose in her guest room."

I snorted. "Yeah, that'd tick her off."

"Usually my existence does," She re-shuffled the papers and picked up a fresh stack. "Since, you know, I'm engaged to her protégé."

I could see where Lady Harper would find issue with someone like Ivy. She liked everything quiet and controlled. Ivy was not proper or well-behaved or good at following rules... not that I was one to talk. I'd never imagined Vance ending up engaged to someone like Ivy either, for that matter, but people changed.

"I'll come back later if Isabel and I find anything," I told her.

"If anyone can figure a way around a ward on a locked door, it's Isabel," said Ivy. "And I've heard you're not so bad at spells yourself."

I didn't miss Vance's raised eyebrow at her comment. The Mage Lord would remember just as clearly as I did that I hadn't demonstrated any talent at witchcraft at all throughout Lady Harper's training. "See you in a bit."

Vance accompanied me to the door, but I didn't break the silence. Anything I said might make it back to Lady Harper *or* the mage council.

"I didn't know you'd learned to use witchcraft as well as the spirit sight, Jas," Vance said.

"I guess not," I said causally. "It turns out I'm much better at magic without Lady Harper breathing down my neck. I was a late developer and she wanted me to be perfect on the first try like you were."

His eyes narrowed a little, not fooled, but I met his stare with a challenge. Most supernaturals discovered their magical capabilities at twelve or thirteen, but it wasn't impossible for witches or necromancers to do so later. Or even mages, like my childhood friend Wanda. Usually there were at least some signs, though. I hadn't displayed any talent in the slightest until I'd started working with Evelyn Hemlock.

"Lady Harper told me you'd spoken with your coven," he said. "The Hemlocks."

I wished the corridor wasn't so long. "Yeah... I wouldn't say we're talking to one another at the moment. You're sending backup tonight, right? Would that include the other council members?"

"Only my second-in-command, and that's because Drake's one of the best combat mages here."

I blinked. "Drake? The same Drake who once crashed your best car into the canal?"

"That's him."

"You made him second-in-command," I said. "You might as well put a necromancer in charge of a wedding."

"You'd be surprised how well he's handled it."

More than you think. Drake had been the person who'd helped me engineer my escape to Scotland when it became clear that the Hemlocks were never going to let me walk away free. I couldn't picture the trouble-making fire mage as a council member, but the idea of working hand-in-hand with the council suddenly didn't seem so intimidating.

"Next you'll be telling me Drake settled down like you

did," I said, a weight lifting off my chest despite my lingering misgivings. Having two people I knew on the local council wasn't bad news, at all.

Vance smiled. "I don't think that's on the cards for him at the moment. I'll tell him about the meeting tonight. He'll want to see you. Wanda, too."

"Sure." Maybe memory had over-exaggerated how much of a condescending dick Vance had been when I was a teenager and Lady Harper had put him in charge of my magical training on occasion. Or maybe he was trying to get on my good side to get answers out of me on my Hemlock witch status.

Either way, I couldn't afford to get too close to the mage council. After all, if Evelyn Hemlock broke out of my trap, we might end up on opposite sides of a battlefield.

6

By the time I reached Isabel's coven's headquarters again, the rain had stopped. I'd picked up a few ingredients from the market, dodging the efforts of a guy calling himself the "Warlock Extraordinaire" who pursued me down two streets trying to sell me some piskie wings for a pound each. I bought a sandwich from a stall and ate it on the way—after applying two tests for poison, that is. I used the hand-made spells every time I ate or drank anything outside of the guild cafeteria. Nearly dying of poisoning had made me cautious, to say the least.

Isabel let me into the house, where she'd taken over the living room with so many chalk circles that it was like playing twister trying to walk through them all.

I stepped around carefully to find a clear spot on the floor. "Got enough spells, Isabel?"

"I'm preparing for every possible eventuality," she said, checking on a bubbling pot on the stove in the adjacent kitchen. Her hair frizzed from the steam, and there was a slightly manic expression on her face.

I laughed. "You're annoyed you couldn't get past that ward on the door, aren't you?"

She moved the boiling pan to the side. "More concerned than anything. You can't buy that spell type on the market. It's a custom job."

"There's a witch involved?" I asked. "We're not far from the market, though. A human might have bought it."

Isabel sniffed at the pan, then stepped back. "There's got to be something seriously valuable hidden in there, then. A custom job like that would cost a small fortune."

"If this Ley Hunters Society is operating up and down the country, they must have money and connections," I said.

"If they have money, what the bloody hell is the point in committing mass suicide at key points, then?" Isabel gave the pan's contents a stir. "Unless the vampire in Edinburgh didn't mean to die."

"Or he was being manipulated, too." She was right, though… it didn't add up. I found a clear spot on the floor and dumped my bags of ingredients from the market. "Who knows why anyone would want to turn off a key point. Unless it was an accident." But there were ways to harness the energy from spirit lines that I knew little about. Necromancers and witches were more tuned into the lines than most, but that didn't mean we knew all their secrets.

I sat cross-legged and sketched out my first chalk circle. Magic tingled in my fingertips, as though being so close to Isabel's work had sent my Hemlock magic into overdrive. *Behave,* I told my glowing hands. Isabel moved in behind me, but I kept my attention on the spell.

"One sneaking spell, coming right up," I said.

"Sneaking spell?" she asked. "I was thinking shadow spells would do."

"Good idea, but I think the ward might cover the whole downstairs floor, in which case, we'd need to get in through the upstairs window." I chopped leaves off stalks and tossed them into the circle. "Not sure if you have a ladder or not, but I had a brainwave the other day while I was making a stealth charm."

"Do I even want to know?" asked Isabel.

"If I know you… yeah, you do."

"Guilty." She grinned as I leaned over the circle. "Let's see."

I tapped the circle's symbols one at a time. Each sent a shiver through my palms and the smell of burning herbs rose as the circle's contents were engulfed in flames. The embers danced through the circle but never went over the edge. I'd nearly burned my flat down the other day when I'd left a gap in the circle, so I'd been extra careful this time around.

The flames faded, leaving two band-shaped spells behind. I picked one up, wincing when it singed my fingers, and slid it onto my wrist. Then I did the same to my other wrist with the second band.

"I need somewhere to practise that isn't covered in circles." I trod through the room to the hall. "Also, if this doesn't work, I might need you to catch me."

"Okay…" Isabel sounded sceptical, but played along.

I gave each band a twist and spread my palms against

the wall. It was still splattered with faerie blood from when Ivy had killed one here the other week.

Then I jumped, and my feet left the ground. Isabel watched open-mouthed as I crawled up the wall and onto the ceiling, hanging upside-down. "Spider-Man, eat your heart out. I could do the same to my ankles, but I think this should be enough to get through the upstairs window."

"Wow," said Isabel. "Okay, I've never thought of that one before."

"I can make you a matching set." I shimmied down the wall. "What're you working on, the shadow spells?"

"Shadows for the break-in, and disguise charms for tonight," she said. "Also, silencing spells in case we trip a burglar alarm, cleansing spells in case we leave a mess behind…"

I detached my hands from the wall. "I think that's more than enough. Let me throw another set of these together and we'll leave."

———

In the end, I had to drag Isabel away from her spells so we could break in with plenty of time before the Ley Hunters' meeting. I had to admit I was tempted to stay indoors and experiment, too, but the rain had stopped, and I was more than ready to see what the Ley Hunters were hiding behind that ward.

We started off by turning on the shadow spells Isabel had concocted. Shadow spells were the most basic form of illusion spell, effectively turning our bodies into human-shaped shadows. In dark rooms, we'd be invisible, and under the cloudy sky, all we had to do was avoid stepping in puddles. I cast a glance in the direction of the raiders' shop, and heard a distinctive squeaking noise from inside, suggesting the owner had walked into Isabel's spell. *Ha.*

Pausing outside the Ley Hunters' shop, I reached for the door and felt the buzz of the wards against my hand. The downstairs window remained boarded up, and moving the boards would give the game away.

"The ward doesn't cover the upper floor," Isabel whispered. Her shadowy palms rested on the door's edge as she stood on tip-toe. "It stops just above the door."

"All right," I whispered, twisting the bands on each wrist. "I'll go in first."

"I'll catch you if you fall." Isabel was thinner than I was, but also stronger. I barely had the upper-arm strength to pull myself up onto the windowsill even with my sticking spell working. At least being smaller than average would help me crawl through the window.

"Break-in time," I muttered. I reached the upper level and freed one hand to use an unlocking spell on the window. A moment later, it swung open. It'd be a tight squeeze to get inside, but I could just about manage it. Because of the angle, I had to go headfirst. My head easily went through, and then my knee got stuck. I grimaced, shuffled around, and fell. My hands shot out to break my floor, the sticking charm working its magic, and I shot to the opposite wall and stuck fast.

Isabel's slim shadowy form jumped down, laughing at me.

"Very funny," I muttered. My body was sprawled against the wall like a fly in a trap. Freeing my hands, I landed on the dusty floorboards. Someone had once lived above the shop, but not for a while, judging by the thick layer of dust.

I left the room with Isabel at my heels, pausing at every creak in the floorboards. At the top of the stairs, I checked the spirit realm. No people here… but a weird flicker caught my eye. It came from downstairs.

I'd expected a trap, but the flickering… wasn't human. Or a vampire. Twisting the spells on my wrists, I nodded to Isabel, took the lead and trod carefully and swiftly down the wooden stairs into the room below. The space ahead had clearly once been divided into rooms, but someone had removed the doors, so it was one big wooden-floored space with chairs set out. Like a meeting room. This was our place, all right.

So what's the deal with the ward?

Isabel looked sideways at me, her shadowy form almost invisible. "Anything?"

I shook my head. "If there is, it's well hidden. Hang on."

Checking the spirit realm, I homed in on the flickering. I tiptoed through to the back and paused, looking up at the ceiling. We hadn't covered the entire upper floor, but the spacing didn't add up right. A tingle in my fingertips gave it away.

"There's a room hidden back here," I muttered to Isabel. "Warded."

She inhaled sharply. "I know. Step back."

She reached forwards with a purple device in one hand. "Spell sensor. Only works on minor ones, but—"

A flash went off, and the spell sensor beeped faintly.

"I don't think that's minor."

The flash expanded, and the ceiling collapsed.

I threw up a shield charm above our heads, but the

shattering pieces of plaster and wood fell *through* the spell. I ran for the door, then skidded to a halt. The damned ward—

Wait. I skidded to a halt and spun around. The ceiling above this part of the room remained where it was, despite the intermittent tingling of magic against my palms and the convincing sound of collapsing floorboards. "That's an illusion? Damn. I could have done a better job."

I raised my hands, feeling for the edges of the spell, and switched it off. The collapsing pieces of plaster disappeared, and the space behind me looked as good as new. Threads of magic caressed my hands, and I gave them a sharp tug. The illusory wall fell away, revealing a box-sized room. Empty, dust-covered, and… warded.

"Nice try." I searched for the warding spell and tugged that one undone, too. The air rippled, as though an invisible curtain had parted. But there was nothing behind the curtain except a small metal-looking device the size of my palm, lying on a table.

I checked the spirit realm, and the flickering stirred again. It came from the direction of the metal device.

Weird. The only items that caused an impact in the spirit realm were generally necromancers' candles. I reached for the device, felt no other hostile spells ready to grab me, and picked it up. The smooth surface was cool to touch, while it easily fit into my jacket pocket.

The door rattled. Someone was here.

I ran for the stairs, throwing down a sound-proofing spell to muffle our steps. With Isabel on my heels, I took the stairs two at a time and careened into the room we'd climbed in through.

"I closed the window," Isabel whispered, tugging on my arm. "If we climb out that way, they'll see us."

"Back window?" I suggested, making for one of the other rooms. In the second room we tried, a dusty window overlooked a garden overgrown with weeds. Not ideal, but it'd do.

With a crash, the door opened downstairs. Isabel threw an unlocking spell at the window and urgently beckoned me to go first. I shook my head, but she grabbed my arm insistently.

Not about to stick around and argue, I climbed onto the windowsill and pushed the window as wide as it would possibly go. A child could probably crawl out. As a full-grown adult, even a vertically challenged one, this was going to hurt.

I squeezed my head through the gap, manoeuvring my body at an angle. Reaching down with my sticky-charmed hands, I pulled my legs out, wincing when my knee cracked against the glass. Once my legs were out, I awkwardly climbed sideways to stand on the sill, freeing one hand to help Isabel climb out. She crawled head-first, too, and I shuffled to the drainpipe to make room for her.

Isabel remained upside-down, using her spell-enhanced hands to pull herself down the wall. *Good plan.* I attached my hands to the drainpipe and did the same, but the stickiness began to fade. Then the house trembled, and my Hemlock witch senses shrieked a warning.

Biting my lip to avoid screaming, I fell, pain screaming through my hands, and crashed face-first into a bush.

"Ow." I groaned, blood dripping from my nose. My wrists burned, and when I yanked off the sticking spells, the skin was burned red. "What was that?"

"Anti-magic spell," said Isabel, pulling herself out of another bush. "Ready to run?"

I held a hand to my bleeding nose as we ran for the fence, climbing into the neighbouring garden. Three gardens later and we found an alley leading back to the main road. Hoping I wasn't leaving a trail of blood behind me, I sprinted alongside Isabel back to the witches' place.

Once inside, Isabel made for the spot where she'd put her healing spells, and I applied one to my smarting wrists and bleeding nose. The owner of that shop had some seriously nasty defences.

"I think I dripped blood all over someone's garden." I groaned when the pain vanished from my hands. "This is why I'll never be a professional spy."

"You weren't that bad at breaking in," said Isabel.

"If you forget the bit where I hugged the wall."

She gave me a grin. "Okay, there is that. What did you find?"

I pulled the metal device out of my pocket. "It looks like a spirit sensor, but I don't think it has ectoplasm inside it. I knew it was there because it kind of… glowed, in the spirit realm."

"Definitely not a witch spell," said Isabel leaning to examine the device. "Hmm. Man-made, I'd say for sure. Best get the mages to look at it."

"Are you sure bringing them into this is a good idea?" I asked. "Vance is already suspicious that I'm hiding something."

"It's worth checking out what that thing is for," Isabel said. "Does it have a switch?"

"Apparently not." I checked every angle, but it didn't seem to come with any way to activate it. Or an instruction manual. "All right. Let's go and see what the Mage Lord has to say."

————

Once we'd cleaned up some of the mess on the floor, the two of us walked to the mages' headquarters again. Neither of us had been able to pry the device open to see how it worked, and like it or not, the mages were the ones who had the expertise when it came to most types of magic. I was more inclined to think it was a new necromancy creation—the weird flicker I'd seen around it in the spirit realm proved that—but despite its competency, the guild wasn't what I'd call modern.

Isabel knocked on the door while I examined the glyphs on the walls, their swirling lines ever-flickering. Security wards, anti-faerie wards, several more I couldn't identify. My Hemlock magic itched to unravel them to see how they worked, and I couldn't tell how much of the fascination was mine, and how much was the remains of Evelyn's influence when her emotions trickled through to me. Even though most of the time we'd been separate people, when we'd used magic, I'd felt some of what she did. Or I thought I had.

Vance answered the door. "You're back."

"Yep." I nodded to Isabel. "We didn't get any conclusive answers, and the person who owned the shop showed up so we had to run. But we do have something to show you."

We went into the living room, where Erwin flew at me again. After swatting at my face and hissing at me, he sat on top of Isabel's head, playing with a strand of hair.

"What's his issue with me?" I muttered to her.

"I think it's the piercing," she said.

"Ah." Being faeries, piskies hated and avoided all iron, and I had a thin band attached to my lower lip. I'd been lucky not to damage it when I'd fallen headfirst into the bush.

Ivy waved at us from the table, where she'd moved her stack of papers. "Hey. Word of advice: never save all your paperwork until the weekend before a major council meeting. Also, Vance, your handwriting is *awful*. What does this even say?"

"Let me look." He lifted the paper from her hand. "You need to sign here."

"Again?" Ivy groaned. "Bloody mages… What did you find, anyway?"

I put the device on the table. Vance picked it up carefully, turning it over in his hands.

"Isabel already tested a spell sensor on it," I said. "I think it's necromancy-related, but I can't get it open, and it doesn't seem to have any switches or buttons."

Vance looked up. "This is made of the same material as a spirit sensor."

"Yeah." I'd thought so. Of supernaturals, only witches and necromancers used handmade props. "If I took it with me to the guild, I'd be able to get a definite answer, but the Ley Hunters' meeting's in less than two hours."

"I'll ask for a necromancer's confirmation to see if they've lost any of their props lately," said Vance.

Ivy made a sceptical noise. "Half of them can't even make a candle circle the right way. I don't see them playing at being scientists and inventing a new device. Maybe it's an import from somewhere else. But it's weird that it has no switch or anything."

"It did give off this sort of flicker, when I looked at it in the spirit realm," I admitted.

"Flicker?" asked Ivy. "Maybe you need to be in the spirit realm to use it."

"Perhaps you're right." I reached for the device, and Vance handed it to me.

As I tapped into the spirit realm, grey light filled the room. Ivy, Isabel and Vance shone within, and Ivy's spirit had the same slightly blue-tinted glowing sheen that Ilsa's did. Weird. Her sword glowed, too. *That* was unusual.

As for the device in my hand… nothing.

I shook my head, switching off the spirit sight. "I can't tell anything from here. Might be the wards."

"Maybe it'll work if you check outside," said Isabel, getting it. "Ivy, Jas managed to invent a spell I hadn't come up with yet. Want to see it?"

As she moved in to demonstrate the sticking spell, I left the living room and made my way down the corridor to the front door again. Slipping outside, I checked nobody was on the street before pulling out the device. It wasn't impossible for ghosts to bypass wards, but they tended to avoid heavily protected areas, and the spirit realm was usually quiet in places like this. The poltergeist who'd haunted Lord Bentley had been an exception.

When I tapped into the spirit realm this time, it was to see the faint shapes of ghosts floating towards the distant gates. I looked around for a moment, and I gave myself a mental slap for half-expecting to see the shadowy form of Keir waiting there. A ghost floated close by, watching the faintly glowing device with curious eyes.

"Don't stop," I said to him. "Go on, float to the gates."

The glow brightened, and I stared as it spread wider. The ghost's hand reached out—

And it vanished.

The device continued to pulse, brighter. I shut off my spirit sight, my heartbeat kicking up. The device's glow remained, fainter in the waking world. My skin crawled, and I ran for the manor's partly open gate.

When I reached the living room, flushed and breathless, the others turned to stare at me.

"Jas, what is it?" asked Isabel.

"I think," I said, "it sucks in spiritual energy."

"And does what with it?" asked Isabel.

The light pulsed. "Very good question. It sucked a ghost inside it. Reduced it to nothing."

Ivy's mouth fell open. "Seriously?"

"Seriously. If you see it through the spirit realm, it's brighter. But I didn't even activate it."

"Don't do it in here," Ivy said. "If it stores spiritual energy, unleashing it would be like sending a poltergeist through a china shop."

"Spiritual energy," I repeated. "What if... what if it doesn't just draw on energy from ghosts?"

Like a key point.

Ivy's expression told me the same had occurred to her. "Shit. Okay, that thing definitely isn't a guild creation. Even they have more sense."

"So it's what, a necromancer rogue's?" I asked.

How had it ended up here? Were these Ley Hunters harnessing spiritual energy up and down the country, and for what ends? Necromancy was widely regarded as the weakest and least useful form of magic to everyone except for the highest ranked among us, and more to the point, the spirit energy from the other key point couldn't have gone nowhere. Which meant there must be another, similar device somewhere in Edinburgh. Unless they'd used up the energy killing those people…

"Uh, how do I get it out?" I asked, turning the device over. "Does the energy just… stay in there?"

"I don't know," Ivy said. "Not an expert."

"All right," I said. "How about this? I take it to the meeting and if they catch us there, use it as leverage to get answers from them. It's valuable enough that they probably want it back."

"Wouldn't they be able to sense it, if they're necromancers?" Isabel queried.

"Right, I knew that." I bit my lip, thinking hard. "Fine, I'll leave it here, then, but put it under protection, and for god's sake, don't tell the other mages."

Vance narrowed his eyes at me. "It's a dangerous device that shouldn't be left unattended."

"Then I'll take it to Edinburgh's guild," I said. "They have the expertise. Look, we can talk about this after the meeting. I don't know about you guys, but I'm curious to know what the person who owns this thing has to say."

7

Our plan didn't come without its issues. For one, Vance insisted on arranging backup, so I had to talk him out of sending a dozen mages to tail us. Isabel and I used disguise spells to give us generic human faces that wouldn't stand out in a crowd, but there was another slight problem.

"If the person behind this is a necromancer, won't they sense you when we come in?" Isabel said, as we walked past the witches' headquarters towards the meeting point.

"Only if they're powerful. But yeah, that's a good point." Most people couldn't hop into the spirit realm while talking at the same time, but if the person running the show was one of the exceptions, I might be better off staying out of the meeting. "Are you okay going ahead and I'll show up fashionably late?"

"That works," said Isabel. "Wish there was a walkie-talkie spell so we could eavesdrop from outside."

"If the owner is working with a witch, he might be prepared for that."

I hated sitting out on the action, but when we crossed the road, I knew I'd made the right choice. A steady stream of people entered the Ley Hunters' place, while a tall, broad man stood outside, looking everyone up and down. Isabel, who wore the form of a generic red-haired man, hesitated.

"Go ahead," I whispered. "I can use the spirit realm to eavesdrop if I want to risk it."

I tensed as the security guard turned in my direction, then looked away. Even if he twigged I was a necromancer, it wasn't like he'd know I was the one who'd stolen the device, since I'd left it at the mages' place.

I walked casually down the road until I was a safe distance away, then tapped into the spirit realm. Sure enough, I spotted the unmistakeable bluish glow that marked him as a necromancer.

The others, though… they were human.

I turned off the spirit sight, burying my cold hands in my pockets. The man hadn't directly seen me—I'd been too quick for that—but if he did spot me in the spirit realm, he might think I was just someone from the guild walking home. Luckily, this was a part of town where supernaturals lived pretty close together.

I counted down the seconds until five minutes had passed, then I prepared to make my 'fashionably late' entrance. When the door closed, I began making my way down the street. With the spell on, I looked like a homeless guy, which wasn't all that different from some of the other people going into the meeting. Looked like my suspicion that they'd targeted only non-supernaturals was dead on. But what could they possibly want them for?

I crept up to the building, hoped the necromancer's

attention was on his audience, and halted, out of sight of the boarded-up window. While the buzzing of the wards remained, voices trickled through the gap.

"If I may have your attention," said a nasally male voice that, judging from the authoritative tone, belonged to their leader. "You've come here because you saw one of my adverts, or you were invited here by a trusted member of my cadre. It's an honour to talk to you all."

Cadre? What the bloody hell was this setup? I hoped Isabel was playing her part well, because my hands itched to yank the wards off the door and demand to know why the speaker had lured a bunch of humans into an abandoned shop. What independent necromancer started a cult of humans? I remained still, my spells at the ready.

"Something was stolen from our meeting room today," he said. "Nobody outside of this room knows what the meetings are about, nor would they have any reason to stop us. One of you betrayed our cause."

There was an uneasy pause. Then, whispers rose among the group. Accusations. Was he going to make them turn on one another? Isabel was trapped in there, and would be the only person not in the know.

Time to get the humans out of there and interrogate the bastard alone.

The boarded-up window meant I couldn't toss a spell inside, so I'd have to go with Plan B. Firstly, I threw a fire-cracker spell into the air to draw his attention, then I tapped into the spirit realm, searching for the bright glow of the necromancer's spirit.

He turned in my direction. I gave him a ghostly wave, and in the real world, he yelled, "There's an intruder outside! Kill her."

Ah, crap.

The door flew open, and the humans poured out, some of them armed with knives. Killing them would play into the cult leader's own strategy, but they'd taken him at his word, advancing on me with murder in their eyes..

I threw a knockout spell first, hitting a heavyset man square in the forehead. Isabel moved among the group and several humans dropped their weapons, scratching at their arms as they erupted into a rash. Glad we'd adapted some spells with non-fatal side effects, I deployed three more knockout and shield spells and zeroed in on the leading necromancer. He'd hidden himself at the back, and if not for my spirit sense, I'd have thought he'd fled. Coward. It didn't hurt that I'd stolen his only weapon.

I grinned and threw an illusion charm. Spiders materialised on the ground in a raging swarm, sending several other humans fleeing into the night.

"They're illusions, you fools!" yelled the necromancer. "The supernaturals are weak. We are superior."

"You *are* one, remember?" I yelled, ducking under someone's arm to get to him. I collided with Isabel's illusory form instead.

"Backup's here," she hissed.

"Crap." If the mages were here, then their fearless leader wouldn't stick around.

Sure enough, the necromancer turned tail, pursued by several humans. I sprinted after him, tracking him through the spirit realm. He might be quick on his feet, but I'd had years of practice chasing down ghosts, and I was faster than he was. A spell flew from my hand, striking him in the small of his back. As he stumbled, I slammed into him, tackling him to the pavement.

"Gotcha."

"Who are you?" growled the necromancer, writhing beneath me. "You're not from the guild."

"Neither are you. Tell me who you are and why you lured a bunch of humans into your weird cult meeting. What is the society of Ley Hunters?"

"You won't take me, necromancer."

"Fine, you can tell the authorities, then." I made for the trapping spell on my wrist, but his eyes glowed blue-white and kinetic energy blasted into me. I lost my grip and he wriggled free, making another run for it. I flung a shield spell into him, knocking him to the pavement once more. "Tell me. What did you plan to do with those humans? Kill them?"

"They volunteered themselves for a worthy cause." He fought against my hold, and I snapped on the sticking spell.

"You're not going anywhere."

"You bitch," he growled, fighting my grip, but I'd bound our hands together. Who needed handcuffs when you had magic? Bloody amateur. Really, the necromancers were the people who I ought to hand him to, but necromancers as a rule would rather die than be locked up in jail.

Sure enough, his body went slack and his eyes slid closed. Swearing, I shifted into the spirit realm and grabbed him before he could flee his body. "Nice try. You're staying put."

"What *are* you?" he growled, fighting my grip. He was tenacious even as a ghost, but I held on fast.

"A necromancer with more sense than you have. Tell

me what you planned to do with those humans." He was as good as dead anyway, if he left his body for much longer. "I stole your weapon. You planned to suck their souls into it, didn't you? To what end?"

"To harness the spirit line," he said, his ghostly form fading. "To open the veil…"

His eyes flashed grey-blue. The light lingered, gleaming with intelligence, and a smile curled his lip. Then another blink and the ghostly form of his spirit was gone.

I stared at the spot where he'd vanished. For an instant, someone else had looked at me through his eyes. I was sure it hadn't been him. Yet no sign remained of either of them.

Was that a vampire? I scanned the spirit realm for dark shadowy shapes, but found none. *Weird. Really weird.*

I blinked the grey away, the necromancer's dead weight still stuck to my wrist. Detaching his limp hand from mine, I began dragging him back to the shop. Flickers of light told me the mages had been their usual subtle selves and set the place on fire.

Sure enough, when I dragged the necromancer across the road, I found several cloaked mages standing before the humans who'd been knocked unconscious by my spells. By now, all of them had been handcuffed and several had woken up.

"The bastard died before he told me who he's working for," I told the mages, throwing the necromancer's dead body down.

"Tame the fire," Vance ordered another mage. "There's nobody inside the building."

"Feel free to let it burn down," I said to him. "There were raiders in the shop next door. Earlier today, the owner tried to proposition Isabel and me, so we turned him into a mouse."

"He did *what?*" said Ivy, raising her sword. "All right, I'm going after the stragglers. Vance, feel free to knock some heads together."

"Hang on," I said. "Not all of them might have known what they were getting into. The necromancer lured them in. It sounded like he was trying to teach them how to fight supernaturals off." That would definitely attract a crowd, especially people who didn't want to train as mercenaries but who also wanted to learn to defend themselves. Pity all he'd wanted to do was sacrifice their souls.

Harness the spirit lines? What did that even mean? The lines were like currents of energy, invisible to most people. As for what he'd said about opening the veil? Bringing back a swarm of ghosts or zombies didn't require human sacrifice. Not in my experience, anyway.

"Is this the person responsible?" Vance enquired, eyeing the dead necromancer at my feet.

"Yeah," I said. "He killed himself by hopping over the veil. I should have bound him first, but there was no time."

"Help!" yelled one of the humans, a blond male no older than eighteen. "Don't set me on fire!"

"Tell me who you are," Vance commanded.

"I'm nobody."

"You were caught meeting with a criminal, then tried to kill two people," said the Mage Lord. The air stirred, a gust of wind kicking up and raising the hairs on my arms. "Explain."

The kid raised his cuffed hands to his face and sobbed. "They said… they said we had to expect to defend him at any costs. That people wanted him dead."

"And you didn't think he was breaking the law?" I asked. "He was going to sacrifice all of you."

"No, he was teaching us to kill supernaturals."

I tried to get them off easy. I left Vance to deal with the humans and walked to the blazing house. A tall lanky mage with coppery hair tended the flames, which leapt closer to the raider's shop by the second, and winked at me when he saw me watching.

"Drake," I said, approaching him. "Don't burn that place down. It's full of stolen property."

"And rats," Ivy put in, holding a struggling rodent by the tail.

"Technically, it's a mouse," said Isabel, who looked very pleased with herself.

Ivy gave the rodent a shake, and it squeaked with terror. "Looks like a rat to me. That's what he gets for being a creep. Anyone want to volunteer to play pest control?"

"Can I burn him?" asked Drake.

Flames leapt from his hand and singed the creature's tail, and it yelped.

"Drake, cut it out," said a female mage wearing a long, hooded cloak. "Criminal or not, he's still human."

"Throw him into the sewer, see how he likes that," I said. "What's Vance going to do with those humans?"

"Scare the living shit out of them, probably," said Drake, grinning at me. He had a long, thin scar running down the side of his face that hadn't been there the last time I'd seen him.

Sure enough, Vance's voice rose above the crackling flames burning down the shop. "You are all extremely lucky not to have caused any damage to anyone," he said. "As it is, if you're ever offered an 'opportunity' like that again, run away or you'll find yourself giving up more than your lives."

That's that, then. At least I wouldn't have to fill out a stack of paperwork like I would if this was an official guild mission. It was about time I headed home.

As I shifted my weight, a hand rested on my arm. "Gotcha," said Drake. "Nice try, but you're not sneaking off without saying hi. Mage politics aren't my thing either."

"I thought you were Vance's second-in-command now."

"More like a glorified bodyguard," said the fire mage. "Hey, Wanda, Jas is sneaking off."

The female mage returned to his side, her hood falling back to reveal thick dark hair framing a heart-shaped face. Wanda was Lady Harper's granddaughter—half witch, half mage, and the closest to a best friend I'd had living with the mages, before her grandmother had packed her off to a fancy boarding school a year before I'd left. She was the only person in existence Lady Harper had actually been nice to, being her only surviving grandchild, and it'd taken her long enough to develop her mage powers that she'd acquired a group of bodyguards. Drake being one of them.

"Jas!" Wanda hugged me. "I heard you were here. My grandmother had me running errands all day."

"She's the person I'm trying to avoid." So much for making a quick getaway. "Not that I'm trying to run out on you guys, but you might have noticed there's an epidemic of amateur necromancers creating cults to sacrifice humans. My boss at Edinburgh's necromancer guild sent me here to investigate, and I have to get back."

"Unless you've learned to teleport like Vance, you're not going back tonight," said Drake. "I can create another diversion if it's Lady Harper you're worried about. She was pulling spiders out of her hair for days after you left last time."

"You conjured *actual* spiders?" I shook my head at him. When I'd fled to Edinburgh seven years ago, I'd needed a reliable way to distract Lady Harper, so I'd begged Drake to create a convincing diversion to keep her busy long enough for me to make it to the coach station.

Drake grinned. "It was a spider-attracting spell. Worked like a charm."

Wanda snorted. "Yeah, she was pissed off at you for about two years. I figured that was why you never came home."

Guilt twisted into a knot in my chest. "I wanted to," I admitted. "But you know Lady Harper and I don't get along. The only magic I had was the spirit sight and it wasn't like I could have made a career out of it here."

"She's seriously pissed off *now*," said Drake. "Not that it's anything new. I swear she gets worse with age."

He wasn't wrong. Lady Harper had reduced me to tears on more than one occasion when she hadn't been able to force some Hemlock magic out of me as a teenager. Now I'd unlocked that magic, outright turned my back on my calling and insulted her to boot? She'd be mad at me for the rest of her life.

"She's spending way too much time in that forest," added Wanda.

Oh… bugger. "She is?"

Wanda shrugged. "Yeah, you know she never tells me anything. What made her decide to start mentoring you again?"

"I learned how to use my witch magic about ten years too late," I said, glancing at the mages. "She decided it was her duty to muscle in. Er, I really do have to get home, and I have my own transport."

"Is it to do with your witch magic?" Drake asked. "So you're a witch *and* a necromancer now? Jealous."

"Isn't being a human fire hazard enough?" I waved Isabel over, and she made her way through the crowd.

"They caught them all," she said. "Ivy threw the mouse into the sewer, too."

"I'm almost certain the person behind the attack is up in Edinburgh," I said quietly. "Not in the city, anyway."

Isabel's eyes rounded with understanding. "I'll ask Vance to fetch the you-know-what. But you should be careful near half-blood territory at this time of night."

"Did she say half-blood territory?" asked Wanda, as Isabel turned away to approach Vance. "Oh—you're going into the forest?"

I nodded. "Don't worry, my magic can get me home from there. Just… don't spread it around."

"The Hemlocks don't like tourists?" Drake asked. "Don't look so shocked. I know you're a Hemlock witch. Lady Harper—"

"Told everyone except me," I finished, rolling my eyes.

"You weren't here last year," said Wanda. "There was a huge kerfuffle in the forest and word leaked out that they were still alive. My grandmother didn't even tell *me* she worked for the Hemlocks until then."

Isabel walked up behind me and pressed the spirit device into my hand. "The council doesn't have to know. That goes for you, too, Drake."

"Oh, is that the spirit thingymajig?" he asked. "Can I push the button?"

"No, you may *not* push the button. There isn't one, besides." I stuck it into my pocket. "I'm heading off, but I won't disappear for seven years this time. Promise."

"We'll bodyguard you," said Drake. "The Mage Lord can handle the humans. Seriously, Jas, I don't know who's chasing you, but I'm not letting you go out alone."

"Are you sure?"

Fire sprang to his hand. "The half-faeries' territory is covered in snow at the moment. Trust me, it'll be fine."

"All right," I said. "Thanks."

"And me," Wanda put in. "Don't look at me like that, Drake. If it's safe for you, it's safe for me."

"Vance would have my head if I let a faerie take a bite out of you," Drake said, but he let Wanda follow us across the road. Out of all the mages, I'd missed Wanda and Drake the most. Wanda and I had bonded over our mutual lack of magical talent as teenagers. The witch side of her family had all died in the invasion and she hadn't inherited any of the gift, but the instant she'd managed to use her frost mage skill, Lady Harper had yanked her into accelerated training and refused to let us see one another most of the time. Losing my closest friend had been the catalyst to my eventual decision to leave home.

"You guys probably won't be allowed into the actual

forest," I told them. "The Hemlocks don't like unexpected visitors."

"We're talking about the creepy tree people, right?" asked Drake, dropping his voice as we walked. "I've never met them, but we know about Fionn and the—"

"Keep it down," Wanda hissed.

"Who's Fionn?" I asked. The name rang a bell, and I vaguely remembered hearing it at the council meeting a few months ago.

"A faerie who tried to cause a second invasion by attacking the forest," Drake answered. "Ivy killed him."

This Fionn must be the reason they'd broken their secrecy. "It was nice of Lady Harper to tell me that. Any other enemies I should know about?"

Wanda's brow furrowed. "No... I don't *think* so. My grandmother didn't actually tell me what she spends her time in the forest doing."

"She doesn't tell me most things, and I'm supposed to be the Hemlocks' heir," I said, quickening my pace. "Hence why we're not speaking. I'm sorry I never got in touch. I lost my phone in the move and I wanted a fresh start."

"Yeah, she did say you were the worst apprentice she'd had," said Drake.

Wanda elbowed him in the ribs. "Drake."

I shrugged. "It's true. The guild's much more stable." And with that, I dived into the subject of my necromancer training. At least I didn't have to lie, since I'd had seven blissful drama-free years before the Hemlocks had bull-dozed through my life and wrecked everything. Even Drake and Wanda would be freaked out if they found out about my extra soul.

We parted ways at the forest's edge. The eerie sounds

of the half-faeries' music pursued me into the dark, and when a figure appeared on the path ahead, I instinctively dug in my pocket for a weapon—the spirit device.

And I found myself face to face with someone far more terrifying than soul-sucking monsters in the darkness: Lady Harper.

8

"Going somewhere, Jas?" Lady Harper asked, her voice deceptively calm.

"I'd rather not do this now," I said, tensing as she reached out a hand.

"Give that here."

I gripped the spirit device tight. "This is the property of the necromancers' guild now, since I found and confiscated it."

The air stirred with the merest hint of her mage power. The trees trembled in response, and magic sparked to my hands.

"The forest is set against you," I warned. "I still don't know my power's limits, but I wouldn't want to be on the receiving end. Get out of my way."

"I'm not your enemy, Jas."

"If Evelyn Hemlock gets out of my trap, anyone is a potential enemy. And I reckon she'll go after my allies first, especially the people responsible for her being bound to me. Let me take this to the guild and you can air your grievances with my decisions later."

"I told you, I'm not your enemy." She leaned on her stick with one hand, the other resting against a tree. "I have spent the last few weeks trying to work out how to correct your little problem."

"What, you mean Evelyn being a power-hungry maniac? Can't work out where she might have learned that."

"Not here," she said sharply. "You may be linked to the Hemlocks by blood, but they won't hesitate to turn on you if you refuse to give them what they want."

"They can't hurt me." My voice sounded quiet, small. "You know that. Also, you do realise they're listening to every word you say, right? Why corner me here?"

"Because it's the only place I can talk to you without being overheard," she said. "We're being watched, Jas, by more than the witches."

"That's funny. I thought it was you who sent witches to spy on me for seven years without telling me."

This was the woman who'd personally killed two Sidhe, for god's sake. What did she possibly have to fear from the Hemlocks? She'd worked for them, on a voluntary basis as far as I knew. She'd been complicit in their quest to force me into the role of heir. Now she was implying I needed to avoid them?

"I spent years out of contact with the coven, and it's changed much in my absence, Jas," she said.

"Yeah, same here. Unless you're jealous I got the magic and you didn't?"

"Certainly not," she said, with a sniff. "My mage abilities are more than sufficient. Don't be ridiculous."

"You can't say you aren't jealous without admitting that it was wrong for them to make a creepy spirit take up real estate in my body, huh?" I wasn't sure she *was* jealous, but I'd driven her attention away from the spirit device, which was the plan. "Keep telling yourself you're in the right, then."

I walked past, pointedly ignoring her, and the forest's path changed, masking the former Mage Lord from sight.

"That is a dangerous power you hold in your hands," rumbled Cordelia Hemlock's voice.

"Let me guess, you know the person who made it," I said, continuing to walk. "It's another of our distant relations, who just happens to be working on a soul-sucking device to yank depraved witch spirits out of my—" I tripped headfirst over a root that definitely hadn't been there before, and swore. "That was underhanded."

The device, though... *could* it take in the spirit? I doubted it. Evelyn had required a full-sized necromancer circle with enhancements to contain, and even then she'd probably have broken free eventually. But damn, the possibilities. I wished I was as creative as Isabel and could pull the device apart to see how it worked, but witch spells were our area, not dubious spirit devices.

"That thing is made by humans," said Cordelia, as I climbed to my feet. "That makes it dangerous."

"Really." I kept walking. "Are you admitting you know what it is?"

"No," she growled. "I do not know what it is, and that's precisely why you shouldn't use it. Many have tried to harness the spirit lines' magic. Few have succeeded, and most have perished in the process."

"Luckily, I'm planning to hand it over to the authorities," I said. I didn't add, *and I think there's a vampire behind this.*

Silence answered, which I took as agreement. I hurried on through the darkness, towards home.

————

It was midnight by the time I'd finished updating Lloyd on the events of the past day. I'd put my cloak back on before sneaking back into the guild so nobody would question how quickly I'd returned from my trip, but there weren't many people hanging around at this time.

Lloyd sat cross-legged on his bed, gaping at me. "And to think I spent today watching Mega Shark Zombie Part Two for the fifth time and missed all that. Now I'm questioning my life choices."

"Only now?"

He swatted me with a hand. "Seriously, Jas. How do you travel home to visit family and still end up in trouble?"

"That was kind of the point. It was an investigation, to see if the people who messed with the spirit line weirdness here were operating in England, too." I stifled a yawn, the dimmed light in Lloyd's perpetually dark room making me sleepy. Full-length posters adorned the walls, which occasionally fell onto our heads when we held movie nights in here, while his TV and DVD collection occupied the entire desk.

"And they are?" he asked.

"Possibly. But the person I saw must have been a vampire." His creepy smile and grey-blue eyes couldn't be anything else, even if vampires usually looked like shadows. Nobody else could influence people over such a long distance.

Lloyd shifted position. "I thought Lady Montgomery had them all under watch."

"That's what I thought, too." I rubbed my eyes wearily. My return through the woods had cost me a few hours and I hadn't eaten since noon, but I didn't have much of an appetite. Tomorrow was free, so I could sneak off to the vampires' territory if I wanted to, if I avoided running into the boss. "Suppose it's worth asking their king and hoping nobody has set up an ambush this time."

Generally, if someone indicated they didn't want to speak to me again, I left them alone, but I'd been glad to have Keir with me when rogues had attacked the last time we'd been to see the vampires' leader. There was at least one vampire involved, aside from the one Ilsa and I had banished. I was certain of it.

"So what's the thing you confiscated?" he asked.

I pulled the metal device out of my pocket, putting it between us on the bed. "It absorbs spiritual energy—including ghosts. I think the people behind this must be using these devices to harness the energy they pull out of their sacrifices—and out of the key points, too, I'd guess. God knows why."

Lloyd kept a sensible distance from the gleaming piece of metal, not reaching out to touch it. "Yeah, that doesn't sound like a sane, normal-person hobby. So the guy who you took it from died?"

"Not before I saw a vampire possess him," I said. "I'm sure that's what he was, but it was over too fast to be certain. Looks like I'm going to have to visit the king again to see if he's lost any rogues recently."

Lloyd fidgeted. "Are you gonna hand that over to the boss?"

"When I make my dramatic return tomorrow," I answered. "Since I'm supposed to be on holiday. I don't understand why she's suddenly so concerned about me."

"You're her valued assistant and you're cracking up. When was the last time you slept through the night?"

"Before someone possessed and took over my body," I said. "And I'm not cracking up, I've got it under control. Anyway, I'll go and see the boss when I'm sure she won't get suspicious. Appearing to teleport across the country would be a ridiculous way to blow my cover."

The slightest crack in my story might expose the lies I'd told. And then? Evelyn Hemlock might get her way after all.

———

The following morning, I walked through the cobbled streets to the vampire king's house, armed with every weapon Lloyd and I could sneak out of the guild's storeroom. The guild had stationed lookouts throughout the vampires' territory and there were more patrols than usual, so avoiding them was a task and a half in itself.

"Are you sure it's this way?" asked Lloyd, after we'd walked in circles for fifteen minutes. "You didn't get the street name?"

I was so sure I remembered the route. "It's the road with one working streetlamp on." This one didn't have any. Stone buildings washed out from the rain sat under a sky the colour of damp cardboard, bathed in so much fog that the spirit realm didn't look all that different. The vampires would be in their element.

"That'd work if the lights were on during the day," said Lloyd. "Which they aren't."

"You're being extra annoying today," I said to him.

"You're just snippy. Did you even sleep last night?"

"A bit." I'd been reliving Evelyn's possession every night since she'd taken over my body, and despite my exhaustion from the day before, sleep refused to claim me until dawn. And then I'd had to leave the spirit device locked in my room under a warding spell, which was preferable to carrying it on me. "I need a lamp to see through this bloody fog. I hope the vampires are in a better mood than I am."

"Are there any nearby?"

I tapped into the spirit realm. I'd been certain we were close, but if we were, I should at least be able to sense a few vampires beneath my feet. Even if the vampires' king was alone, I'd detect him. But not a single vampire pinged on my radar.

Weird. Seriously weird.

I halted, and the intermittent flickering of a lamp drew my eye. "Hey, you were wrong," I said. "This is the one."

"Creepy," he commented, eying the flickering lamp. "They can sense us, right? Maybe this was a bad idea."

"I should be able to sense *them.*" I scanned the tall, thin houses through my spirit sight. "Maybe he moved house."

"Hmm. Which house?"

I found the right one, and using my spirit sight, I scanned beneath the street level again. The guy lived in the basement, but I didn't pick up on anyone in the house —vampire or human.

Oh, boy.

Fists clenched, I walked to the stone steps leading to the basement door. Lloyd hovered over my shoulder. "Uh. Aren't you breaking and entering?"

"I can say it's guild business." I rapped my knuckles on the door, and it swung inwards. "Oh, damn. I think he's done a runner."

"So he does live in a tunnel," said Lloyd. From behind us, the weak daylight seeped into the hall, illuminating murky walls painted the colour of earth and revealing unstable foundations that hadn't been obvious while walking in here with Keir at night time. It was lucky that digging the tunnels hadn't caused the whole house to collapse. Had every vampire fled the place all at once? The tunnels extended far beyond a single house. They must cover the entire street. I'd bet they all belonged to vampires, too, so they could sneak in and out of each other's houses without ever seeing daylight. For vampires who didn't drink blood, they did seem to make a careful effort to match all the stereotypes.

"Right." I pulled a candle out of my pocket. "Nobody living in here. That means…"

"Dead. Got it." He yanked a knife from his pocket. "I swear you owe me hazard pay for coming with you on your wild schemes."

"You chose to be my Second."

"Er, Second?"

Where had that come from? "Witch thing. It means you'd get my powers if I died, if you were a witch and I was an actual coven leader."

"Wow, really?"

"Didn't Isabel tell you?" I walked further into the hall,

shining my candle's light onto the walls. "It's not the same for me, anyway. Mine's the only coven in existence that passes on the power by bloodline and not a democratic vote. Makes sense that they ended up with a lunatic like Evelyn as their heir, really."

"Still badass," he said.

"It's overrated." I paused as we reached the main room, or cave. "I think he ran into the tunnels."

"Jas!" He grabbed my arm. "Did you hear that?"

I dropped the spirit sight and inched towards the tunnel entrance. A faint dripping sounded from ahead. I inched forwards, my gorge rising at the faint coppery smell.

My candle's light found a dead body sprawled on the tunnel floor, throat torn out in a spray of blood. "Ugh. I knew it."

I moved closer. The vampire's wounds were thick, ragged, so deep that he wouldn't even be able to stand if someone reanimated him. Behind, more thick blood splattered the tunnel walls and floor, and more bodies lay sprawled, shredded to ruins.

"Uh." Lloyd pressed a hand to his mouth. "I take it that's your runaway vampire king?"

I gave a brief scan of the bodies. "Yes. That's not good."

"No shit,' said Lloyd. "I'd say the odds aren't looking good for the people living upstairs, either."

"No... I would have thought at least one of them would have left a trace behind." Their deaths had been quick and brutal. I turned away, tapping into the spirit realm. Ghosts floated on either side of me, not speaking, approaching the gates. The vampires who'd died would have had control over dozens of zombies collectively, and yet… nothing.

Lloyd grabbed my arm as a faint sound came from upstairs. Maybe footsteps.

"Not undead," I muttered. "Too coordinated. Maybe a vampire's vessel, but I didn't sense one."

"That's not very helpful, Jas."

"I'm doing my best." My spirit sight wasn't as good without Evelyn amplifying it, and my head felt weirdly fogged. Wait a second. "I think we're on the wonky spirit line. And we never did find out where that energy went."

"What?" said Lloyd. "Crap, you think they have a magical device thingy, too?"

"Maybe." I pulled out my phone. "I can't even report the deaths to the guild and ask them to help catch who did this. It's out of our area." But whoever—or whatever—had killed the vampires was not human.

"The mercenaries are usually good at hunting down monsters," said Lloyd, though he sounded uncertain. "I don't know. This guy was their leader, right? Isn't there, uh—a backup king, or heir?"

"Nope. They don't even have a council. They're mostly independent and I'm pretty sure half of them didn't give a shit about the king. Obviously, the guild needs to know, but I don't want to step outside the lines on this one."

More footsteps. My heart dropped. "Looks like back-up's arrived."

I sprinted into the main tunnel and ran smack into someone solid, and human. *Now* my spirit sight decided to inform me he was a vampire.

Keir.

9

"Keir?" I said in disbelief. "How'd you get in here? Did *you* kill him?"

"You think so little of me?" He stepped backwards, the candle light flickering on his sharp-edged features. "The monsters that did this are still in the tunnels."

"Let me guess. Furies." Nothing else could cause wounds that savage. Which meant someone else was messing around with blood magic.

Keir stepped in the direction of the tunnel. His black jacket was caked in dirt, and so was one side of his face, like he'd fallen headfirst into a tunnel. Maybe he'd spent the last three weeks chasing monsters underground, but a call would have been nice.

"You, Lloyd," Keir said. "Stay back. You can't fight these."

"That's lovely," he said. "Maybe I can outdo you, vampire. Jas loaned me some spells."

"Necromancy," said Keir, "doesn't work on furies."

"Iron does, but they're fast," I told Lloyd. "Also, don't look directly into their eyes, otherwise you're dead. We don't want to fight them in a confined space—"

Rustling and the sound of wingbeats came from ahead. "We can't always have what we want, Jas," said Keir.

What is that supposed to mean?

A flurry of wings echoed off the tunnel walls, and a screaming beast entered the cave. Seven feet long and covered in black and red feathers, it looked like cross between a giant monstrous bird and a pterodactyl. Its long, curved talons were slick with blood. Vampire blood.

"Hello, ugly," I said, flinging a spell into the beast's eyes. The stickiness spell covered its entire face in gluey black tar. "That's one way to avoid looking at its eyes."

Keir shot me a half-bewildered, half-impressed look. "That's new."

"Yes, it is." I ran to stab the flailing beast, but Keir got there first. With a practised swipe, he lodged the blade between its scales, cutting downwards. Furies' skin was harder than concrete even without the scales, but they did have weak spots. I ducked under its flailing talons and stabbed the underside of its wing, causing it to unleash an agonised squawk.

Lloyd shouted a warning as more wingbeats sounded. The fury had brought a friend over from whatever hellish dimension it'd come from. Yanking my knife free, I left Keir to take care of this one and ran to help.

Lloyd threw a spell at the oncoming winged monster, which exploded in a shower of sparks. The fury flew back, barely fazed. My spells might be volatile, but furies were covered in so much armour that it was impossible to reach their organs without going through several layers of scaled skin first.

Detaching itself from the wall, the fury turned its simmering, pitch-dark gaze in our direction.

"Bloody hell," Lloyd yelped. "Is that what you meant by 'don't look it in the eyes'? I can't move."

"Stay down!" As the beast flew at us, I grabbed Lloyd and pulled him out of reach of its talons, swiping wildly. The knife bounced off its rocky skin, and Lloyd yelped, diving for cover.

"Get me instead, you big scaly dickhead," I yelled, waving my knife.

The fury screeched, a bone-chilling noise that shook up my senses, and Evelyn's magic hummed in my skin, sudden and intense. *All right, then.* I didn't have to hold back this time.

My hands glowed white, and a whipcord of magic shot from my palms, yanking the fury away from Lloyd. Another swipe severed its head from its shoulders. This time, the weapon didn't vanish after I used it but remained in my hands, shimmering with iridescent light. Glyphs swirled up and down its length, glimmering faintly green-white. *Whoa. That wasn't there before.*

A snarling noise drew my attention to Keir and his own attacker. I readied the whip, but Keir had already lunged in for the killing blow. The fury's death rattle rang through the tunnel, fading to silence.

I breathed out. "That was close." I turned to Keir. "Tell me you saw where they came from?"

Someone—a witch—must have used the same ritual as before. Maybe word had spread before Leila Hemlock had died.

"I imagine they came from the same hellhole as usual." Keir shook droplets of blood from his knife, but aside from a few scrapes and scratches, he looked unhurt. "They tore a hole through the wall of my apartment. Someone sent them to hunt vampires."

My mouth went dry. "What? Who would do that?"

The same someone who thought they could switch off the spirit lines using a handmade weapon?

Lloyd release a shaky breath. "Jesus. How many?"

"I killed three, not counting this one." Keir shook his head. "It's an epidemic. I couldn't find the site of the summoning either."

"What, you don't think there's another Hemlock running around?" Lloyd said.

"Just what we need." I wiped my bloody knife on my sleeve. "Any more of those bastards? Which direction did they come from?"

"I've been up and down this street and all the neighbouring tunnels and these are the last of them," said Keir. "The furies must have all come out of the same place, but they can't be tracked."

"But—Leila's dead," I said. And Evelyn was gone. Yet the cold feeling persisted, and the fuzziness in the spirit realm bothered me more than the pile of dead vampires in the tunnel.

"Great," Lloyd said. "I take it back about missing out on the fun. I vote we leave the vamps to sort out their feud alone, Jas, while we deal with the spirit line. That's our business, not… this."

"We're *on* a spirit line," I pointed out. "I don't know, it feels like it's all linked."

"What's that about the spirit line?" asked Keir.

I glanced at Lloyd. "We should probably get out of here first. But who are we supposed to report the bodies to? The vampires have families, right? They should know."

"I'll take care of it," Keir said. "There's a procedure. Vampire bodies make potent hosts, and the guild leaves us to handle their deaths ourselves."

"Even if your leader is brutally murdered by a beast from another dimension?" I asked. "Have you even spoken to the king recently?"

One of the dead vampires abruptly sat up. Its flesh hung off in in tatters, and I tasted bile in the back of my throat.

Keir sighed. "John, I told you not to follow me."

The undead's mouth moved, speaking the words, "You will pay for what you did."

"I didn't kill him, you fuckwit," Keir responded.

Footsteps came from behind us, and several more undead ran into the tunnel. Keir made an exasperated noise and threw a knife at one of them, spearing it through the eyeball. "John, this is your last warning."

"You murdering bastard," said the zombie, the knife still sticking out of its glowing eyeball. "You will pay for that."

"Not again." Keir slipped another knife into his hand.

The undead charged. I threw a blasting spell, which took a zombie's head off, and set another ablaze using one of the warmth spells that'd accidentally turned into an inferno. Beside me, Keir grappled with another zombie, flinging him into the wall of flames I'd created.

He wasn't using his vampire power. Why? Usually he finished the fight in seconds by ripping out the soul of the person possessing the vessels. Maybe he didn't want to kill the person attacking him, but he seemed unusually cautious.

I tapped into the spirit realm, searching for the fading threads connecting the vampire to its vessels. "Hey, dickhead!" I yelled at the retreating shadowy figure. "Keir didn't kill the vampire king."

Blue light blasted back at me, and I ducked as kinetic energy shot over my head. "Oh, you want to fight, do you?" I grabbed the threads of light, tugging the vampire towards me.

"Hemlock bitch," he growled.

He wrenched loose from my hold, and Keir's shadowy form appeared at my shoulder. "I wouldn't pick a fight with him," he said.

I blinked back into my body. "He knows my coven," I retaliated. "That generally means he wants to kill me."

"Not necessarily," said Keir. "You've acquired something of a reputation. The vampires who worked with Leila Hemlock spread word of your name before their deaths."

"Yeah, thanks for just standing there while she nearly died, dickface," Lloyd put in.

"Lloyd," I said warningly, though he had a point.

"I know where he is," Keir said. "He's not half the vampire I am, and while he might think I killed our king, he'll come to his senses when I don't claim the position."

"Can you just do that?" I said dubiously. "I mean, I know there's not a literal crown involved. Not even a metaphorical one."

"Any of us can decide we're the new leading vampire if there's an opening," he said. "Whether we get to *keep* the position or not depends on how many followers we've managed to gather."

"And the size of your zombie armies."

"Yes." He raised his hands, which glowed with white light. "I'd strongly advise you to duck."

Kinetic energy blasted through the tunnels, turning to fire, which engulfed the furies and undead all in one.

"What was that for?" I looked down at the blood-stained tunnel floor. "You just burned away all the evidence."

"Exactly," Keir said. "Let's get out of here. I need to search the house, but I suspect I won't find anyone alive in there."

"There were humans living upstairs." Who could have set the furies on the vampires, and why?

"I'm aware of that," said Keir through clenched teeth. He walked a little unsteadily, and though he had no visible injuries, I recognised the signs of a vampire on the brink of exhaustion.

"Hey," I said as we climbed the stone steps. "Why not drain that other vampire?"

"I didn't need to."

"You look like you need it." His form was a little faded in the spirit realm, while in this one, he was in dire need of a haircut and shave.

"I'll feed later." He shrugged. "It's good to see you again, Jas."

"You two can catch up later," said Lloyd, opening the door before I could figure out how in hell to respond to that. "Want to check out the house?"

Keir moved behind me. "You should, considering there's a guild patrol two streets down, coming this way."

"Oh, *shit.* The house has a back exit, right?" I climbed the stone steps to the surface and jumped to the doorstep, ignoring Lloyd's protests. The fire in the tunnels would have destroyed all the evidence, and if we got waylaid by the patrol, we'd have to give eyewitness accounts. Considering furies were covered by the same geas as the Hemlock Coven and I'd never been able to tell anyone about them, it'd be impossible for me to adequately explain what I was doing here when I was meant to be miles away. Especially with no bodies left behind.

I used an unlocking charm to let us into the house rather than forcing the door, and Keir closed it behind us once we were inside.

"Why are you avoiding the guild?" asked Keir.

"Long story." I ran through the hall into a kitchen. The scent of rot pervaded, but there was no time to check for bodies. The guild patrol would find them soon enough.

"They won't be able to take action," Keir said, as though he'd guessed my line of thought. "It's out of their area. If the person who summoned the furies wanted to destabilise the vampires' society, they didn't need to go to that much trouble."

"No, you're not exactly a united front," I said. "Who do you think will be the next king?"

"Whoever gets there first."

I used another unlocking spell on the back door, which sprang open onto an overgrown yard. The ongoing theme of the weekend was unintentional trespassing, apparently. The back garden was overgrown with weeds, suggesting the person who'd lived in the house hadn't been a keen gardener. With one last look back at the house, I broke into a run towards the fence.

"At this rate, we'll get caught by the police instead of the guild," Lloyd said from behind me.

"The owners of these houses were all vampires, and dead." Keir climbed up the fence ahead of me. "The guild will likely send in an investigation, but as I said, the evidence is gone, and they don't want to get any more involved with us than they already are. The enemy is picking us off one at a time."

"So talk to the guild." I vaulted the fence, landing beside him in the neighbouring garden.

Keir pushed his mud-streaked brown hair from his eyes. "I'd rather not."

In the daylight, he looked even worse than he had in the tunnel. I'd thought I had the sleepless look down, but dark smudges underscored his blue-grey eyes and his cheekbones were more prominent than the last time I'd seen him.

If people had been trying to kill him, why hadn't he called me? Was it vampire pride at work, or was there something else going on?

"We can get out that way," said Lloyd, pulling his lanky form over the fence and pointing across the garden. "No necromancers?"

I checked the spirit realm, but it remained fuzzy. "I can't see any."

Keir took the lead, sprinting for the next fence and leaping over like he broke into people's gardens every day. He waited expectantly as I jumped down to join him. "Aren't you going to tell me why you wanted to speak to the king?"

"You're assuming that's why we were there?" said Lloyd.

"You don't have a death wish," he answered.

"And I do?" After his long absence, he didn't deserve my trust, yet someone had set a swarm of furies on him and his fellow vampires. What if my coven *had* been involved?

Keir listened in silence as I ran through an abbreviated version of the weekend's misadventures, while we crossed more gardens until we reached an alley leading out onto the street.

"You should show me that device," he said. "I might be able to help you figure out how it works so you can shut it down."

"It's at the guild," I said. "Since it's a product of illegal necromancy, it's their property. If you cooperate with the guild, though, they might let you help. Unless it's them you're avoiding, not me."

"I'm not avoiding you."

Lloyd made a sceptical noise, while I said, "Not at this precise moment, you aren't."

He didn't dignify that with a response, and we exited the alley onto the street. No patrols in sight. Mission accomplished. Except for the fact that the only vampire I was on speaking terms with was about as reliable as the sun in the Highlands.

"I need to go back to my apartment," said Keir. "Before someone breaks in through the hole in the wall and steals my things."

"Aren't you being followed by furies?" I asked. "Look, are you positive you don't know any vampires who are in the business of conning humans?"

"Not that I'm aware of," he said. "I'll talk to you later, Jas. I'll message you."

I'd heard *that* before. "Sure, whatever." I turned to Lloyd as the vampire walked away, not even bothering to clean the dirt and blood off his face beforehand. "The king's dead, and our contacts are a bust. What are we supposed to do now?"

"I think the real question is, what's *his* problem?" Lloyd jerked his head in the direction of Keir's retreating back.

"I wish I knew." It wasn't like we'd parted on bad terms, unless he hadn't enjoyed kissing me on the guild's porch as much as it'd seemed. Whatever his problem was, it was entirely on his end, not mine.

Except for the fact that someone had had the vampires' leader brutally murdered at the claws of a fury. Even if the king had been a temporary title and didn't necessarily command respect, who in the world would summon a monster like that on purpose? Another vampire? Their society consisted mostly of loners who didn't care to draw attention, and I'd thought all the ones who'd known the fury-summoning ritual had met unfortunate ends. Unless they'd taken up a new hobby running a local cult to sacrifice helpless humans.

Just for once, I'd like my wild theories to be wrong.

I released a sigh. "Never mind him. I'm done. Want to go grab a drink?"

10

The rain began in earnest by the time we'd left the vampires' district behind, and we ran for the nearest pub. The space inside was packed with people sheltering from the rain, and the only free table was by the door. I ran a brief check of the spirit realm to make sure there were no vampires inside, then made my way over to the bar.

"Is now an acceptable time to start day-drinking?" I asked Lloyd.

"Morgan seems to think it is," Lloyd remarked, pointing at a dark-haired figure at the table I'd thought was empty.

"Ah, never mind." I backed up. "We're supposed to be *avoiding* the guild."

"He's way too far gone," said Lloyd. "Come on, we nearly died in a tunnel. Live while you can."

"Spoken like a true necromancer." Who knew, maybe Morgan had sensed the vampire who'd killed the king. I

121

didn't have much cash, so I opted for a glass of 'witch's brew', the cheapest option on the drinks menu.

Lloyd shook his head at me. "That tastes like feet, Jas."

"Sorry I'm not as sophisticated as you are."

"I have no idea what you're talking about." He lifted his glass of 'elven lager' and clinked it against mine. "To surviving near-death experiences."

"To staying on the right side of the veil." I tipped back my glass. Ugh, maybe he had a point about the taste. With any luck, by evening I'd be drunk enough not to care.

We walked over to the free table, where Morgan was asleep with one head resting on his hand. Lloyd poked him in the shoulder. "Training getting to you again?"

The psychic blinked at us. "What're you doing here?"

"You know you're sleeping on a table, don't you? Have you seen any vampires?" asked Lloyd.

"No. What do you want a vampire for?"

"We're tracking a criminal," said Lloyd, and I elbowed him in the ribs. "C'mon, we're going to have to tell the boss as soon as she gets back to her office tomorrow morning."

It would help if we knew where the criminal was. The only vampires aside from Keir within a mile's radius were dead, except for the dick who'd set his zombies on us.

"What criminal?" Morgan dug in his pocket for his wallet, which he was lucky nobody had stolen while he was asleep, and counted out change on the table.

"Someone decided to kill a bunch of vampires." I said. Now Lloyd mentioned it, maybe I should have done more poking around at the market to find if someone else was screwing around with dark magic. "Have you seen Mackie today?"

Morgan grunted. "I went to talk to her because she's still refusing to wear the iron, and her dreams are keeping me awake all night. Stuff about being chained up in the spirit realm. This is the only place I can get any peace."

I stared at him. Those were *my* dreams. Or Evelyn's. My Hemlock nightmares were infiltrating the nearest psychics' minds? That must mean Mackie was able to hear them, too. And if she ended up in the enemy's hands again, they'd almost used her to break the spirit line once already without the need for a necromantic device.

Cold fear washed over me. Maybe the vampire king's death was connected, maybe not, but Mackie was in more danger than even she knew if the person harnessing spirit energy got hold of a psychic. People would notice if necromancers started disappearing, but a girl who'd once lived on the streets…

"Morgan, please try to convince her to stay at the guild," I said.

"Do you think I'm not trying?" He tugged at his over-long hair. "If she doesn't want to, nothing'll keep her there."

That's what I'm afraid of.

"We'll help her," Lloyd said. "We're on the dawn patrol tomorrow, right? Tell her about the vampires then. If we tell her the truth, she's less likely to run."

"I wouldn't count on it." I downed half my glass of witch's brew, shuddering at the taste.

If my nightmares had ended up in Mackie's and Morgan's heads… what else might have sneaked in?

Dawn came with another burst of fog and a lot of regret, but luckily, I had a spell for every occasion. One hangover-cure charm later, I hummed as I pulled on my cloak and skipped out of my room.

Lloyd met me outside. "How'd you sleep?"

"Like the dead. Which, in my experience, involves a lot of flailing around and trying to poke people's eyes out."

He gave me a bleary-eyed stare. "Why are you in such a good mood?"

"I may have brewed up a hangover cure and put in too much of a mood booster." At least, I hoped that's what I'd put into it. The fourth round of shots yesterday had seemed such a good idea at the time, and I sincerely hoped the part where I'd sung karaoke had been a dream.

"Give me some of that, Jas. I'll pay you for it."

"I'm not turning it into a business, believe me." But I handed him a purple band-shaped spell. "Think of it as payback for dragging you into danger yesterday."

"I wouldn't say you dragged me into it," Lloyd said, activating the spell. "I did volunteer. And you bought the drinks."

"Oh, shit." I groaned, my good mood evaporating. "I was supposed to save some cash to buy some more marigold leaves from the witch market."

"Speaking like a true witch. Eye of newt and cauldron bubble."

"Keep it down," I said. "Does my memory deceive me or did you and Morgan duet at the karaoke with that awful faerie ballad?"

"Was that before or after I threw up on his shoes?"

"Remind me never to buy you two shots again." Even after using the hangover spell, my head still felt decidedly fragile. If we ran into an undead patrol today, we'd have less brains between us than the zombies. At least I'd fallen asleep in an instant thanks to the alcohol in my system, but furies and Evelyn Hemlock were never far from my thoughts. I'd received no contact from Keir either, which came as no surprise. Whatever other issues he had going on, the vampire was too damned stubborn to accept help from the guild.

"Have you seen the boss yet?" Lloyd asked as we headed downstairs.

"It's the crack of dawn," I said. "I can give her the you-know-what after the patrol. One disaster at a time."

Mackie and Morgan waited in the lobby, the latter looking as rough as Lloyd did.

"Dawn patrols should be illegal," Mackie said.

"We wouldn't be on this one if you did one bloody thing I asked," said Morgan, his eyes bloodshot and his hair dishevelled. "Did you at least wear the iron yesterday? Considering I got to watch you struggle in a net all night, I guess not."

"Get out of my head," she shot at him.

"I wouldn't be in your head if you used basic protective measures," he said.

"Guys, it's way too early for this crap," Lloyd interjected. "Come on. We're on patrol, and that means no diverging from the route. Also, Jas has a secret hangover cure."

I trod on his foot, but not hard. "It's not a secret. I got it at the market."

At this rate, my friends would expose my Hemlock powers before Evelyn did. I reluctantly handed over the last spell to Morgan, figuring that having to put up with

Mackie's disobedience was punishment enough without a hangover on top of it.

The street was quiet, the city wrapped in fog beneath a barely-risen sun. Cold shadows washed the ancient buildings, and silence followed our steps. Mackie walked alone, her body tense. I wondered where she'd lived before the guild. If the vampires had found her, maybe she'd have some idea of who'd try to bump them off. Or maybe I was better off not poking that beast.

Hmm.

Caution urged me to tread carefully. "So do you know how to track vampires?" I asked her.

"No. Should I?"

"It's advanced level," I said. "But you can probably skip some of the basics. You saw the vampires at the station, right?"

"I spent the whole time trapped in a witch's net, so no." Her voice was brittle and angry. *Okay, change the subject.*

"They look like shadowy people," I told her. "I didn't have a clue what they looked like until I saw one."

"I know," she said. "Like Keir. I saw him last night, too."

Oh, damn. So much for keeping my thoughts to myself. A psychic being able to read my mind was the least of my problems this week, but was it too much to ask to be allowed some peace?

"You should put the iron on," I said. "I'm going to start doing the same. There's… there's another vampire trying to recruit people. You know how dangerous they are. You can't trust them."

"Then why do you want to sleep with one of them?" she asked, entirely too loudly.

Lloyd and Morgan both cracked up laughing, while my face flamed to my collarbones.

"Mackie, it's not polite to dive into people's thoughts," I said, shooting a look at Lloyd that dared him to keep laughing.

"It's not polite to lie either," she said. "Which every single one of you has been doing to me since the start."

Morgan and Lloyd both stopped snickering at me.

"What?" I said to Mackie. "We've never lied about the guild. We're here to help you."

"You took me in because you're scared I'll wipe you off the face of the planet."

"Mackie," I said warningly. "We took you in because the alternative was sending you to rot in a jail cell for what Leila Hemlock made you do."

"Maybe I did it because I wanted to." Her voice deepened, and anger flared in her grey-blue eyes.

As Morgan took a step in her direction, she whipped something out of her pocket, and magic blasted the three of us off our feet. My elbow cracked off hard stone, and stars swam before my eyes. Then she screamed, and the spirit realm dissolved into a blur. I rolled over on the stones, my head throbbing.

"Dammit, Mackie, get back here," I yelled.

Lloyd was on his feet first, chasing her down. Of the three of us, he was probably the fastest, but she'd disappeared down a side street. I swore and pulled myself to my feet, my elbow and head throbbing with every step.

"She used your metal thing," Lloyd shouted over his shoulder.

"Shit!" I picked up the pace, with Morgan on my heels. "The vamps got to her. I *knew* it."

I hadn't expected them to act this fast, much less tell her to steal something I hadn't even owned until two days ago. If ever I needed proof that the same Ley Hunters were operating up and down the country...

The alley halted at a dead end. I tapped the spirit realm and it came up murky, still fuzzy from her screaming. And—we were on the spirit line, the one that led from the guild to the station.

"I can't track her," I said. "She's gone."

And she'd taken the spirit-absorbing device along with her.

"I tried telling her," said Morgan. "She wouldn't listen."

"I don't think she's alone in her head." One of the vampires had contacted her, poisoned her mind, and turned her against us. Unless she'd never been on the guild's side to begin with... but her desperation had seemed so genuine.

Whatever the case, Mackie had just walked headfirst into a death sentence. And unless we got that device back before she activated it on the spirit line, so would I.

11

"You *lost* the psychic?" said Ilsa.

For want of a better plan, we'd agreed with Morgan that bringing backup was the best move to quickly track down Mackie. Which meant letting the Gatekeeper in on our little mishap.

"Worse," I said. "She stole something of mine. A device that stores spiritual energy. It's what switched off the key point, I think, and it can absorb ghosts."

Ilsa's eyes widened. "Tell me more."

I explained Saturday's discovery as we hurried out of the guild's headquarters and retraced our steps. If the rest of us couldn't track Mackie, then maybe even the Gatekeeper couldn't, but short of telling the boss and winding up locked in a jail cell while Mackie ran amok with a dangerous weapon, our options were limited.

"Who, exactly, told her to steal it?" said Ilsa, a step behind me on the cobbled street.

"I have my suspicions," I admitted. "But I don't know for sure. I saw someone… before the necromancer died, in Birmingham. I think he was a vampire. I think it's safe to say the person orchestrating this can project over a long distance."

The vampire must have seen I'd stolen his device, worked out where I lived, and used Mackie to get back at me.

"The place is a maze," said Lloyd over his shoulder. "And she ran fast, right onto a spirit line. Jas said that makes her harder to track."

"Does the device itself leave a signal?" asked Ilsa, pausing behind us when we reached the alley where we'd lost her.

"A weak one," I answered. "It's easier to track Mackie herself, but they probably told her to run this way on purpose. She screamed, jolted the spirit line, and that's all it took for her to escape."

"She screamed again?" asked Ilsa. "It didn't knock anyone at the guild out, so she couldn't have used as strong a blast as before."

"No, she *is* stronger," said Morgan. "I kept trying to tell you. She's learned to control that attack of hers—hell, she might even have already known how to do it. She hit us just hard enough to stop us tracking her. She's way too smart."

Ilsa swore. "And now the enemy has her. Do you think they've been recruiting her through the spirit realm, the same way that fetch got to you?"

"Fetch?" I asked.

Ilsa glanced over her shoulder. "A faerie creature with a fixation on psychics. It could get to Morgan by connecting with his mind, but it stopped when he moved into the guild and started carrying iron everywhere."

"That sounds awfully familiar," said Lloyd. "So the vamp's been whispering in her ear the whole time?"

"If I had to guess—yes, he has," I said. "I warded my room, but I guess I didn't put a strong enough protection spell on the device. It wasn't like I thought anyone would break into my room and steal it." I hadn't exactly been at my most observant yesterday.

"It isn't your fault," Morgan said. "It's that damned fetch all over again. Look, when something is speaking to you through a psychic link, it's kind of like... hypnosis. You can't resist. You're almost sleepwalking. She probably doesn't know why she took it and was hardly aware of doing it. That voice she used before she left—it wasn't hers."

"So she's possessed?" asked Lloyd, backing out of the alley onto the street.

"Nope," I said. "I think it's more... the enemy is speaking through her, like a vampire, except she's still alive."

"There were vampires involved in the battle, right?" asked Ilsa. "Lady Montgomery told me a witch was there, too."

Ah, crap. I'd planned to keep the details of the battle to myself, and as far as anyone knew, the fighting had taken place entirely within this realm. It didn't sound like the vampires were taking any influence from Leila Hemlock any longer, considering she was dead. But on the other hand, the spirit line was right under our feet.

"A witch was," I confirmed. "But she died. They all did. And the vampires. I'm not sure if this is linked to the same rogues, but that device—I should have handed it in from the start." I'd been too set on keeping up the deception and not giving away my Hemlock powers that I'd let it fall right into the enemy's hands.

"No, I'd have done the same," said Ilsa. "I've never heard of a handmade device that can store spiritual energy before. Must be a new creation, and definitely not guild-approved."

"There's at least one more out there, considering the number of people killed in the first attack we found," I said. "The vampire… I don't know how he managed to trace me back here. Vampires can't generally pinpoint a person's exact location, especially that far off. Except when it comes to their vessels, I guess." I'd need to ask Keir how it worked.

Ilsa stopped walking. "I don't think we can go much further without actually leaving the spirit line, and I'm guessing she's still on the line."

Yeah. Because the vampire has a new target. Guilt squirmed inside me. In chasing down his vessel, I'd brought him right to the guild's doorstep, and now Mackie might lose her life for it.

"Right, I'm going in." I ducked down, setting up candles in a circle. "This line is way too obvious a target. There are guild people stationed all over the place since the battle. Which means she can't be at the train station, at least. She must be closer."

The others didn't argue, nor when I entered the circle and tapped into the spirit realm, searching for the glint of the psychic's spirit. Within the candles' glow, everything was brighter than before even with the fuzziness. Ilsa was beside me. Morgan on my other side, with Lloyd just behind. But no signs of Mackie remained, and even the guild looked like a blur when I moved in that direction.

"There's an easier way for me to find her," said Morgan's voice from my left. "I'm wearing iron, too. If I take it off, there's no barriers. I can mind-link her and find her that way."

"But—that'll make you a target, too," Ilsa protested.

I blinked away the grey and stepped out of the circle. "Okay, get in the circle. If you're sure."

Ilsa's expression said *she* wasn't sure, but psychic links were not my area of expertise, and if anything brought us to Mackie, it was worth a try.

I stepped away from the circle as Morgan took my place within the candles. He pushed his sleeve up, where a thin iron band was wrapped around his wrist, and he pulled it off.

Immediately, he dropped to his knees, his ghostly form rising from his body. Lloyd exclaimed in alarm, but Morgan's ghost shrugged. "It's okay, I'm still alive. So's Mackie." He rotated on the spot as though searching for something close by. "That way."

I turned in the direction he pointed in, tapping into the spirit realm. Fuzziness surrounded me, but I pushed forwards, reaching out for a familiar presence.

Mackie's spirit shone within, just off the spirit line. My heart contracted. *There she is.*

And she wasn't alone. Faintly glowing blue lines indicated at least two—no, three—vampires, and an uncountable number of humans.

The buzz of my phone jolted me back into the real world.

"I know where she is," I said, reaching into my pocket and pulling out my phone. Keir had responded to my message from yesterday, asking where I was. He must have sensed I'd left the guild twice in a short space of time.

"Who's that?" asked Lloyd.

"Keir. I'll ask him to back us up. There are three vamps in there, I think."

Ilsa nodded, her eyes slightly glazed from the spirit sight. "Three… and humans. Get the candles."

Morgan and Lloyd scrambled to pick up the candles while I dashed off a message to Keir telling him where we were. Unless he was close, he likely wouldn't catch up to us before we got to Mackie, but those vampires weren't messing around.

"Humans?" echoed Morgan, straightening up. "The guild's laws say don't hurt humans, don't they?"

"Get that device out of their hands by any means possible," I said. "And Mackie, of course. The vampires don't seem that strong, but there might be others hiding nearby." None of them pinged on my radar as the guy I'd seen staring through the necromancer's eyes before he expired, but I'd bet he was close by.

Candles retrieved, we hurried across the road towards where I'd sensed Mackie's signal. "I didn't see what the actual place looked like, but a crowd that big isn't hard to miss. We can take them. Just get that device off the spirit line before it blows up."

The device might not contain that much power, but on a key point, with a dozen innocent humans in the room? I shuddered to think what it might do. Especially with the Hemlock witches a mere step away.

We turned the corner into an abandoned street, which came as no surprise either. They picked derelict locations for a reason. And people who wouldn't be missed.

"There," Ilsa whispered, pointing at a squat, dilapidated house on the corner.

Morgan's body tensed. "Right. I'll get her out—"

"Don't just walk in there," I hissed. "Tell you what… someone put up a candle circle around the place. That'll contain the spiritual energy if it explodes and stop it from affecting the whole spirit line. It'll also protect Mackie."

"And trap her," Lloyd said. "Right?"

"Not if we get her out first." But he was right. All someone would need to do was activate the spirit device and it might easily kill anyone who touched it. "Look, I'm trying to think. Those people are going to die unless we get in there, but they might sacrifice her life if they realise they're cornered."

Mackie, of course, would have sensed us coming the instant we got within range. It was up to her whether she wanted to alert the enemy or not.

"I think we're best off going in through the spirit realm," said Ilsa. "The humans won't panic because they won't be able to see us."

"And we can take out the vamps that way." I nodded. "Just… don't be too obvious about it. We have the element of surprise as long as Mackie doesn't give us away."

Lloyd shifted in position. "What you said about candles," he said. "I can booby trap the outside of the house in case she makes a run for it again."

"Good idea. She'll be watching me, and probably Morgan, so you can probably sneak under their radar. Just don't get caught."

I tapped into the spirit realm again. Mackie appeared floating before me, her gaze panicked and pleading. She mouthed *help.*

That was all I needed to tell me she had no control over what she'd done.

I scanned the spirit realm for the device, and spotted its glow, brighter than before. Too bright. A human held it in his hands. *Crap. It's switched on.*

The glow grew brighter, covering one human, then another. The vampires planned to suck in all their souls in one go.

"Let go!" I yelled at the human gripping the device, not that he could hear me through the spirit realm. The device continued to glow, mirroring the glow in the vampires' hands. *Oh, god. It's the vampires—they're the only ones who can activate it.*

One of the vampire's heads snapped in my direction, and I lunged through the spirit realm, blasting kinetic energy into the human's back. The device fell from his hands as he turned around in confusion and alarm, and a shadowy vampire surged on the device, scooping it up.

"Hey!" I shouted. "Put that down before it blows your head off."

He ignored me. Either he had a death wish or someone else was telling him what to do, over a distance.

The device sparked in his hands, its blue light glowing brighter.

Mackie screamed.

The noise blasted me back into my body, shaking the spirit realm. I heard Morgan and Ilsa both exclaim in pain from beside me. *Not again.*

Dim candle lights at the house's perimeter told me Lloyd had managed to complete the circle. *At least one thing's going according to plan.* Now to get Mackie out of there.

Head swimming, I sprinted the rest of the way to the doors and kicked them open. I was the only one of the group still on my feet, but the vampires would be equally off balance.

Inside the room, a dozen bewildered humans stared at me, in front of the three blank-faced vampires at the back.

"Give me that device!" I snapped, shoving the nearest human aside. Mackie's hands gripped the piece of metal, and her wild gaze met mine. She hadn't screamed in pain. She'd been diverting them on purpose, and had taken back the device for herself.

"Mackie," I said, elbowing another human out of my path. "Give that here."

A vampire struck her from behind, snatching the device out of reach. My hands tingled with static as its blue glow grew brighter, expanding to cover the room.

"Get out!" I yelled at the humans, shoving two of them in the direction of the door. Sure enough, one of them dropped a 'Society of Ley Hunters' business card on the way out.

The vampire raised the device, his face to the heavens, and I tackled him, taking him off his feet. The spirit realm rose to meet me, grey blurring the world, further blurred by the aftereffect of Mackie's scream. Tremors rocked my body, and Evelyn Hemlock's magic rose to the surface.

Magic poured from my hands and the device shattered, pieces of it flying in all directions and striking the walls and ceiling. I fell backwards, blood soaking through my shirt. An urgent male voice—Keir?—broke through the fog, but my spirit was already slipping free of my body.

Ah, crap. I was dying all over again.

12

I'd probably spent longer than the average person imagining how I'd die. I mean, being a necromancer, it kind of went with the territory. Being blown up by a spirit device made by an amateur, though? That was pathetic. Not to mention undignified. I floated through the spirit realm, propelled by the impact of the blast. Even the vampires had vanished, and I hoped the others had caught them in time.

Perhaps if I floated over into the forest, I'd get to avoid passing through the gates, but the idea of spending an eternity with Cordelia Hemlock wasn't any more appealing as a ghost, to be honest.

Don't be ridiculous. You can't die that easily.

The voice sounded almost like Evelyn. If I died, she'd never escape her prison… and even if she did, she wouldn't have a body. Maybe this was how she'd felt when she'd been ripped out of her body and bound to me. *Really, Jas.* I had no business feeling the slightest bit sorry for her. Maybe I was growing soft in my almost-dead state.

Blue threads of light caught my vision, reminding me of the voice I'd heard screaming my name. *Keir.* It would have been nice for him to tell me what was bugging him before I took a one-way trip into the afterlife, but death was never simple, and always left a mess for the living to clean up.

A scream jolted the spirit line, snapping me to alertness. "Mackie?" I called, realising that I'd stopped flying and started hovering instead.

I concentrated on the screaming, seeking its source. The spirit realm grew clearer as I floated, and Mackie appeared before me, struggling in the grip of a tall shadowy figure.

Vampire.

"Let her go," I warned. "Now."

"It's nice to finally meet you, Evelyn Hemlock," said the shadowy man. It was *him...* the man who'd looked at me through the necromancer's eyes.

"Jas," I corrected. "Evelyn's dead. Very dead."

"Not as far as I can see." His form became more distinctive, and less vampire-y. His eyes glittered, silvery grey, and his grip on Mackie tightened. "Why are you hiding?"

"I have no idea who you even are," I told him. "Do you have a name?"

"They call me the Soul Collector," he said.

Mackie struggled against his grasp. "You won't take *my* soul."

"Let her go," I warned. "I was the one who destroyed your little contraption, not Mackie."

"Yes, I suppose you did," he said, looking me up and down over Mackie's flailing arms. "Luckily, you did me more good than harm… thank you for that."

Mackie squirmed, freeing one of her arms, and I lunged to grab her. My hands glowed white-blue, as I took her arm, pulling her away from the vampire. He remained still, a shadow in the shape of a man, and didn't try to stop me.

Why would he need to? He could reach her, mind-to-mind, whenever he wanted to. Unless I finished him off.

I pulled Mackie behind me, my other hand reaching to grasp his throat. My hand passed through thin air, and not so much as a shadow remained of the vampire. It was like he'd evaporated into thin air.

"Get back here, you bastard," I shouted at the spot where he'd vanished. I'd never seen a vampire disappear so quickly.

"He's not really here," Mackie said from behind me. "He's everywhere—everywhere at once."

"Mackie," I said. "Get back to your body. To the guild."

She shook her head, silent tears spilling down her ghostly cheeks. "I can't shut him out. He's always there, always. Please… help."

My heart wrenched. I was dead. There was nothing I could do—*I think.* "Go back to the guild. I'll be right behind you."

Mackie quietened, and I remained floating on the spot. Death seemed a long time coming, but a familiar chill rose at the sight of the gates on the horizon, transparent and endless. Mackie's presence slipped away, and a thousand ghosts surrounded me. *Dammit. There's got to be a way out of this.*

A pair of shadowy hands gripped mine. I fought, kicking out, and a familiar sensation brushed against my spirit. "Keir?"

"Jas," he said, his voice quiet, his shadowy form barely there. "Don't let go of me. I'm going to get you out of here."

"I think you're a little too late." God, it was good to feel something familiar, even the coolness of a vampire's lethal touch. My spirit pulsed like a heartbeat, aching to feel again…

The spirit realm turned transparent, the gates fading away as I tightened my grip on him. Hazy greyness smothered the world, and unbearable cold gripped my arms. Not pleasant vampire-related cold, but the chill of Death itself.

I gasped, jerking upright, my body stiff and frozen like I'd dived into the sea. My body. *I'm alive. I survived.*

Keir's face swam above me, then solidified. "Hang on," he said. "Don't move too fast. You lost a lot of blood."

"I should… be dead," I said through chattering teeth, shivering violently. Keir leaned in and pulled a blanket over me. Oh, right. I was lying on a bed… and not in the guild's infirmary. The coppery smell of blood mingled with laundry detergent.

"I barely got to you in time," Keir said. "You had a healing spell on your wrist, but you were already in Death. I had to pull you back here."

"I remember." I licked my numb lips, clinging to the now-blood-covered blanket. "Where am I?" The compact bedroom with its expensive-looking wooden furniture didn't fit the same layout as one of the guild's flats. The ceiling was high, two of the walls lined with bookshelves.

A set of odd-looking hand puppets faced me. Their stitched, lopsided faces were kind of creepy.

"This is my apartment," he said. "It was closer than the guild, and I needed to get you away from the debris before I brought you in. Your friend threw a shielding spell up, but that explosion brought the ceiling crashing down. The humans barely got out."

I screwed up my forehead, thoroughly disorientated. "Your apartment? I don't see any holes in the walls."

His jaw tightened. "This is—was—my brother's room. I'm in here now, since the furies trashed my own room."

"Oh. Sorry, I've got blood all over the bed…" I lifted the blanket. My clothes were a shredded mess, and my necromancer coat was in tatters. "I look like I stole from the Grim Reaper's wardrobe."

His mouth pinched together. "I thought you died."

"I did die. I have nine lives, Lloyd says. Crap, where is he?"

Keir pushed his hair back with one hand. "He's not hurt. He helped those two other necromancers banish the vampires, after the house collapsed on them. They got the humans out first."

Right. Of course. Ilsa and Morgan were more than a match for the vampires. Mackie had survived and escaped the Soul Collector… but he'd let me go on purpose. *This isn't over. Far from it.*

"At least there's that." I didn't want to take off the blanket, but I couldn't stay here all day. "I need to report to my boss. Should probably leave the *nearly died* part out, considering it's happened enough times that she's probably suspicious by now."

"You were in Death a long time, Jas," Keir said, his eyes unusually serious. "I thought—I was too late."

"I had to get Mackie out." I looked away, his intent stare making me feel—something. Whatever it was, I had no time for it at the moment. "The person behind this scheme, the one who forced her to betray us—it was him. I *think* he's a vampire, but he has some serious glowing going on. Maybe he's eating all the souls he captures."

"A vampire?"

"Yep." I swung my legs over the side of the bed, and he took a step backwards—not too fast, but enough to catch my attention. Like yesterday, he looked a little worn, to say the least. His skin appeared stretched too tight over his bones, and in the spirit realm, he hadn't been nearly as shadowy as usual.

I frowned. "Something wrong? You didn't feed on anyone yesterday, did you?"

"I was too busy repairing the damage to my wall," he said. "I also had to tell John that attacking us was a bad idea, so I stole his vessels and turned them on him."

"Vampire warfare. Fun." I felt less than charitable towards vampires in general now I knew several of them were in cohorts with this so-called Soul Collector, but Keir's subdued demeanour bothered me more than I expected. I had to admit, I'd had a moment or two when I hoped he was wallowing in guilt for not getting in touch with me, but it wasn't like he'd given me a reasonable explanation. "I guess I should head back to the guild. Will you be joining me?"

He paused for a moment. "I'll walk you."

"You should probably grab a snack on the way. Not that I'm encouraging ambushing more humans, but if people sign up to join a murderous death cult, they probably deserve it." I searched the spells on my wrists for a repairing charm, which I applied to my shredded clothes. I'd need to change them later, but at least now I looked less like I was on my way back from a Halloween party. "What's with the puppets?" I indicated the row of crudely stitched faces on the bookshelf opposite. "They kind of look like they're plotting to murder me."

"Ah, they were my brother's," said Keir, not catching my gaze. "He made them so he could teach me how to pilot vessels from a distance."

"Oh. Sorry I said they were creepy."

"They are," he said, in an attempt at an offhand tone. "Especially when he used them to practise ventriloquism."

"So that's how you learned to throw your voice and speak through a vessel?" I'd kind of figured that type of thing came naturally to vampires. Like feeding on souls.

"He was better at it than I am," he said.

Silence fell, and I returned my attention to my newly repaired coat. "Cleansing… eh. I'll deal with that later. The Lynns will get suspicious if I show up squeaky-clean."

"You've certainly grown proficient with witchcraft." His gaze followed my movements as I tugged my cloak shut. My skin heated at the memory of his hands on my soul, his vampire's touch. I'd wanted him to drain me, even when I was dying. That was one lethal power they had.

I looked at him. "My soul is in one piece and I don't want you snacking on another necromancer. Go on."

He shook his head. "I shouldn't."

"Look, it's that or get kicked out of the guild. And you want to tell my boss what you know… right?"

"No, I don't," he said. "The guild is effective, but too slow. If you hadn't gone behind their backs today, Mackie would be dead."

"They're fast when they want to be," I countered. "Also, there's a vampire behind this. Several. Look, I have no idea what your problem is, but the guild could use the help and I'm not going to blow our chances of catching the villain just because you blew *me* off."

"I said I didn't *want* to help the guild. Not that I wouldn't." He stepped towards me. The air felt charged as his hand reached out to brush my cheek. "I'm sorry I didn't return your messages, Jas. I'll explain later, but I have to…" I felt the cold touch of his spirit against mine. "I apologise. It's been a while since—"

"Go on." I remained where I stood, my head turned pointedly downwards. *This is nothing. Vampires do this kind of thing every day.*

He placed both hands on my shoulders, carefully, as though afraid I'd snap in two if he pushed too hard. I held my breath as his mouth moved down my neck, and all the coldness of the spirit realm melted away.

I'd forgotten how it felt to be fed on by a vampire. It felt more like a full-body, or full-spirit massage—and then some. Coldness turned to warmth, trickling down my spine to my toes, and there was that *openness*—like he was giving something to me rather than the other way around. I found my hands slipping around his waist. His strong arms held me tightly, trembling a little, as his spirit fed on mine like a starving man.

Whoa. He was draining me, too fast. "Slow down."

He wasn't listening. Just how long had it been since he'd fed on someone?

"Keir!" I shoved his shoulders backwards, breaking the connection violently enough that he slammed into the opposite wall. Several books fell from the shelves, the clattering noise seeming to bring him to his senses.

Keir pressed a hand to his forehead. "Jas." He squeezed his eyes shut. "Fuck. I'm sorry."

"What the hell?" I gasped out. My skin burned, my soul burning brighter, if anything, but the outright panicked look on his face kick-started my heartbeat. "Keir, what is it?"

"Fuck," he said, again, replacing the books roughly on the shelves. His hands were visibly shaking. "Something is wrong with my vampire abilities."

"Wrong… how?"

He shook his head. "I don't understand how. Maybe it's because you have two souls, but whenever I feed on anyone else, it has next to no effect, compared to yours. My vampire's ability seems to have latched onto you—or your shade. It's been driving me to distraction for weeks."

"Oh, come on." I rolled my eyes at him, though my heart continued to pound. "I'm not *that* unique."

"No, you're deadly to vampires," he said. "Any other vampire who tried to feed on you would experience the same. I nearly killed two people the day after you left for the forest."

"You're serious. Oh, bloody hell. I didn't know." How could I? It wasn't like I'd looked up the effects of a vampire feeding on a shade, since I'd only discovered both of them existed in the same week. *Deadly to vampires?*

"No, it wasn't a pleasant surprise, I'll give you that." His mouth curved, though his eyes remained shadowed. "None of my usual coping mechanisms worked. I usually lift weights or spar with other vampires as an outlet to take the edge off the hunger, but my concentration levels are fucked. I even tried feeding on a necromancer or two, but it's like my abilities shut down. I thought I was dying."

"Clearly you're not," I said, but my heart beat faster.

He picked up a folder that'd fallen from the shelf bearing the name *Aiden Langford,* and returned it to the bookshelf. "I should have checked if there'd be side effects before I fed on you. A less experienced vampire might have killed you."

"I have nine lives, remember?" I buried my own shaking hands in my pockets. "Why not just *tell* me?"

"It's hardly a conversation topic for a first date," he said. "Besides, I've been searching all my contacts trying to find a solution without giving away your secret."

"Oh, damn."

It barely registered that he'd said *first date.* Because there was no way to solve his dilemma, short of letting someone else in on my second soul problem. But Keir couldn't end up dependent on me forever. Right?

"Exactly." He ran a hand through his overgrown hair. "I think I'm satiated for now, but I generally need to feed every two or three days, and that's assuming I haven't been drained by another vampire. Let's just say it's been a while since I visited the king."

Now I had to add 'deadly to vampires' to my 'Jas's weird powers' list. Great. "Do you think… do you think Evelyn might have done it?" A final 'screw you, Jas' before I'd sealed her away?

"No," he said, his voice husky. "I mean—possibly. But I only remember you."

I stared at him for a moment. A flush brightened his

prominent cheekbones, and his eyes were positively fever-bright. I swallowed hard. I couldn't afford to be distracted, and god knew we had enough dilemmas to solve already. Not to mention, I didn't entirely trust his vampire side.

I looked away. "I'm sorry, Keir, but my boss is probably going mad. I hid that spirit device in my room and nearly got Mackie killed."

"That wasn't your fault," he said. "You said yourself the boss wasn't around at the weekend, and technically it wasn't a guild mission you acquired the device from."

"The rules are kinda fuzzy when it comes to running into necromancy issues while off the clock," I said. "Usually we're advised to report in anyway. But obviously, most people don't have sentient forests, extra souls or forbidden covens to contend with. And Mackie herself hasn't told the guild everything. Probably for the best, considering she knows all *my* secrets."

"She can read your thoughts?" he asked.

"No, but she can see into my head when I leave an opening and she happens to be linked into the spirit realm at the time," I said. "So basically, when I'm sleeping, or my defences are down. Then she gets impressions and thoughts of whatever I'm projecting. Morgan—he's the guy who was with us at the house—is the same, but he wears iron and actually bothers to control the link. Mackie is wide open."

"So someone lured her to the house?" he said. "I got your message, but I was in too much of a rush to read it all."

"The vampire behind this lured her through their mind link," I explained. "It's like he hypnotised her, almost. And he's still out there. I think he captured her before Leila Hemlock did, or maybe they worked together. I'm not sure."

"And can this vampire read your mind, too?" he asked, his expression wary.

"Possibly, but I don't know. It might only be psychics he can connect to, but it depends if he *is* one. Do psychic vampires exist?"

"I've never met one," he said. "From what I know of psychics, they can pick up on the thoughts of anyone with a strong presence in the spirit realm in the vicinity, but can only link mind-to-mind with other psychics."

Not just psychics. Ilsa mentioned there was a type of fae who could do it, too. But that Soul Collector... vampire or not, he looked human.

"Yeah, I heard the same," I said. "Either way, he might have got anything just from reading Mackie's thoughts, considering how much info she got on me when Leila Hemlock had her captive. Hell, for all I know, she read Evelyn's mind, too, before I locked her out. I mean, we're two separate minds, technically. And she was their prisoner for weeks."

His mouth thinned. "Did you see nothing of where the vampire who spoke to you actually was?"

"Nope," I said. "He didn't really have an accent and he never shows up to the crime scenes in person. On that topic—how did you control that vessel halfway down the country without knowing I was there?"

"I extended my spirit sight in your general direction then grabbed the nearest corpse and shoved some of my consciousness into it," he said. "It wasn't a very neat job."

"Sure you're not still sore that Isabel and I beat you?" I said, trying to lighten the mood.

His mouth twitched. "I have to say, it was a pleasant surprise to find that you weren't the dangerous rogue shade I was expecting."

"Not dangerous?" I said. "You certain about that?"

A grin widened his mouth. I wouldn't lie, it was a relief to see it at this point. "No, you're dangerous, Jas. I forgot how much I like having you around."

Me, too. Unfortunately. "So… want to come and introduce yourself to my boss?"

13

The necromancers on guard duty outside the guild's headquarters looked suspiciously at Keir when he walked alongside me into the lobby, but none of them stopped us. The absence of familiar faces fuelled my certainty. "I think the others have been hauled into the boss's office for a grilling. Still want to come?"

"He'd better," said Lloyd, approaching us. "The only reason she's not yelling at me for letting Keir take you away is because she's more pissed with Morgan and Mackie."

Sure enough, Lady Montgomery's voice drifted down from the upper level. She didn't yell so much as project her voice so the walls rattled and everyone in a mile's radius ducked for cover. No wonder all the novices were hiding downstairs. I glanced at Keir, whose mouth quirked in an inexplicable smile.

"What?" I hissed. "If you think this is amusing, half the reason she's so mad is because I nearly died."

He shook his head. "It's not you. I was... forewarned about the guild's leadership approach. I'm glad to see they're taking the threat seriously."

"Of course we are." Lloyd glared at him. "If you hadn't brought Jas back in one piece, we'd have strung you from the ceiling."

"Lovely sentiment," said Keir, taking a step forwards in the direction of Lady Montgomery's strident voice. "I think I can find my own way upstairs."

"Now is not the time to pick a fight, you two. We're *all* deep in the shit."

Lloyd scowled at Keir and turned back to the stairs. Several novices stared after us—or more specifically, at Keir's expensive-looking jacket and jeans, and the absence of a hooded necromancer's cloak. Most of them wouldn't know a vampire by sight, but I could see them putting his presence together with Lady Montgomery's shouting and drawing their own conclusions.

The upper corridor, by contrast, was empty, and the boss's voice drifted towards us. I winced at the sound of Ilsa's name. Of the group, she was the person who least deserved to be yelled at, considering we'd dragged her in to help undo the mess we'd created.

"Jas," said Lady Montgomery, through the closed office door. "Come to say your piece?"

"I also bought an ally." I opened the door and entered. Ilsa, Morgan and Mackie gathered around her desk, all of them looking noticeably chastened.

"Keir Langford," the vampire said smoothly, reaching out a hand. Lady Montgomery shook it, her sharp eyes appraising the new arrival.

"Keir is the vampire who helped us out," I said. "And he helped us save Mackie the first time around, too."

"And did he know about this illegal device?" she enquired.

"Not until yesterday," I said, my shoulders tensing at the warning hint in her voice. "And I didn't know they existed until I found one."

"Yes, I've had to listen to an extensive explanation from your partners-in-crime."

"It wasn't really a crime," said Morgan. "It's a non-guild matter, right? She wasn't on a mission when she got the thing. It wasn't like she knew someone would hypno-tise Mackie into breaking into her room."

Wait, since when was Morgan defending me? Someone must have put him up to this... and the person in question was hiding behind Keir and me at the back. *Thanks, Lloyd.*

"Yes, I'm aware that the situation isn't covered by our usual procedures," said Lady Montgomery. "But the fact remains that the council will want an explanation as to why a device outlawed by the guild ended up in the hands of a new recruit who then handed it over to a criminal. Are the vampires all dead?"

"The ones from the scene of the crime are," I said. "Uh... outlawed by the guild? Has someone made one of these things before?"

Lady Montgomery's nostrils flared. "There have been incidents in our history where necromancers have met unfortunate ends through trying to create weapons that can harvest souls. Like most experimental necromancy, it never ends well."

Ilsa straightened upright, and I could almost see her

mind ticking, wanting to get her hands on the guild's entire history on the subject. I had zero academic interest in the device. I just wanted the damned thing out of my life and people to stop trying to screw up the spirit realm.

"Just wondered," I said. "This is… it's a collective effort. The person behind it is a vampire and I'm almost certain he's within this city. He called himself the *Soul Collector*."

The air seemed to vanish from the room as Lady Montgomery turned to me. "Is that so? Would you be able to describe this individual?"

"I only saw him as a ghost," I said. "I can draw a picture of him, if it helps, but he was kinda blurry, and shadowy. Only his eyes were clear—sort of blue-grey."

I dug in my pocket for a pen and paper, since nobody else was forthcoming, and leaned on the end of the boss's desk to sketch the vampire's face.

Lady Montgomery turned her attention to Mackie. "I'm sure I don't need to tell you that you've put your future in the guild, and your safety, in a very precarious position. We've taken in one other psychic in the last year and the only reason he was allowed to stay is because he cooperated with the law, for the most part."

Morgan shifted from one foot to the other. "Not exactly. What that vamp did to her is the same as what happened to me when I first joined up here. It's just I never got my hands on a spirit… thingy. That's all."

"And Mackie only knew about it because her mind accidentally ended up linked with mine," I added, tapping my pen on the notepad. If nothing else, I wanted *that* little problem out in the open. The enemy's info on me had come entirely through her, and even if it wasn't her fault, she was almost as much a wild card as Evelyn Hemlock.

"What I don't get is how the Ley Hunters have been luring in humans without being traced."

"Humans are good at not seeing what's in front of them," said Keir. "It's what makes them such willing victims."

"Yes, including every one of you," Lady Montgomery interjected, taking the notepad from me as soon I was done sketching. "You're not infallible, and you've made my life incredibly difficult. This is likely to take weeks to resolve. I'm going to send out patrols to scour the vampires' known haunts to find this individual. Mackie, you're to stay at the guild with Morgan. Ilsa, find River and ask him to help you organise some extra patrols."

Ilsa, Mackie and Morgan left, but when Lloyd tried to follow, Lady Montgomery beckoned him sharply. "I want a word with you, too."

Lloyd froze. "What did I do?"

"Failed to inform me of the presence of that device, for one thing," said Lady Montgomery, tearing off the vampire's picture and handing me back the notepad. "It's incredibly lucky that it had a limited amount of energy inside it when it exploded, and your candle circle prevented it from damaging the spirit line."

"Jas nearly died for it," Lloyd said. "Trust me, we were backed into a corner."

"Yet you chose to act alone."

"It was my idea," I said quickly. "I knew Mackie's life was in danger and we were already *on* the spirit line. Same line as the guild. We had to act fast."

"I see that allowing Mackie to join you on patrol was a bad idea," she said. "She's too powerful to be allowed to leave the guild."

"But—if you lock her up, she'll run," I told her. "Trust me, I know." Or Evelyn Hemlock did, anyway.

She looked at me for a moment. "Luckily for all of you, nobody was seriously hurt. But this city has a high number of spirit lines and if this vampire intends on repeating the performance, he may have other devices hidden, too."

"I think the best place to look is with the humans," said Lloyd, then shrank under the boss's glare. "Uh. Not that you're wrong. But they lured the humans in by handing out flyers, and no supernaturals knew it was happening. We don't move in the same circles."

"Yes, you're correct," she said. "But you have human family, don't you?"

"I do," he said warily. "I have a little sister at uni. I can ask if she's seen any flyers lying around, I guess."

"Do that," she said. "You have the rest of the day off. Jas, stay here with your... friend."

Lloyd left, while the boss finally turned to Keir. The vampire maintained a calm expression, and it struck me that the boss didn't seem bothered that he'd heard everything. She knew this was the second time he'd helped us, after all.

"What exactly have you come to give me?" she asked him.

"Information," he said. "I have a number of vampire contacts I can ask about this criminal. It might interest you to know that someone has been murdering vampires, too."

"Yes, it would. Tell me the details."

"I woke up to an attack yesterday morning," he said. "A wild fae seemed to have been set upon me. When I killed it, I went in search of my allies. I found a number of them had also been slaughtered. The vampires' king included. None were, as far as I know, working against the guild."

He hadn't mentioned the furies by name. Maybe he couldn't, like me, or maybe he was being cautious.

"So you were the one who disposed of the evidence my patrol found at the vampire king's house?" she asked.

"It's our method," he said. "Vampires become unstable after death and I didn't want another person reanimating them afterwards. I questioned several other vampires I suspected of being involved, but found none of them knew who'd orchestrated the attack."

"And why do you believe you were targeted?"

"I'm known to be an ally of the king, at least on paper," he said. "These rogues care nothing for the laws, and they may have tried to take me out because they knew they'd never win me over. I don't care much for luring humans into lethal traps."

"Except as a vampire," she said. "You've had several brushes with the law yourself."

"Merely in passing."

Oh, great. Maybe inviting him here hadn't been the best move. He was one of the few people I'd seen stand up to the boss, but it didn't bode well for their professional relationship. And if he spent too long around Mackie, she'd probably end up eavesdropping on *his* thoughts, too.

Lady Montgomery gave him a long look. "It's lucky Jas trusts you, otherwise I would invite you to spend some time with our council."

Wait, she trusted my word? Since when? I'd made a monumentally bad judgement call *and* was keeping some fairly major secrets. Then again, as I'd found out today, so was everyone she'd yelled at in the last hour.

"As it is, Keir," she said, when neither of us responded, "assuming you didn't suffer any damage in the battle, I'd like to request that you speak to as many of your vampire contacts today as possible."

"That may be difficult," he said. "Several fled the city after the attacks yesterday. Others fear they might be targeted next. And there's the matter of the leadership position. We're typically loners, but it's likely that it'll take a while for someone to step into the position. But I can speak to everyone I know."

"Do that," she said. "Jas, go with him. You're dismissed."

I foresaw a mountain of paperwork waiting when we got back. So much for her taking it easy on me after my near-death experience. A pounding headache threatened, probably the come-down from nearly dying coupled with my improvised hangover cure, and I'd rather take a nap than wander around interrogating vampires. But I'd promised the boss, and if I let on how bad the damage had been, I'd give away that I pretty much *did* have nine lives.

Once I'd closed the boss's door behind me, I turned to Keir. "Sure *you* don't want to be the new king?"

"No," he said. "If I make a bid for the leadership position, I'll never get a moment's peace for the rest of my life."

"Because you obviously have such a peaceful existence." I turned the notepad over in my hand. "Hang on, I'm going to draw another sketch of the guy I saw." My view hadn't been that clear, but I wouldn't forget that face in a hurry. "I need to change my clothes, too... I'm still covered in blood under here." I made for the stairs to the upper level. "Lucky I had that repairing charm. I can't afford another coat."

"I'll buy you one," Keir said, as we turned into the corridor which housed most of the novices. At least nobody was up here at this time.

"You can't buy back my trust, Keir. It doesn't work that way." I paced down to my room and unlocked the door. "Also, this place is a mess. I haven't cleaned it in weeks."

"I won't judge," he said. "And I'm not trying to buy back your trust. It was wrong of me to disappear without any explanation, but I expected you to react badly when I told you."

"You thought wrong," I said shortly, opening the door to my room. Spell ingredients scattered everywhere, clothes discarded after yesterday's drunken escapades, and…

"Is that a fury?" He indicated one of the sketches on the wall.

"Oh, fine, come in." I scooted inside, tossing my notebook onto the bed. Walking to the desk, I retrieved a blue cleansing spell. I'd rather shower instead, but not with Keir hanging around. When I turned on the spell, all the dirt and blood vanished from my clothes, leaving me refreshingly clean. "Now I know what to do when the guild runs out of hot water."

"I take it you don't normally have visitors?" Keir indicated the monstrous drawing of a fury in full battle mode. "Or you're trying to give yourself nightmares?"

"Nah, I like to draw out my fears. If they're on the page, they're not in my head." I didn't let on that I had *not* added Evelyn Hemlock to the collection. I had enough nightmares about her eyes watching me from her prison as it was. "But no, I don't tend to invite people in here. Lloyd and I hold our movie nights in his room, since he's the one with the expensive TV."

"Hmm." His gaze flicked to the notebook on the bed. "Is that me?"

"Ah. That must be the first sketch I drew when I found you in the spirit realm." I picked the notebook up, glad I hadn't left any other sketches of him lying around. I'd been honest when I said I drew out the thoughts in my head so they'd stop bugging me, but his face wasn't easy to exorcise. "I'll just quickly draw the vampire guy again, since Lady Montgomery took the other picture. So I'll know him when I see him."

He looked at the upside-down drawings as I turned the pages over. "Is that Lloyd?"

I examined the more recent picture. I'd spilled elven beer on the page, and my drunken scribbling revealed that I had not, in fact, imagined the karaoke part of last night. Nor the part where the three of us had taken a full hour to stagger back to the guild. "That's... yeah. I don't remember drawing it, to be honest."

"When was this?" Keir asked.

"Yesterday." I turned the page over and began sketching the vampire again, entirely too conscious of Keir's touch a whisper away, reminding me of what we'd started earlier. "Our brush with death turned into a wild night out."

He tilted his head. "You didn't invite me."

"You ran off." I finished the sketch, suddenly wishing I'd just walked out in my bloody clothes instead of bothering to come back here. There was a high chance I'd end up covered in blood again before the day's end, anyway.

"I'm going to find Ilsa before we head out. I assume Lloyd returned the candles to the training room."

"Which one was Ilsa?" he asked.

"The… right, you won't know who the Gatekeeper is. You've probably seen her in the spirit realm, though." I shoved the notepad into my pocket and made for the door.

"She was there today?" said Keir, following close behind.

"Yep. You'll like Ilsa, I think. She's a former academic and knows more about vampires than even I do, since she borrowed every book on the subject." I locked the door and turned away.

"Really?" His brows rose. "Does she know about…?"

"Nope," I said, dropping my voice. "I mean, it's pretty well established that I'm weird even by necromancer standards by now, but only Mackie and Lloyd know everything. And I can't say I have a bloody clue if my coven is linked to this or not, except through Mackie. This Soul Collector person definitely had his claws in her for a while, but he didn't show up when Leila made her play for power."

"That suggests the vampire either isn't in the city, or isn't as powerful as he seems," Keir commented. "So he's hiding behind weaker servants."

"What, you think he's doing a Leila Hemlock and hiding in a liminal space?" I hadn't considered that, but he *had* showed up at the scene when Mackie had thwarted him. He didn't need her, any more than he needed the other vampires whose lives he sacrificed. But what was the point in sacrificing humans? What did he have to gain from it?

"No," he said. "We're not capable of using our abilities outside of this realm, as far as I know. Even liminal spaces, I don't think. I can't say I've ever tried."

He had a point. He might have cornered me when I'd been in the Hemlocks' forest that one time, but he hadn't actually known I was there, and I doubted his abilities worked in the Hemlock witches' domain.

"He can still reach anyone, anywhere. Throughout the spirit line." He might have a dozen other Ley Hunters branches up and down the country, backed up with lives to sacrifice for his cause, and not everywhere had a functioning necromancer guild. I shook off the thought and headed downstairs. As frustrating as it was that the bastard had slipped through my grasp, we had thwarted him—twice. We'd catch him.

With Keir beside me, I followed the sound of voices to the weapons room. Sure enough, Ilsa, Morgan and Mackie were arguing loudly, with Lloyd looking on from the side.

"This," Ilsa said to Mackie, "is why Morgan kept telling you to keep iron on you at all times. Did you know he nearly got killed by a faerie beast like that one when he joined the guild? Only iron stops you from being lured into traps and possessed. Even if that vampire bastard was already linked with you, you could have stopped him from getting that far."

"God, all right!" said Mackie. "I fucked up, okay. It's not like anyone *taught* me this."

"We tried," Morgan said.

"And Jas is the one who almost died for it," Lloyd interjected. From his positioning, I gathered he'd returned to the room to put his weapons and props away and ended up boxed into a corner by the others' argument.

"Don't worry, I've learned my lesson about storing dangerous objects in my room," I said lightly. "Won't happen again. Ilsa, can I talk to you for a moment?"

"Sure," she said. "I was just on my way to take a patrol out. *Not* you two," she added to the psychics. "You stay here and try not to drive the boss into an early grave."

She passed the others and looked between Keir and me, a frown puckering her brow. "We haven't met, have we?"

"I'm Keir," he said, his gaze cool. "I'm here to assist Jas with questioning some vampires. I heard you had an interest in the subject."

She gave him an equally cool look in return. "Just curiosity. Was it the books you wanted, Jas?"

"If you have them handy, I wouldn't mind having a look when I get back," I said.

"I left them in the locker room, but I can hand them to Lloyd," she said. "I don't usually keep my stuff at the guild, but since they're from the archives… haven't you already read them, Jas?"

"Some of them. The boss still doesn't let me get at the top-secret stuff."

"Is there anything specific you're looking for?"

"Just vampires and any variations thereof," I said. "You know I ran into the guy behind this scheme in the spirit realm, right? He was way stronger than any vampire I've faced. I feel like I'm way out of my depth."

What I *really* needed was a way to undo the link between Keir and me, but getting an answer without giving away the fact that my soul was linked to another seemed impossible.

"We all do," she said. "If you need anything else, let me know. Including… the secret stuff."

She went back down the corridor, leaving me blinking after her. Wait. Had she…?

"Damn." I glanced at Keir. "I think she just implied she swiped Lady Montgomery's secret books. Or her brother did, I guess." I'd bet it was probably Morgan's idea.

Despite my misgivings, my heart lifted a little. The Lynns were on my side. And at this point, I desperately needed allies. Ones who weren't bound to my soul.

14

The first four addresses Keir and I tried yielded no results. Apparently, their owners had all left. Keir didn't seem fussed about allowing me to see the vampires' secret haunts, but with each missing vampire, he grew more tense.

"Is it normal for them to leave the city like this?" I asked.

"A lot of us move around a lot," he said. "The street where the vampire king lived was an exception, and mostly because he was paranoid about security. Now those tunnels are off-limits, there are going to be more and more vampires relocating near the guild, partly for safety reasons."

"The guild was a target last time," I reminded him.

"Yes, but from the looks of things, even furies would have a hard job getting in there," he said.

"I bloody well hope so." I dug my hands into the pockets of my coat, wishing I'd picked up another warmth spell from my room. "Unless someone screws with the wards again, but I think I fixed them." Or Evelyn had, anyway.

"Yes, you did. Have you used your magic a lot since then?" he asked.

"Oh, I have," I said, but it wasn't strictly true. Up until the last few days, I'd held off from using it outside of creating portable spells, the way I had when I'd let Evelyn take the wheel. Even in my own hands, the power felt unwieldy, too much. "I've invented a few dozen spells in the last week alone."

"Your mentor isn't here, though?"

"I saw her at the weekend." I assumed he meant Isabel, not the other Hemlocks.

"Right, you said." He nodded. "And the two of you attempted to intercept the Ley Hunters' meeting."

"If you're going to lecture me for not telling you—"

"I'm not," he said. "I'm trying to get a sense of the time-line here. These Ley Hunters are clearly answering to a single individual. This... Soul Collector person. He likely has people stationed throughout England and Scotland, and if I had to guess, the attacks on my fellow vampires are an attempt to take out the people most likely to be able to intercept him."

"The same might apply to any gifted necromancer," I pointed out. "Half my friends can track across a distance through the spirit realm, if they know who they're looking for..." Should I even be telling him this? Oh, well. It wasn't like he hadn't witnessed it in person earlier today.

"You have interesting friends, then," he said. "I wasn't under the impression the guild had a significant number of members with such a gift, but the vampire was attempting to operate under the guild's eyes. Thanks to you, he's had to change his plans."

"Yeah… but it sure didn't sound that way when he spoke to me after I got Mackie out of his hands."

He shot me a sideways look. "What exactly did he say to you?"

"He said I did him more good than harm, which was weird," I said. "The exploding device, losing his allies, not to mention Mackie breaking free and coming back to our side… that sure didn't look like things were going his way."

"No, it doesn't." He took a left turn down a side street. "What was his goal, cause a disturbance on the spirit line? Because he certainly succeeded in doing that."

"Not really. The candles we used stopped him doing any damage. Unless he still has Mackie under his spell, but she was already his."

"Right." A grimace curled his mouth. He looked tired and beaten down, not at all like the slightly cocky and exasperating person who'd hijacked a corpse to annoy the shit out of me a few weeks ago. "I suppose she fell in with the wrong crowd. They're recruiting." He paused outside a tall brick house. "And he's gone, too."

"Gone as in dead?"

"Let's find out."

He walked through an overgrown garden to the front door, which he kicked sharply with his heel. The hallway within smelled stale and musty, but not the sickly rot associated with corpses, nor the coppery tang of blood. You'd think necromancers would build up an immunity to the stench after a while, but no such luck.

Keir scanned the rooms inside, which contained dust-covered furniture and not much else. "He packed up and left. I suspected as much. Most of us have vessels scattered throughout the city to give us ample warning if a threat presents itself."

I gave one last scan of the spirit realm as we left the vampire's house. "You're talking like people have targeted the vampires before."

"We're powerful, unique, and have abilities nobody else can match. Of course we're walking targets. If not for my brother, I'd have died before I reached my fifth birthday."

"Really?" He hadn't been willing to volunteer information about his family before, but I couldn't help being a little curious despite everything that had happened between us. All he'd told me was that his family were dead, save for his brother, who'd been kidnapped by people claiming to be connected with the Ancients.

"Yes," he said, burying his hands in his pockets as a few raindrops began to fall. "We'd better hurry up and check the last of the houses."

"You lead the way." I pulled up my hood, sensing he desired a change of subject. Maybe it was for the best that I didn't learn too much about him, in case he pulled another disappearing act. It seemed to be a vampire trait, after all.

The drizzle turned into rain soon enough, and still, no vampires. By the time evening arrived, I was about ready to pass out on my feet.

"One more house," said Keir. "Then I'll take you back to the guild. This way." He ducked down yet another side street. Today had been an education in the back alleys of

Edinburgh's vampire's haunts, but I'd been too tired to commit them to memory.

The house he approached wasn't deserted. Two men stood outside, both blank-faced and hulking. Undead.

"Not the enemy," Keir murmured. "They're his vessels. He must have left them to guard the property in his absence."

"I have to admit, that's not very reassuring."

The two men moved to block our path, for all the world like living bodyguards.

"We're not here to rob you," Keir said.

"Begone, shade," said the man, and lunged at me.

I raised my arm to block his strike, kicking out on instinct. He barely stumbled, grabbing my arm when I hit out. He was as strong as any living person of his size, while I was exhausted and freezing.

Evelyn's magic whispered to the surface and I broke free of his grip. Keir tackled him into his neighbour, tossing the man over his shoulder in a martial arts throw.

"He's not here," he said to me, slightly breathless, and we half-ran from the house. "You're making them uneasy for some reason."

"How the hell do they know...?" I didn't say the word 'shade'. Nobody had called me that in a while. And I'd thought to most people, I looked like... me.

Evelyn? She couldn't have woken up. Right?

Keir slowed his pace as we reached the street's end. "You were definitely you. I've seen what happens when she's controlling you, and you don't look like that now."

"Right." I was losing my grip, apparently. Or the vampire controlling those vessels needed his eyesight testing.

"I can come with you to the guild," Keir said. "But I won't be able to share details of my fellow vampires' addresses."

"She won't expect you to," I said. "But I won't lie, it doesn't look great for us that they all ran away at the same time."

"Some would call it moving strategically out of the line of fire," he commented. "We're a little paranoid, even when there aren't people setting beasts from beyond Death on our tail."

No kidding. It didn't help that the vampires seemed disinclined to ask anyone else for help. Keir's reaction to our dilemma made a little more sense now. Vampires didn't strike me as the sort who opened up to people... other than in the *feeding on people's souls* sense, anyway.

I'd figure out how to deal with *that* later.

———

Luck was with me, and the boss was on the phone to the council when I returned. After I'd hovered outside her office for ten minutes, I resigned myself to a night of filling out paperwork and went back into the lobby with Keir. "It's your lucky day. You get off unscathed."

He didn't move. "If you're free, I'd like to take you out to dinner."

"I... don't think that's a good idea."

"Jas, you look like crap," he said. "I don't want you to be stuck doing paperwork all night after the shitty day you've had. At least let me make up for my part in it."

"Well..." My resolve weakened. "Only if it's Cassandra's Café. And you're paying. I have no money."

A grin swept his mouth. "Of course. Your choice."

Cassandra's Café wasn't exactly high cuisine, but I was too starving to care. I hadn't exactly been doing a spectacular job of taking care of myself lately, and it was only when the food showed up that I realised how hungry I was. I devoured half a burger before pausing to breathe.

Keir raised an eyebrow at me. "Did you even taste that?"

"Don't judge. It's been a long day."

"It has." He cast a glance around at the other patrons.

"Are you using your spirit sight? Now?"

"Habit," he said, with a shrug. "I find it helps to see who has the strongest spiritual presence in any given area."

"Keep your enemies closer?" I suggested. "Relax, this place is fairly well warded. Besides, there are at least two guild necromancers in here."

Meaning, Ilsa and her boyfriend, River, who sat a few tables away. The golden-haired half-faerie was Lady Montgomery's son and probably knew about the latest debacle by now. I hadn't seen Mackie or Morgan, so I assumed both had survived training in one piece and without Mackie making another break for it. Not a bad end to the day, all things considered.

"So you've never been here before?" I picked up a few fries and ate them.

"We have a tendency to draw attention," he said. "From necromancers, if nothing else. Also, crowded places... some of us don't react well to the presence of so many spirits. It muddles our senses if we're not well-practised, and a lot of us aren't. If another vampire doesn't teach us coping strategies, we find it difficult to be around a lot of people at once."

"But you learned."

"From my brother, yes." He nodded, sipping coke through a straw. "He taught me how to handle crowds, how to touch people without draining them… everything."

"Huh. I didn't know." Even the necromancers' vampire-related guidebooks seemed to be written from an outsider's perspective and gave no hints as to what it was actually like to live with the constant need to devour people's souls. I reeled my curiosity in, figuring that was probably what he least wanted to discuss.

"No, I expect not," he said. "Do you have siblings?"

Or maybe not. "Nope. Orphaned witch, remember?" I kept my voice low. "I had a few close friends growing up, though. Is your brother older than you?"

"Three years older, yes." He waved over a waiter for the bill. "We can head somewhere for drinks, if you like."

"I had enough of that yesterday. I'm still not sure if I actually sang karaoke or if it was a dream."

He grinned. "Do you usually sing?"

"Hell, no. I'm tone deaf."

He tilted his head, studying me. "No, you're an artist. I'd like to see those new spells you invented."

"Right here." I lifted my wrist, my stomach swooping when he ran a finger over the spell's curved edge, delicately brushing the underside of the skin.

"What does this one do?" he asked.

"Don't touch that if you don't want it to blow your testicles off."

He dropped his hand sharply. "Really?"

"Nah, that was a joke. Isabel does have a spell that causes you to get boils down there, but that's not much use on an undead."

He chuckled under his breath. "No, I suppose not. I have to say, this is the first time I've ever heard testicle-exploding spells mentioned on a date."

"I'm a winner at conversation, clearly." I rolled my eyes. "I don't date. Not really. Work is busy, and… never mind. This isn't actually a date, right?"

"Depends if you want it to be." He turned a plastic straw over in his hand. "I don't typically date either. I— and vampires in general—have difficulty settling down in one place."

"I'll bet."

He looked at me. "Jas, I don't want to give the impression that I'm going to just disappear again. It was a shitty thing to do, even considering the circumstances."

I raised a hand. "Say no more. Just give me a little warning if you decide to leave town like the other vampires."

"If I were sensible, I would," he said. "Considering I've had to redo the wards on my flat to stop any more furies tearing holes in the walls."

"Oh, crap, I forgot about that." I pulled up my sleeve. "I have another warding spell here, if you need one."

He smiled at me. "I might take you up on that offer. Want me to walk you home?"

"Sure. Thanks for this." I waited for him to leave the payment on the table before heading out into the darkening street. Then I handed him the warding spell. "I'll have to brew up some more of these tonight."

Once I'd dealt with Lady Montgomery's paperwork,

that is. As tempting as it was to invite Keir to help out, there were several reasons why it was a bad idea, even if I'd had a genuinely good time with him this evening. For one, I might wake up in the night to find him chewing on my soul. Never mind that it might even be worth it.

"Thanks, Jas," he said, pocketing the spell. "I fixed the damage, but since I own the property, I'm responsible for security. It's a little difficult to explain monsters that can tear through brick and plaster to the neighbours."

"You own the place? Seriously?" He must be even more well off than I assumed. Thanks to the invasion, property prices had skyrocketed, while most survivors had lost everything. I was lucky the guild's salary covered my accommodation costs, otherwise I'd have had to live out on the street.

"My brother used to own the property, and it became mine after he disappeared," he explained. "I'm pissed that the bastards tore the wall down, but it might easily have been my skull they tore open."

"Yeah." Worry crawled up my throat. The furies hadn't initially gone after me, but after the vampires. "I can give you a defensive spell, but they don't work on furies. And the vampire—the Soul Collector—I'm sure he can contact other vampires the same way he can psychics. What if he comes after you next?"

"He can't when I'm wearing this." He pushed up his sleeve, revealing an iron band. "It somewhat dampens my own ability to control my vessels, but I've been having considerable trouble keeping a grip on them for a while."

"Since me, right?" I said. "I don't know if those books Ilsa gave me have any useful information in them, but I'm going to read them tonight. Might sneak into Lady Montgomery's secret library, too, since apparently Ilsa and Morgan managed to and got away with it. There must be a way to undo what Evelyn did."

Keir shook his head. "Shades usually disappear fairly quickly or take over their host for good. Nothing I've read about them has ever mentioned vampires."

"That doesn't seem like it'd end well for you either."

"No, I suppose not." A smile bloomed on his mouth that didn't reach his eyes, and coldness grew in the pit of my stomach. In letting him feed on me, I might well have ended his life.

"Keir, I'm going to fix this," I found myself saying. "I don't know how, but I will. I haven't given up on the idea of getting her out of my body. When she's gone… maybe it'll help. Do you know what exactly it is that caused your vampire abilities to bond to me? Is it just her, or me?"

"I have no idea," he said. "I wouldn't say I was thinking particularly clearly at the time."

"No, you were half dead when we were in the tunnel. Maybe I should have let you snack on a human instead."

"That's not what I meant." He met my eyes again, and his were bright, intense. "I'm not blaming you for this."

I poked him in the chest. "It's hardly your fault, either. If anything, I'll lay the blame for this one on Evelyn, too. And the Hemlocks."

He caught my wrist. "Evelyn isn't you."

My skin warmed as he traced the spell-bands on my arm. "No shit. I'm not a murderous power-mad spirit trapped in the body of a necromancer."

"I'm glad I can tell it's you I'm talking to." He smiled at me and my heart dipped a little. Oh, boy. This was why getting attached was a bad idea. It made me forget things like common sense and oh, the slight issue of him being addicted to feeding on my soul.

"Yeah, I'm way more charming than she is." I didn't move, not when his fingers moved to my neck, then trailed along the edge of my jaw. His fingers were cool to touch, but not freezing. Warmth pooled deep inside me as he leaned in.

Oh, Jesus. Did I want to do this? Really?

His face was inches from mine, and I closed the gap. He kissed me, his strong hands carefully cupping my face. His lips caressed mine, soft and inviting. I deepened the kiss, barely noticing when his hands dropped to my shoulders and the touch of his spirit swept over mine. He stiffened and broke his mouth from mine, an apology on his tongue, but I cut off the words with another kiss.

"I have twice as many souls as most people, Keir. It's fine."

He smiled against my mouth. "Good."

Coolness massaged my body down to my toes, and I gasped into his mouth. Maybe doing this in public was a bad idea after all. A shiver racked me from head to toe, a sense of opening, of release, and when he stepped back, his eyes were positively glowing.

He breathed out, his chest rising and falling. "It's lucky I still have some self-restraint."

Yeah, I'm not so sure I do. But did I want him, or his vampire's touch? Or both?

Equally breathless, I said, "Let me know if you need my help. I don't want you to get chewed on by a fury."

"Sure, Jas." He stepped back, his eyes still glowing with silver-grey light. "I'll talk to you tomorrow."

"Bye." I turned my back before I lost what little control I had left.

I walked through the lobby in an exhausted daze, climbed the stairs, and stopped at the weapons room to grab an iron band to wear on my wrist. No psychics would get into my thoughts that night—I'd make sure of it.

Lloyd waylaid me in the upper corridor. "Jas, you left one of your sketchbooks in my room again."

"Oh. Bugger. Did I?"

"Yes, you did. Must have left it there after our last movie night."

I released a breath. "I suppose at least Mackie didn't get hold of it when she ransacked my room. She's done enough riffling around in my head anyway."

He snickered, opening the door to his room to let me in. "Yes, since she knows you like Keir. Did you two have fun tonight?"

I let the door close behind me. "There's not much to tell." Or rather, there was too much. Because I still hadn't told Lloyd I'd accidentally messed up Keir's vampire powers. "We wandered around looking for vampires. Had a run-in with some vessels and then picked up some food at the café, since the boss wasn't in. And now I get to spend the night doing paperwork."

"You don't," he said. "I dealt with it for you. Asked the boss to let you off for once."

I sagged against the wall. "Lloyd, I could kiss you."

"Not after you locked lips with that vampire, you won't."

"Lloyd—" I began, but he cut me off.

"It's fine. I don't like the guy, but it's not personal. I have something against people who suck out souls for a living. But I don't exactly have a great track record when it comes to relationships either."

I frowned at Lloyd. "What, you like someone?"

He half shrugged.

"Someone *living?* Who, me?" I doubted it. We'd established early on that neither of us harboured any romantic feelings for the other, but there was a lot I'd missed over the last few weeks.

"No, you're not my type. Too many souls."

He yelped as I shoved him in the shoulder. "Lloyd, it's lucky I like you. Otherwise I'd have punched you in the nuts for that comment."

He mock-punched me back, turning it into a wrestling match which ended with me pinning his arms above his head on his bed. "Now you have to tell me who it is. River?"

"No. He has Ilsa." He attempted to free his arms from my grip, but I was stronger than I looked.

"The guy who cleans the training room?"

"He's half troll."

"I have no bloody clue what your type is." I climbed off him. "Never mind. I'm not one to talk."

He tossed my sketchbook to me. "Yeah, your type is the living dead."

"He's not exactly dead. Did I mention things are a little complicated?"

Lloyd stuck his tongue out. "Please, Jas, keep me out of your romantic drama."

"It's not romantic. Believe me." I pocketed the sketchbook and told him about Keir's revelation.

"You broke the vampire?" he said. "Jesus. Is there anything you haven't broken this week?"

"Lloyd."

"Okay, just saying. Considering I found out about vampires the day after you did, this is not my area of expertise. But I do have those books Ilsa told me to give you." He walked to his desk and picked up three dusty volumes.

"Thanks." I took the textbooks from him. "But Evelyn isn't like most shades. The rules don't seem to apply to her. I don't know if the issue is her being a witch, or stronger than normal shades, but how do you go about undoing a link with a vampire?"

"Nope, there's no cure. Luckily, I know a dozen ways to help you hide the body."

"Lloyd!" Keir would kill me for laughing. Oh, who knew, he might find it amusing as well.

"Joking," he said. "Want to watch Zombie Armageddon Part 3?"

"I think I'll get an early night, to be honest." I tucked the books under my arm, stifling a yawn.

"Right, you have some new reading material."

"Yep." I also needed to replace my spells, and check that Mackie hadn't moved anything else when she'd swiped the device from my room.

I wasn't sorry the illegal contraption was gone. I *was* concerned that the vampire who'd orchestrated the attack hadn't seemed to care he'd been thwarted. While the iron band I'd borrowed ensured nobody would see into my dreams that night, a sense of foreboding followed me to my room.

After dumping the books on my bed, I cleared a spot on the floor to sketch out some chalk circles and re-make some of my most valuable spells. Healing spells, knockout spells, locking, unlocking, shielding, shadow spells for illusions… I knew each pattern by heart. I'd cleaned out half my stash of ingredients by this point, but Isabel had taught me you could make a variation of most spells with almost anything if you knew what you were doing.

Mechanically, I moved through the well-practised motions for a fire charm. Let's face it, I wasn't planning to hang up my metaphorical broomstick anytime soon. The Hemlocks' magic felt as natural in my hands now as it had when Evelyn had moved my body like a puppet, and—

A sharp breath tore through my lungs as my hands jerked sideways, glyphs flowing from my palms to the circle. The spell ignited, and when the light faded, the band-shaped spell lay in the circle. Yet for a second…

Evelyn?

Nothing. The feeling had gone as quickly as it'd hit me.

I shook my head. "Evelyn?" I whispered.

Silence answered. I got to my feet, shaking spell residue from my hands, and sank wearily onto the bed, my head resting on the textbook I'd thrown onto the pillow. I needed to read up on vampires… but my eyelids were too heavy.

Blissful oblivion claimed me.

15

Frantic knocking on my door woke me from slumber. "What?" I groaned and rolled onto my back, and the spine of a textbook dug into my ribs. Right, I'd crashed before I'd had the chance to read them, and I'd left a mess of spell ingredients all over the floor.

Another knock. "Lloyd, I swear if you don't have a good reason for this, I'm test driving my boil spell on you."

"Jas," said Lloyd. "Your friend's here."

"Keir?" I reached for my phone and saw a message.

Not from Keir. Isabel.

Oh shit. Did something else happen at home?

I scrambled off the bed. "Tell her I'll be down in five."

"Will do."

I stripped off yesterday's clothes, threw them in the laundry basket and tugged on a fresh outfit, grabbing my necromancer coat for good measure. Leaving the books

Ilsa had loaned me on the desk, I left the flat and locked up.

Pulling on my coat as I walked, I hurried downstairs to find Isabel waiting in the lobby with Lloyd.

"There was another spirit line attack," she said. "In Glasgow. The Mage Lord has been watching the official channels for anything odd, and it seems this attack was a mirror of the one you saw in Edinburgh. The mages found fliers advertising the Ley Hunters at the scene. Seven dead humans, one dead vampire."

"Crap." My stomach dropped. "We never could have warned them in time."

"I know," she said. "I expected the news to reach the guild, but I thought I'd come here and tell you first. In case you need a witch handy."

"I might do." I rubbed my tired eyes. "Not sure what the boss wants us to do today, but we're not patrolling."

"You can start by explaining why you keep bringing your friends to the guild," said Lady Montgomery, approaching from the stairs. She looked Isabel over. "And you are?"

"Ah, I'm Isabel. I came here because Jas told me to let her know if there was any other spirit line trouble."

"You heard about the attack, then?" asked Lady Montgomery. "Yes. I have a meeting with the council at the Mage Lords' headquarters today. Jas, if you aren't on today's rota, it would be a great help if you could write me a list of places where the next attack is likely to occur. I'm assuming you have some idea of the patterns the attacker is using."

"But it could be anywhere in the UK," I said. "At a key point. Wait, was it the same spirit line as before?"

"It was," confirmed Isabel. "I borrowed a map from the necromancer's guild at home, and checked."

"Use the guild's resources to look for the other key points which are likely targets," said the boss. "And do try to stay out of trouble."

And she was off, thankfully without asking Isabel any more questions.

"I take it I'm allowed to stay?" asked Isabel. "She doesn't know I came up from England..."

"Best not clue her in on that one."

With no choice but to do as the boss said, I headed to the archives, where the guild's biggest map of the spirit lines was fixed to the wall. Ilsa was on desk duty this time, and waved at me when I entered with Lloyd and Isabel.

"Hey," she said. "Who's your friend?"

"This is Isabel, my mentor," I said. "Isabel, this is Ilsa."

Isabel nodded to her. "I saw you at the council meeting in October."

"Speaking of council meetings, that's where the boss is," said Lloyd. "So we're meant to use our powers of deduction to figure out where the next attack on the spirit lines will be. Where's a psychic when you need one?"

"Not even a psychic could predict the pattern," said Isabel.

If they have a direct link with the enemy, maybe they can. But I doubted the boss wanted Mackie to end up close to the enemy again. "We can start by marking where the last few attacks took place." I moved to the map on the wall. "Ilsa, can you look in the desk drawer and see if there's anything I can use to mark this?"

"Sure." She dug in the drawer and handed a box of

drawing pins to me, while Lloyd sat on the edge of the desk to watch. "Need me to look anything up?"

"If there's a historical reference for 'Ley Hunters' or the 'Soul Collector', it would help if we knew," I said. "Maybe the perpetrators are taking inspiration from an old scheme."

"What, you think it might have happened before?" Ilsa obligingly walked to the book-lined shelves.

"Maybe." The soul-sucking device wasn't a new invention, or so Lady Montgomery had implied, anyway.

Ilsa started pulling books off the shelves, and Isabel went to help her. I wasn't convinced we'd find anything in the archive, though sticking pins into a map didn't seem much help against an elusive vampire, either. To complicate things, the spirit line itself fluctuated like they all did, so a few years ago, the key points wouldn't even have been in the same place as they were now. Not to mention the Ley Hunters seemed to be moving at random. How was anyone meant to predict what they'd do next?

"Ley Hunters," said Ilsa, already neck-deep in a book. "I haven't found the name, but people have been tracking the spirit lines for centuries. The first maps of the spirit lines were drawn by hand."

"This one is, too." I traced the lines on the map with my fingertips. The spirit lines divided Earth from Death, but they might also contain an infinite number of liminal spaces. The humans being sucked into this scheme didn't have a clue what they were messing with.

"Any recorded cases of humans tapping a spirit line?" I asked.

"There wouldn't be," said Ilsa. "Humans can't touch them. Necromancers, though—too many to count."

I thought so. "And vampires?" Lloyd put in.

"Vampires, I'm guessing, would fall under the same category as early necromancers," said Ilsa. "It's only since the guild's inception that they existed separately."

"Yeah, they aren't fond of rule-following," said Lloyd. "Maybe using those spirit devices gets them more souls to feed on. That's got to be why there's a vampire behind this, right?"

"Maybe." I squinted at the map to find the local key points. His theory was plausible, but didn't explain the enemy's efforts to take out the other vampires. Much less why they'd used furies to do so.

The furies had come from another dimension. The spirit lines divided the realms…

"They only want that spirit line," said Isabel, walking to my side and sticking another pin on the map. "If you look. All the attacks have taken place on the same line, including today's."

"Except yesterday's," I said, indicating the pin I'd stuck at the top of the map. "It broke the pattern." It had also targeted the Hemlocks' line, which I would have thought would be a more alluring target than the other one. But the attack in Glasgow had hit the original spirit line, the same one that would have been a target if I hadn't intercepted the meeting in Birmingham.

"So are they trying to wipe one spirit line?" asked Lloyd. "Or just hit a bunch of places at once?"

Ilsa didn't answer. She'd stuck her head in the book, skimming through the pages.

"Who knows," said Isabel. "The mages in Glasgow weren't able to get any conclusive answers from the humans they questioned, either. Some subtle brainwashing was going on, but the humans didn't take much convincing."

"Why, though?" said Lloyd. "I think even if I wasn't a necromancer, I'd have a few questions if someone tried to recruit me to a death cult."

"Not if it's billed as giving humans access to magic," said Isabel. "Or self-defence against supernaturals, like the one we ran into before. A lot of humans would want that."

"Exactly," I said. "Lloyd, didn't the boss ask you to poke around yesterday and ask whereabouts they're recruiting these humans from?"

"Funny you should say that," he said. "I was just waiting on a text from my sister. She wasn't on the university campus yesterday, but she said she'd take a look around today and see if anyone was handing out fliers with the Ley Hunters' name on it again. They'll be more careful now, but broke students are an easy target. Make some spare cash in exchange for your soul."

"I seriously doubt that's what they're telling people," said Ilsa, looking up from her book. "I asked my house-mates if they'd seen anything, but they hadn't. They're supernaturals, though. The vampire behind this is targeting humans." Worry underscored her voice. She'd lived among humans for a few years. And most of Lloyd's family was human, too.

"Hey," he said, suddenly, as his phone pinged with a message. "There she is. She found a flyer."

"Let's see." I moved in behind him, looking at the cracked screen of his second-hand phone. The photo showed a flyer, embossed with the following words: "The Society of Ley Hunters is looking for volunteers. Want some extra cash? Come to the church on Frey Street."

"That was yesterday," I said, spotting the date on the flier. "But the location is wrong. Where's Frey Street?"

"Let me look." He took his phone back, while I turned to the map, searching for other key points near Edinburgh. If we intercepted another meeting… this time, with Mackie out of harm's way, we might be able to pin down the enemy. Literally.

Lloyd held out his phone. "Check that."

I looked at the map on his phone screen showing the designated address, then at the spirit line map. "We need a zoomed-in map."

"On it," said Ilsa, moving behind the shelves. "Did the flyer your sister saw definitely say yesterday's date?"

"Yep," said Lloyd. "There weren't any other attacks on the spirit line yesterday."

"Check that out," said Ilsa, holding up a book depicting a map of the city with the key points highlighted. "Yesterday's meeting was meant to be at that church on Frey Street. But it wasn't. It was at the house on the other spirit line instead."

"They moved meeting locations?" asked Isabel.

"Apparently." Lloyd lowered his phone. "Why?"

"Because Mackie came along?" I said uncertainly. "Or because they had that device? That can't have been planned. I only stole the thing two days before."

"The fliers were put on campus last week," said Lloyd. "So yeah, last-minute change of meeting place. Weird."

Why change the meeting place at the last minute? Because they'd found it easier to lure Mackie to a location closer to the guild?

"No, you're right," said Isabel. "But did the fliers say

there definitely wouldn't be a meeting at the church at all?"

"Good question," said Lloyd. "Do you think it's worth checking the original address out?"

"Worth a try," I said. "The enemy might have hidden another of those spirit devices at the scene." I doubted we'd get that lucky, but the location was at a key point north of the one they'd switched off. It was as likely a target as any.

"I reckon it's worth scoping out the place," said Lloyd. "*Before* they drag innocent people there. Leave a booby trap."

"That's our area." I nodded to Isabel. "Might see if they left anything. I know the spirit device was only left in the house in Birmingham because the guy had rented the place, but you never know."

"And he wasn't exactly all there," Isabel added. "Yeah… getting ahead of them might be a good plan. Unless they anticipate it."

"This time we need to capture one of the vampires alive," I said. "The necromancer I met in Birmingham hopped over the veil without giving anything away, but there's got to be a way to lock them down. The Soul Collector… I don't get why he doesn't directly get involved. He's hiding in the background, letting his vampires do all the work. Yet he's powerful. I sensed it."

"This guy needs to collect human souls… why?" asked Lloyd.

"Soul Collector." Ilsa's mouth twisted with distaste. "I can't find any references to him in these books, at all, but vampires aren't *that* different from necromancers, except for their ability to extend their control beyond the usual limits. Otherwise, their link to the spirit realm works the same as ours does. And their souls are worth twice as much."

"Is it vampire souls he's collecting, then?" asked Isabel.

"If it was, he wouldn't have killed them." I stared at the map as though hoping the lines would reveal the truth. Furies didn't just materialise out of thin air… but that spirit device's explosion had unleashed a blast of kinetic energy intense enough to shake the spirit line. Maybe rip open a rift… in which case, there might not be any witches involved at all.

Leila Hemlock was gone, while Evelyn hadn't surfaced, except in those odd moments. If the Soul Collector and his band of vampire minions wanted to open a way into the Hemlocks' forest, surely they would have targeted that spirit line from the start.

Unless that wasn't their initial goal, but their end goal.

"Jas?" said Lloyd. "Something up?"

"I…" Damn. I still couldn't voice the Hemlocks' secrets with Ilsa there, even now. "I think they're building it up," I said. "Each attack gets bigger. Until they have enough energy massed to go after a major node."

"The Ley Line?" said Ilsa, her eyes widening. "Shit. That would break open a way into Faerie, if they hit hard enough."

Damn. I didn't even think of that.

"Why would a vampire want to get near Faerie?" said Lloyd.

Everyone remained silent. It didn't make any sense. There were no faeries involved in this scheme, after all. But if their end target was the Hemlocks' spirit line… that would open another realm entirely.

"Isabel, can I have a word outside?" I said.

Lloyd gave me a curious look, but the geas stopped me mentioning the Hemlocks in front of Ilsa, and it'd look suspicious if I asked just her to leave.

"Sure." Isabel joined me, and we left the room.

"Isabel," I said, lowering my voice. "I know what they're trying to do."

"I know," she said. "That's why I came. It's not the Ley Line they want."

"Did you speak to them in the forest?" I asked. "Face to face?"

"No. I heard Cordelia spouting her usual line about how you're the heir and it's your duty to help protect the realms, et cetera. She wanted you to come and speak to her."

"I do need to speak to her. Later. I think yesterday was a test run."

"And… the other spirit line?"

"Haven't a clue, but if the Ley Hunters are planning anything at that address, we need to intercept them first." I re-opened the door and walked back into the archives, addressing the others. "I think we should head to that church."

"You sure?" said Lloyd. "I really think they'll be onto us. They usually are."

I closed the door behind me. "Keir has already offered to help the guild. He's capable of piloting zombies from a distance, so convincingly that they look like real people. If he sends a couple of vessels to scope out the place, he can watch through their eyes as though he was there. Then if they get caught, they're only zombies, it doesn't matter."

"Not a bad plan," said Ilsa, "but wouldn't a vampire pick up on another one being present?"

"Yes, but we don't know for sure if they're still planning to go ahead and blow up the place," I said. "Checking it out through the spirit realm is more reliable than using disguises. I don't think the last guy was a powerful vampire either, so he might not even notice."

The person orchestrating this was a different story entirely, but with luck, the Soul Collector wouldn't pop into the meeting until the last second. If we scoped out the place first, set up a trap or two and set things up so that we'd be able to capture the vampire or necromancer in charge before any humans got involved, we'd finally have a live prisoner to question. *I hope.*

"I'll get the props," I said. "This time, we'll stop the Ley Hunters before they even get started."

16

"If you're sure," said Keir, when I'd finished explaining our plan. He'd arrived immediately after I'd messaged him, looking much more awake than he had yesterday. He'd shaved the stubble from his face, though his hair was still a little longer than before. "I can certainly help out, but the vessels I'm currently using aren't trained. That means I'll have to drop them if things get too rough in there."

The rest of us had agreed that our best bet was to watch the show from a distance while Keir sent his vessels to booby trap the place. Ilsa and I could project ourselves directly into the church to have a look around if it turned out to be deserted, but I sincerely doubted we'd get that lucky.

The small group of us waited in a deserted street a short distance from the proposed meeting place for Keir's undead to show.

"It's no big loss," said Lloyd. "They're only zombies. Better than any of us getting blown up in there."

"That was a one-off," I said. "I'd like to know how to turn off a spirit device in a way that doesn't blow up in the face of the person carrying it, but I doubt they'll leave another one unguarded. They're smarter now, and they know we're on their tail."

I doubted they'd expect zombies to show up, though. To be honest, I envied Keir's skill at manipulating his vessels. I could raise undead, but they lumbered around in a very obviously dead way. Keir had them walk around and interact like living humans and made it look easy.

Keir turned to me, his mouth lifting at the corner. "Here they are. Three dead people, at your service. Their van went off the bridge last night. They might need a little drying."

Three slightly damp male zombies walked towards us. Aside from their sopping wet clothes, I wouldn't have picked any of them out of a crowd.

"It's lucky I have some quick-dry charms on hand," said Isabel, passing Keir three spells.

I dug into my own spell collection to pass a few among the three vessels. Keir seemed confident he had enough control to order them to use the spells to booby-trap the Ley Hunters' meeting place without any of us having to show up in person. That way, if any humans came nosing around, they'd be frightened into running off. Meanwhile, the vampires would run right into a trap.

On paper, it almost sounded simple.

"It's not that far off the guild's standard approach," I said. "We want to minimise conflict. Not to mention the casualty numbers."

"Because it's bad for the guild's reputation?" Keir asked.

"No, it's to stop people from panicking," I said. "Humans blow things out of proportion when supernaturals go bad. Most of them are already terrified of us as it is." My mouth moved, and for an instant, it was as though someone else spoke in my place. "Nothing in this world is scarier than being human."

Everyone stared at me. Huh. Where had that come from? The words... didn't sound like me. They sounded like Evelyn. Maybe she was rubbing off on me. Or maybe I hadn't imagined feeling her presence last night. I was far from in the mood for another foray into the spirit realm, but I wouldn't leave Keir to face the enemy alone. Even if his vessels would be the ones to take the hit if we failed.

Lloyd pushed a spell onto the nearest vessel's wrist, then jumped a foot in the air when it moved. Keir's voice came from its mouth: "Want me to shake your hand?"

"Fuck *off*," said Lloyd, giving Keir the finger from where he stood innocuously at my side. The vampire grinned at him.

"If you do that to me," Isabel said, handing a spell to another vessel, "I'll unleash my coven magic on you."

"Not to worry," said Keir. "I've had my entertainment for the day. And we're running out of time. The vessels can only move at human speed."

Isabel stepped back from the vessel, and the man turned away. It felt seriously weird to be giving orders to people who weren't technically people in the usual sense. You'd think I'd be used to it by now, but those vessels were creepily convincing. Hopefully they'd fool the vampires, if they ran into any.

"Farewell, my friends." Keir gave an exaggerated wave

to the three zombies as they wandered off down the street.

Ilsa rolled her eyes. "Are you sure they won't get caught?"

"They're well-trained," said Keir. "They'll walk as fast as they can without drawing attention. Then it's on us."

"Yeah." I pulled a candle from my pocket. "Ilsa and I can go ahead through Death, but we should probably use candles. Since we're not on a spirit line at the moment."

"Good. I'm not so keen on watching you float off again." Lloyd moved in to help me set up the candles. "I'm also not expecting this to go without a hitch."

"Nor me," said Isabel. "Keir's zombies can still be detected for what they are by necromancers."

"Yes," said Ilsa, setting candles in a circle of her own. "But our main goal is to get any curious humans out of harm's way, right? It doesn't matter if the zombies get caught afterwards."

"No." At least we were nowhere near the Hemlocks' spirit line this time around.

"It doesn't feel right, sending off a bunch of zombies with no backup," said Isabel. "I know *we're* supposed to be the backup, but we're too far off."

"That's the point," said Lloyd. "Jas and Ilsa are way too recognisable as far as the spirit line goes. And Keir, too."

"It's okay, they have our spells," I said. "And we can fight just as well in the spirit realm. Better, probably."

"Ivy's rubbing off on me," said Isabel. "She's always favoured an all-guns-blazing approach, and it's weird hanging at a distance rather than charging in and making a racket."

"I think there's plenty of time for that later," I said. "Does she know you're here?"

"Of course she does," answered Isabel. "She and the Mage Lord were the ones who told me about the latest attack."

I should have guessed. We weren't the only ones watching the line, but with the enemy able to strike anywhere at any given time, all bets were off. For all I knew, they planned to escalate the situation and go for a more major target while our attention was elsewhere. But this was the closest we'd get to tracking the bastards down.

"Ivy as in Ivy Lane?" asked Ilsa, turning to Isabel.

"Yeah… you've met?" asked Isabel.

"Once or twice." Ilsa fidgeted, shooting Keir a look. He stood with his brow furrowed in concentration, probably jumping between his three vessels to make sure they stayed on track. Sending more would look suspicious, but if anything happened to them, it wasn't like he couldn't seize control of any nearby dead if he wanted to.

Winning a battle wasn't a problem. To win the war, we needed to find the enemy's real location.

"Go in," Keir said, through the side of his mouth. "Jas, Ilsa. Watch the dead."

The candles lit up at my command, I nodded to Ilsa, and we plunged into the spirit realm.

Keir was easy to spot, a brightly outlined shadow. Feeding on my soul yesterday had done him a world of good. Threads of blue light spun from his hands, directing Ilsa and me to follow their trail through the spirit realm to the vessels.

Soon enough, the blue lights came to an end beside the

run-down church chosen as the meeting place. Weird choice, or maybe not. Old churches were often haunted, and it made some sense for humans to feel more connected with the spirit realm at a place of religious significance.

It would be expecting too much to find the enemy's plans hidden inside, but it was nice to imagine. One of Keir's vessels walked around the church, setting down candles. The other two walked to the doors, looking for all the world like an ordinary pair of friends, venturing into an abandoned church on a whim. Nobody else was around, which was probably why they'd chosen this location. I scanned the spirit realm for interlopers, and spotted a faint glow. *Looks like we got here just in time.*

Ilsa floated to my side. "The candles will stabilise the spirit line, but I think the perpetrator's close."

"Shit." I whirled around as she pointed at a blurred figure at the end of the road, approaching the church. From the glow around his spirit, he must be a necromancer. *There you are.* He hadn't spotted us yet, too focused on walking towards the church to notice two ghosts floating above him. The third vessel had disappeared from sight, and I really hoped he'd complete the candle circle before the necromancer reached the church's doors.

I remained still as he drew closer. If he tapped into the spirit realm, he'd see both of us, but if we kept our distance, we might be too late to stop him.

The necromancer reached the doors, putting a hand into his pocket. When he pulled out a familiar shiny metal device, my breath caught. The contraption seemed a mirror image of the one that'd exploded. But this one was whole, glowing with blue-white light.

Oh, man. Judging by the bright glow, the device had taken in at least a few spirits already. Maybe it'd been the device used in the first attack. All that energy must have gone somewhere, after all.

The necromancer pushed at the door, and stepped back when he found it open. "Who's in here?"

The necromancer shoved the door inwards and marched in. Ilsa and I followed close behind, not impeded by the doors, to the sight of the vessels standing silently in the darkness.

"Who the devil are you?" demanded the necromancer. "What are you doing here?"

"Isn't there a meeting?" said one of the vessels, with the barest hint of Keir's voice. "The door was unlocked."

The other vessel moved in front. "That's cool," he said, eyeing the device in the necromancer's hand. "What is it?"

I hope you know what you're doing, Keir.

The necromancer took a step back, and the vessel moved swiftly, catching his arm in a tight grip.

"Vampire," the necromancer hissed, and his body glowed brighter as he tapped into the spirit realm.

"Surprise," I said, right behind him, and gave him a shove, bolstered by kinetic energy. Ilsa did the same, and he tripped backwards—right into the path of the third vessel. The zombified man grabbed the device from the necromancer's hand, leaping over the threshold to the door.

The instant he did so, twelve candles snapped on, imprisoning the necromancer inside the church.

Ilsa and I were on him before he could dive out of the

circle. He yelled and struggled as we grabbed him by the shoulders, wrenching him from his body. Ilsa's expert movements suggested this was not the first time she'd liberated someone from their earthly form.

"Let me go!" he shouted.

"Not until you tell us what you're doing here," I said. "You're not acting alone. Where is your boss?"

He struggled, swearing, but one spirit couldn't overcome two, and the candles held him captive. "I will not bow to you."

"I'm the Gatekeeper," said Ilsa, pinning his arms behind his back. "I will send you through the gates of Death before you even have the chance to use that device of yours. Are you trying to shut down the spirit line altogether?"

"No…" He struggled again, sweat beading on his forehead even as a ghost. "The spirit lines are infinite. So is their power. The more we gain, the more we can use to find what we seek."

"You're brainwashed," I said. "By who? Who is the vampire controlling you? *Where* is he?"

His mouth opened and closed, then a glint consumed his eyes as blue light spread from his form. "Right here, Jacinda Hemlock."

My body stiffened. Ilsa maintained her grip on his shoulders—but she'd heard my birth name. *How does he know?*

"How are you piloting people who are still alive?" I demanded. The necromancer's spirit might be outside of his body, but the Soul Collector was speaking *through* him. Through his spirit, not his body.

"How indeed." The ghostly man's eyes gleamed blue-grey, but no shadow lurked behind him. He was no ordinary vampire.

"You called yourself the Soul Collector," I said, thinking fast. "But that's not what you're doing, is it? You're stealing energy from the key points as well as from people."

And he planned to use that energy to break down the Hemlocks' spirit line. That much, I could guess. But Ilsa's presence made it impossible to force my way past the geas to ask what in hell he wanted with my coven. They hadn't even believed vampires existed at first.

"What's your purpose in tapping the spirit lines?" Ilsa asked. "What is it you're after?"

"What am I looking for?" he said. "The Ancients, of course. And my path to them is through you, Jacinda Hemlock."

What...?

The light disappeared from the necromancer's eyes, and he vanished. The spirit was gone.

Ilsa's hands dropped to her sides, no longer restraining the necromancer. "Where did he go? I didn't see the gates."

"No..." Crap. Ilsa was the Gatekeeper. If even *she* hadn't seen where the guy's spirit had vanished to, I was clueless.

No... the Soul Collector was no vampire. But what *was* he?

"The spirit device!" I spun on the spot, but the vessels had disappeared from the circle. The necromancer's body lay inert on the ground, and I didn't need the spirit sight to know he'd departed when the Soul Collector did.

"Relax, the vessel still has it," said Ilsa.

I'd take her word for it. I felt unbalanced, out of sorts, and not just because my body was a mile away.

I jumped at a sound from nearby, but it was only the other vessel collecting the candles. Trusting Keir to handle it, I floated out through the open doors. "I don't understand. Where did he go?" The Soul Collector couldn't live *beyond* the veil. There was no returning from that place. But Ilsa's weighted stare told me she hadn't missed hearing my real name. The geas hadn't broken, but I was right—the person behind this was linked to the witches. The Hemlocks knew where the Ancients were hidden, if they still existed. That alone was enough reason for him to want to get to my coven.

Then... why did he pick this spirit line first?

"C'mon, Jas. We should head back." Ilsa glanced around, then her transparent form disappeared, leaving me alone.

With one last glance at the church, I closed my eyes, feeling my way back into my body—

I slammed into an invisible forcefield, spinning on the spot, the church wheeling below me. *What the hell?*

Gritting my teeth, I focused again on inhabiting my body, moving my hands... and again, I hit a barrier so hard it was like it was solid.

Icy fear washed over me. *Oh, no.*

I felt my way back to my body, concentrating fiercely. *Let me back.*

Evelyn Hemlock's presence brushed against mine, triumph and anger mingling in conjunction. "You won't shut me out again, Jas."

Once more, I was thrown into the air, spinning above the spirit line. I squeezed my eyes shut, releasing a stream of curses. Ever since the explosion, I'd felt traces of Evelyn, closer than before. When I'd sealed her away, I'd instinctually known it was a temporary solution, and the shock of nearly dying must have woken her up again. And now she was in control of my body. *My friends are there. They don't know.*

I left the church behind, floating as fast as I possibly could. If I couldn't get into my body, I could at least warn my friends through the spirit realm. I floated, the ground disappearing below me, and halted at the alley entrance. My body remained standing in the candle circle, and none of the others knew the person inside it wasn't me. Ilsa stepped out of the circle, while Lloyd stood beside Keir and Isabel.

Evelyn Hemlock lifted her head, her eyes opening. She smiled, oh-so-faintly.

"Let me back," I mouthed at her. "Move."

I concentrated on my body once more, my hands clenching, and this time, sensation came back piece by piece. Ice cracked on my hands, and my breaths came quickly. I needed to seal her away, but not with witnesses. I'd acted on instinct when I'd done it the first time around and wasn't sure I *could* repeat the performance or if I needed to be close to the forest to do so, but whatever the case, I had to get her out of the way before she took control again.

"You won't stop me," she whispered in my ear. *"You were lucky to be on our spirit line at the time, and that's the only reason you were able to bind me. But if you go back to that line, I'll make you pay for it."*

Cold sweat trickled down my back. She had me cornered.

"Where are the vessels?" Ilsa asked Keir. "Hey, Jas, glad you're back."

Yeah, the problem is, it's not just me. "Slight problem," I said.

"You're telling me," Lloyd said.

A tall, cloaked figure walked towards us. Lady Montgomery approached our hiding spot, Keir's vessels just behind her, the spirit device in her hands. My heart dived into my shoes.

The boss's gaze went to the candles at my feet, and then to Keir. "Mind telling me what you're doing?"

Oh, bloody hell.

"Stopping the Ley Hunters," answered Ilsa. "We found an address where they cancelled a meeting yesterday and decided to take the initiative. Again, the perpetrator died on sight when the person calling himself the Soul Collector possessed him."

I nodded mutely, not trusting myself to speak in case Evelyn stepped in. With the boss watching like a hawk, it'd take a miracle for me to get away in time to shut my second soul away.

"So I see," Lady Montgomery said. "Pick up those candles and come with me."

"Dammit, I don't have time for paperwork." The words burst out before I could hold them back. "Erm, I mean, the Soul Collector escaped right in front of us. We have to stop—"

"Our best necromancers are watching the spirit lines," she answered. "The candles, please, Jas."

There was nothing like the sharp tone of an authority figure to snap everyone into action. Even Keir and Isabel moved in to help, the former leaving his vessels behind once Isabel had retrieved the spells they hadn't used. Lady Montgomery watched our every move, then accompanied us back to the guild on foot. Every time I contemplated making a run for it, she was there, her gaze sharp, as though she knew I planned to make a run for it at the first opportunity.

Chill, Jas. The guild's in an iron-covered building. Besides, I'm stronger than Evelyn is. I've had enough practise keeping her out.

Evelyn remained suspiciously quiet while we walked to the boss's office. Between us, we cobbled together an account of the day's events. What Keir had done hadn't been illegal and had clearly worked, so the boss was less pissed off than yesterday, but it took all the self-control I could muster not to scream that there was a mad spirit on the loose in my head, and if I didn't get her locked away soon, she might try to kill everyone in this room.

"I will take this contraption to the council," Lady Montgomery said, indicating the metal device. "I can't say I know how it works, but I can guess. I have also asked if anyone saw the man in the picture you drew, Jas, but nobody recognises his face."

"I only saw him as a ghost," I said, as all eyes turned to me. "This time, he… he was possessing a ghost. I don't know what he is, but I'm getting the impression he's no normal vampire."

"Possessing a ghost?" repeated the boss. "That certainly isn't possible. Not for one of us."

Then what is he? Even Keir looked utterly confused. Only Ilsa's confirmation told me I hadn't imagined what the Soul Collector had done to the necromancer.

"He's not carrying out the attacks in person," Ilsa said.

"He's sending other, weaker people to do the same, people who can be sacrificed. He seems to think he can break *open* the spirit lines."

"Not with this," she said, her mouth tightening. "But I've issued a security warning, and the entire guild will take measures to protect ourselves against this individual. That includes all of you."

"What do you need us to do?" I shifted my weight, hoping for a dismissal.

"Ilsa, tell the psychics to be on their guard. Lloyd, Jas, you're dismissed, but please be careful if you leave the guild. And if any other attacks take place, I'll expect you to be ready at a moment's notice."

"Gotcha," I said, another bead of sweat trickling down my back. For a moment, I expected her to call me to stay behind, but the gleaming device on her desk took priority. I bloody well hoped she had somewhere safe to secure it.

As we left, Lloyd said, "I thought she'd read us the riot act. Guess she doesn't mind if we break the rules and don't royally screw up in the process."

"Yeah." I quickened my steps. "I'm just gonna head up and get something from my room, okay?"

Or rather, sneak out and fix Evelyn's prison before anyone realised she was free. Her quietness was too good to be true, and it was only when I rounded the corner that I realised I hadn't given my body permission to walk that way.

A tingling began in my fingertips and ran down my spine, and my legs continued to move, without my permission. *Dammit, Evelyn, stop that!*

I picked up speed, and nearly walked into Morgan coming the opposite way. A psychic was the last person I needed to be near with a potentially dangerous spirit inside my head.

"Ilsa said you might be interested in getting to Lady Montgomery's book stash," he said. "I assume you've got spells, but just in case—"

My hand shot out of its own accord and grabbed him by the throat.

Evelyn! Stop!

I pushed, hard, and wrenched control away from her. Morgan staggered back, gasping for breath, and Ilsa appeared behind him. "What in hell is going on?"

Morgan gave me a confused stare. "She tried to strangle me."

"I—" Crap. *What the hell, Evelyn? You can't attack the other necromancers.* "Sorry," I managed to gasp, shoving Evelyn's presence aside. "I—I need to get outside."

"What did you do, Morgan?" asked Ilsa.

"Me? Why assume I'm the one who did something?"

"I'm guessing you're the one responsible for leaving that disembodied zombie hand lying around the cafeteria, for one thing."

"What else was I supposed to do with it?"

"Put it literally anywhere else, for a start."

Oops. I'd kicked off another sibling war. "I'm sorry," I mumbled, and then ran for it before Evelyn decided the Gatekeeper was a threat, too.

I have to bind her. Now.

"*Not anymore,*" Evelyn whispered in my ear. "*I won't be contained again.*"

I broke into a sprint across the lobby, out the doors— and ran smack into Keir.

"Whoa." He caught his balance, his eyes wide. "Jas, what—?"

Evelyn pushed into my head, and I pushed her out, my control slipping. "She's in control," I gasped at him. "Take me to the forest—to the spirit line—"

Grey light rose around me, then blackness.

y eyes opened, taking in the sight of the Hemlock forest's endless dark trees all around me. I'd made it over, but where was Keir?

I scanned the path, my heart dropping. Thick tree roots bound Keir's whole body so tightly, I couldn't even see his face, just a tuft of dark hair sticking out and his arms hanging limply between the roots.

"Cordelia," I said. "Cordelia, let him go. He didn't do anything wrong."

I walked towards him—or floated. Oh, crap. I wasn't in my body.

"Dammit, Evelyn!" I yelled. "Where did she go? Cordelia, let Keir out so I can find her. *Now.*"

"He has trespassed." Cordelia's face appeared in the branches, staring down at me. "This one knows the Ancients. We can't let him go."

"Please." My voice cracked, desperation breaking through. "He wouldn't have brought me here if Evelyn hadn't hijacked my body. Can you at least tell me where she went?"

"She left the forest."

I swore loudly. "Let Keir go. If you make me choose between leaving him to die and saving my own skin, then I swear I'll unleash your own power on you sevenfold."

"If you do, then it is you who will pay the price for it, Jacinda," she rumbled. "Your companion here hides secrets that belong to us alone."

"If you mean the fact that you exist, it's your own fault for putting the geas on me to begin with," I said. "As for the Ancients, they kidnapped his brother. That's all he knows. Let him go."

Silence descended. Crap, what if he did know more? There was a time and a place to get answers from Keir, and in the middle of the forest while Evelyn Hemlock possibly went on a massacre using my body was definitely not one of them.

The tree roots trapping Keir shifted, releasing him. He gasped for air, pulling them away from his face with his hands. Small cuts lacerated the skin, but he looked in better shape than I'd feared.

"Keir!" I ran to his side, reaching for his arm. My hands passed right through him.

"Shit, Jas," he said, staring through me. "Evelyn—she took over. I couldn't stop her. I don't know where she went."

I whirled on the tree Cordelia had spoken from. "Tell me where she went. Is she in Edinburgh?"

"She's beyond our borders," said Cordelia.

"It's my body. I should be able to track her." If she was in Edinburgh, she might be back at the guild making trouble. But otherwise? The forest could link to literally anywhere on the spirit line. Who knew where she'd run off to?

"Calm down, Jacinda."

"Calm down?" I said. "Tell me how to get her spirit out of my body. *Now.* I don't care if it leaves you without an heir. She's a madwoman, and she wants the world to burn."

"She does not," she rumbled. "She carries much passion and pain, but her mind is clouded from so long imprisoned. Given the time to heal, she will be able to take over as heir."

"You want her to be heir," I said, my voice shaking. "Not me. I was never a consideration. Just—a vessel."

"Not at all, Jas," said Cordelia. "You're two separate individuals, and I'm sure you'll learn to cooperate in time."

"Oh, you can't pretend you didn't play favourites," I said. "I don't care if you were buddies with her when you were all still alive and kicking: she nearly destroyed the spirit line to get power. And if you can't see that, you're beyond my help. Feel free to have a heart to heart when she does come in here to finish you off. Maybe I'll even watch."

"You used Jas," Keir said, addressing Cordelia. "You do realise that what you did broke the laws of this realm, and you let an innocent person take the fall?"

"They know," I said. "They just don't care."

Cordelia's dark eyes briefly flicked to Keir before moving back to me. "Let it not be said that I care nothing for your well-being, Jacinda. Evelyn was a loyal and dedicated apprentice who died before her time. You have done nothing but run from your responsibilities.'

"I've spent the last month dealing with the enemies *you* brought on my tail," I said, my ghostly fists clenching. "Someone is breaking the spirit lines to get to the Ancients. And if I fail to stop them because of Evelyn's quest for power, you're equally to blame."

"Evelyn is not your enemy, Jacinda. I believe she acted rashly out of desperation, but believe me when I say that I do not believe Evelyn plans to turn on her coven."

I threw up my hands. "You're taking her side even now?"

"Did Evelyn ever use her power to hurt others?" she enquired. "Evelyn does not desire to destroy us, only share in the power she sees as rightfully hers."

"No, she wants *more* power. She implied you gave up most of yours."

"We did," she said. "To create this forest, we poured our lives and our souls into the magic, and as long as we remain, the Ancients will never return."

"That's what the enemy wants, right?" I said. "To free the Ancients. They're... in another realm somewhere. Right?"

The void-like dimension where that winged monstrosity existed... was that what the Soul Collector planned to crack open? He'd already knocked out one spirit line, to say nothing of how he'd freed Evelyn using the knowledge he'd yanked from Mackie's head. He knew everything she did—about me, about Evelyn, and maybe even about the forest. The only reason he wasn't already here was because he needed a Hemlock witch's magic to enter, and now he had one. And Cordelia still had the nerve to act like *I* was the villain.

"The Ancients," said Cordelia, "will never be allowed back into the realm of mortals. And the spirit lines cannot be destroyed."

"But they can be opened," I said. "Some furies already escaped through the gap."

Keir shot me a sideways look. "So that's how they got out? They weren't summoned?"

"I should have told you." I screwed up my forehead. "Keir… is there anything you know that I don't? About the Ancients?"

"It might be that my brother knew things I don't," he said quietly. "I'd never heard of the Ancients before he was kidnapped. After… I went direct to the mages and appealed to them for help. But they shot me down and insisted that the Ancients no longer existed and neither did any realm they might have inhabited."

"They might well believe that. Everyone thinks the Hemlocks are extinct, after all. But what *are* the Ancients, precisely? Come on, Cordelia, at least give me a clue."

"Our predecessors," said Cordelia. "Gods, or so our ancestors believed. It is said that they died out, but they are not so easily destroyed. Tell me the name of our enemy."

"The Soul Collector," I said. "Why, do you know him? He's not… oh, hell."

The Soul Collector wasn't human. He was more powerful than any vampire had the right to be… yet he was weak, hiding behind others and sending them to do his bidding. He couldn't be one of the Ancients, right?

"Cordelia," I said, trying to keep my voice steady. "The

Soul Collector wants to come here, and with Evelyn, he might just get his wish. Put your bias aside and tell me… if Evelyn used your magic against you, would she be able to undo the spells you used to lock the Ancients out?"

Her eyes blinked, once, and I knew I'd lost. She was determined not to see Evelyn for the villain she really was.

"No," she finally said. "It's not possible for a single Hemlock to undo the work of the others. But there's no reason for Evelyn to turn on us. It's thanks to our magic that she survived at all, and if you were to be destroyed, so would she."

"Maybe she doesn't want to destroy me. Just taking my body and leaving me stuck as a ghost forever is enough," I said. "If you'd had your way, I wouldn't have survived at all, would I? You wanted her. Not me."

"If we had our way, we would not have died out," she said. "We would not have been forced to sacrifice ourselves in defence of this realm."

"Spare me the *woe is me* speech. You chose to bind yourselves here." I turned to Keir. "We have to get to Evelyn. But if she's too far off, I might lose all connection to my body."

Keir moved to my side, and I stiffened in surprise as his hand interlocked with mine, through the spirit realm. In the grey fog that briefly appeared, his ghostly form appeared less shadowy, like a veil had peeled back and I saw him the way he really was, behind his vampire form.

"Look," he said. "The rules on shades—hell, the rules of *necromancy*—throw them out the window. If the connection between the two of you was going to break, it already would have. She won't let your body die, not while she needs it, and as long you both live, you'll stay connected.

You've even passed through liminal spaces without your body and the connection still exists. The forest alone is much further from Earth than the distance between two key points."

I drew in a breath I didn't need to take. "Thank you. I think you're right… but I don't like not knowing what she's doing with my body."

"I can find her," he said. "If you cross over, you'll be able to bring me with you. Trust me."

You know what? I trusted him.

Keir's grip on my hand remained steady, and I closed my eyes, pulling both of us out of the forest, back to Earth.

18

Seeing Edinburgh as a ghost was like viewing the world through a grey haze. Anyone who looked at Keir and me would think he was alone—except for necromancers. Best hope I didn't run into anyone I knew before I got my body back.

I focused as hard as I could on the sensation of inhabiting a body, wishing I wasn't so close to the guild, and closed my eyes. *Take me back. Let me in, Evelyn.*

A whisper of a connection, then nothing.

"Nope." I turned to Keir. "I can barely sense her. She's too far away." Or she'd got better at shutting me out.

I closed my eyes, reaching out. Even when she'd temporarily shut me out of my body before, I'd been able to push my way in eventually. Now, it was as though she was nowhere at all. She couldn't be dead, or beyond the veil, otherwise I'd have died along with her. Unless…

"Maybe… maybe she's not in this realm."

Keir's hand brushed against mine. "Keep trying. Maybe she went into a liminal space, maybe not, but she's on the hunt for this vampire. *He's* in this realm, as far as we know. He wouldn't be able to possess anyone otherwise."

"He's not a vampire," I pointed out, opening my eyes. "And—bloody hell. She has my body, which means she has my phone. She can easily call anyone whose number I have and lure them into a trap, or… anything."

His mouth pinched. "I don't think you're giving yourself enough credit—or the people who really know you. They won't believe her for a minute."

"And does that number include you?" A heartbeat passed, then I shook my head. "Never mind."

I turned away, my mind spinning in circles. There must be a way to reach my friends which didn't require having a physical body. Most of them were necromancers, for crying out loud.

"I want it to," he said, so quietly I half thought I imagined it.

I extended my senses through the spirit realm, searching for any familiar people. If I went directly to the guild without a body, the boss would pick up on me immediately. But there *was* one way to communicate with them. "Wait. There are two psychics in that building. If I get their attention, they'll know it's me. You can probably do the same."

"Aren't they wearing iron?" he asked.

"Dammit." Of all the times to regret pressuring Mackie to block out her psychic connection.

"I can go there myself and tell them you're in trouble," said Keir. "Or I can find them through the spirit realm. Nobody noticed when I visited you."

"It's risky," I said. "The guild is on full alert—specifically, for a vampire. They won't let you in."

"Yeah, that's what I thought. I'll check first." He closed his eyes, then opened them again. "No. They have guards outside. Any higher necromancers will sense me the instant I go near."

"Bugger. Maybe they sensed me, too."

"No, they won't have. I'm easier to sense than you are, since it's vampires they're looking for. None of them can project that far, and if that Ilsa is involved, she'll know it's me."

"Let's hope so. I think reaching the psychics is the only way."

Mackie! I thought loudly. *Morgan! It's Jas. I need help. Come and meet us at Waverley Bridge now.* I repeated the thought, over and over. *Mackie!*

Keir tapped a foot. "Are you sure it will work? How do you know they can hear?"

"I don't," I admitted. "Mackie implied that psychics are super attuned to anyone who has a strong presence in the spirit realm, so if you do anything to draw their attention, it hits harder. But I can't link mind-to-mind the way other psychics do. The fact that she saw into my dreams, though… it implies the iron isn't enough to completely block it out. It's only a temporary measure. Morgan said that you have to learn to control the power yourself, otherwise anyone else with psychic abilities can still get around the link." Like the Soul Collector had.

"Maybe they won't let her leave the guild," said Keir, after another minute had passed.

"They probably won't." And for Mackie's own safety, she shouldn't. "You know what, I should probably try to link to my body again instead…"

Keir gripped my ghostly hand. "There they are."

Several cloaked figures approached the bridge, moving fast. Ilsa led the way, with Morgan and Mackie behind Lloyd and Isabel.

"God, stop *yelling* at me, Jas," Mackie exploded. "You nearly blew our cover."

"I didn't know if you could hear me," I said. "Or that you'd bring the others."

"Like we'd stay away," said Lloyd, hurrying down the bridge. "After you ran out on us."

"Wait, you're a ghost," said Morgan. "Am I the only person seeing this?"

"No," said Ilsa, staring through me. "Jas, what in hell happened to you? Where's your body?"

"Yeah, the thing is, I'm kind of not allowed to tell anyone. Pain of death. Suffice to say, it's not where I want it to be, and I can't find it."

Lloyd's eyes bugged out. "But you're still alive. I mean, relatively speaking."

"For now," I said. "I'm stuck like this until I find my body, but wherever it is, there's a strong chance our enemy's there, too."

"Did your body go walking off by itself?" said Morgan. "Seriously, that's *not* normal in my book. Unless you're secretly a vampire?"

"No, she..." Ilsa hesitated, her forehead screwing up. "I'm lost."

Lloyd and Mackie looked at each other, then at Isabel, whose mouth was pinched. All three of the others knew, but the Lynn siblings were in the dark. They were both too smart to stay ignorant for long, though, and getting to the enemy was more important than keeping secrets.

"Just imagine a vampire piloting a vessel and you'll get the picture," I said.

"Shade," Ilsa said suddenly, her face paling.

All eyes turned to her.

"Shade?" repeated Morgan.

"It's what you read from my mind, if you were paying attention," said Mackie. "It's not like I was great at shutting you out."

"Mother-fucker," said Morgan. "You tried to strangle me. That wasn't you at all. Was it?"

"Nope," I said. "Unfortunately, the person hijacking my body is not friendly."

"And she's probably not in the city," Keir put in. "We're assuming she's assisting the Soul Collector, and has cut herself off from the spirit realm so Jas can't reconnect to her body."

Mackie's mouth fell open. "I take back every bad thing I've said about being a psychic. That's crap."

"It is," I said. "I'll be honest and say the odds of me making it out of this alive are slim, but if I don't find my body, then the enemy is likely to break the spirit line. He's been attacking smaller nodes to build up power, and has probably succeeded in at least one place."

Ilsa swore. "He said he wants the *Ancients*. Can the person controlling your body take him to them?"

Oh, bugger. I'd forgotten, momentarily, that she'd witnessed everything the Soul Collector had said to both of us before he'd killed the necromancer and fled. But I hadn't known she'd recognise the word.

Keir took a step towards Ilsa. "I knew something about you wasn't right. You—you know them, don't you?"

Ilsa turned to him, her eyes narrowing. "Do I know

that the Ancients are the former gods of the faerie realm? Yes, I do. And I wasn't aware any of them were still alive."

My mouth fell open. Ilsa knew? And Morgan, too, judging by his lack of surprise. Well, that made explaining easier. "The Soul Collector is one of them," I said. "At least, I think so. He's almost like a vampire, but not quite. And he looks human, except he seems to be able to possess ghosts."

"He might not have his own form," Ilsa said uncertainly. "Uh. I don't know. It's not like I run into ancient gods every day, but as far as I know, a lot of them are, or were, shapeshifters. They can take on human form if they like. But maybe this Soul Collector is different."

"Jesus," said Lloyd. "And he has your body?"

"No, Evelyn's seeking him out. I assume he has a real body somewhere."

Mackie cleared her throat. "I know how to reach him."

"Nope," said Ilsa. "I've been through this with Morgan already. Don't you even *think* about encouraging her."

"She's mind-linked with him," said Morgan. "I don't like it either. But I can't think of any other way to get his attention. He wants her, not me."

Oh, shit. The only one of us with a direct link to the Soul Collector was Mackie. But if she used that link, she risked him taking over her mind and either turning her against us or killing her.

Mackie scowled. "Look. You all know I'm right, and there's no other way to track him down. He thinks I'm terrified of him, he won't expect me to seek him out willingly. I'll take off the iron, find him, then put it back on—you've done this before, Morgan."

"Yes, I have," he said. "It also nearly killed me. You told

me he tried to kill *you* the last time you met in the spirit realm."

Mackie's hands curled into tight fists. "Yeah, because I betrayed him. He's a monster. But I can reach him, and when we link minds, I sometimes get impressions of where he is. I think it's the only way to know."

"It's true, but you're taking a huge risk," I said. "If we can lure him here, though, we might be able to force him to face us. He's after this spirit line we're standing on, one way or another."

"What's so special about this line?" asked Ilsa. "Wait—don't tell me. It's to do with the Ancients, isn't it?"

I nodded. "I don't like the idea of Mackie risking her life, especially when the person on the other end is so damned unhinged, but it's the best we've got. And if she's absolutely certain she wants to do this..."

"I am," said Mackie. "The bastard used me as his pet for two years. I won't be controlled again. This time, I'll bring him right to us."

19

Within ten minutes, Mackie stood in a circle of candles, down by the abandoned train station. We hadn't been able to find a better spot, and besides, the enemy was likely on the spirit line already.

Mackie's face was ashen, her hands shaking as she clenched her fists at her sides. "Are you sure you can get the iron on me as soon as he realises I'm close to him?"

"Yes," said Ilsa, standing next to the circle with Morgan at her side. "We've done this before."

"We've linked mind to mind," he said to Mackie. "If he takes over you, I can stop him."

The corners of her mouth turned down, and she didn't look particularly convinced.

Lloyd hung back with Isabel, while I joined the Lynn siblings beside the circle. We likely had only one shot, and everything was riding on Mackie. I hoped she knew what she was doing.

Holding out a hand, Mackie let Ilsa remove the iron

band from her wrist. Then she stood within the circle, hands stretched out, eyes closed.

"You've been awfully quiet, my pet," said a male voice through her mouth, and her eyes opened, glowing blue-white.

"Go fuck yourself," said Morgan.

A smile stretched Mackie's lips. "I do like breaking psychics. Almost as much as I enjoy bending necromancers to my will."

"You're sick in the head," I told him. "Mind telling us where you are so I can come and knock the stuffing out of you?"

Mackie stumbled to the circle's edge, her eyes still glowing, and Morgan grabbed her shoulders, pushing her back. "I've got you," he said. "Bugger off, you twisted scumbag."

Lloyd ran to his side, looking panicked, as both Morgan and Mackie half-fell into the circle. Ilsa grabbed Mackie's arm and shoved the iron band back onto it, while Morgan kicked over the nearest candle, breaking the circle.

"He's gone," gasped Mackie. "God—he was in my *head*."

"Did you see where he was?" I asked.

Mackie sucked in a breath. "He was... it's blurred. Before he came here, I think he was in London. I saw through his eyes for a moment there and I'm sure I recognised the place. A huge park in a city."

Isabel swore suddenly, her eyes on her phone. "London?" she said. "I just heard from the Mage Lord. There's been a few incidents on the spirit line, and they heard from the London Mage Guild that at least one of them took place there."

"Shit," I said. "Where in London? I've never been."

Could the forest take me there? If not, there was the spirit line, but I'd never travelled along a line without my body before.

"I can check," said Keir. "Now I know what city he's in, I can grab a few vessels and poke around. I guarantee that any supernaturals close by would know where the nearest damaged key point is. They'll have felt it. London is a hotbed of key points and spirit lines, same as here."

"All right," I said. "If he's there, so is my body. You guys alert the guild, and Keir and I will find my body and get it away from the enemy. The Soul Collector might be based in London, might not, but chances are, he'll be back here before long."

Mackie nodded. "He's here… he's everywhere, all at the same time. Once you've linked to him, he'll never leave."

A chill crawled down my spine. "And can he come back to you, even when you're at the guild? Seriously—if there's anything you can tell us… it's life or death."

Her jaw clenched. "Don't you have a world to save?"

"Yes, but he's holding my body hostage, and the person inside it is on his side. I could use a little direction."

"He can't get into the guild," she whispered. "He's stronger than before, but he can't get through the barriers. But he's—not human. I'm not sure he even has a body."

"He must do," I said. "He's an Ancient…"

"He never called himself that," she said, looking at her feet. "He did call himself a god."

"The egotistical little…" Lloyd began.

"He has no body," Mackie said. "Or if he does, I never saw it. He linked us, mind to mind, and sometimes I get impressions of other people he's linking to, but never any physical body. I don't know where he is, or if he can just hop from one body to another, but he's not like any other necromancer or vampires. And he's clever. He lured me in by teaching me to mind-link, and to use my powers to affect the spirit lines. There's nothing he doesn't know."

I shook my head. "That's not true. He's not all-knowing. He's adept at using the spirit realm, but the same can be said of any vampire."

"That's why he tried to kill us off," Keir said. "Jas is right, nobody can be all-knowing. He must use his psychic linking ability to gather information from anyone who leaves their mental shields open."

"And possessing them," I added. "Possessing ghosts? It doesn't seem possible."

Except, perhaps, for a god.

"I'm pretty sure he's not been alive in a while, if he ever was," said Morgan. "I linked to his mind just then, and all I can see is a mess of other people's thoughts and memories. He's been in the spirit realm forever."

"Can gods survive death?" I asked, not really expecting an answer. But the Soul Collector sounded almost like Evelyn, but without a host to grab onto. And if you spent long enough in the spirit realm, you lost all connection to the land of the living.

Maybe he *had* been alive, once. And, like Evelyn and me, gods didn't easily die.

"Maybe," said Ilsa. "Soul Collector... I'm sure Lady Montgomery seemed to recognise the name when we told her. But it's not like I can go back and ask her."

"You can," I said. "You three—and Lloyd, I won't be

able to bring you with me, either. Keir, too—sorry. I don't think you can come. But you can link from a distance."

Keir's mouth tightened. "Do what you have to, Jas."

"Tell the boss I've been kidnapped," I said to the others. "It's close to the truth. If the Soul Collector can hop around, he'll try to get to you through the psychics anyway. Warn her. She has to know—the guild needs to be prepared for a potential attack from the inside."

"She's right," said Mackie. "I don't like it, but I can *feel* the bastard trying to push through the iron to get to my head. One slip and the damn thing will be off my wrist and he'll be in control again."

"We won't let it happen," said Ilsa. "Jas—are you going to try to get back into your body?"

"Yeah. I have to stay outside the guild for it to work. Sorry, guys. You too, Lloyd," I added. He looked about as unhappy as Keir did at the prospect of leaving me behind.

Lloyd gave a tight nod. "We'll take care of the psychics, make sure the fucker doesn't make it to the guild. Okay?"

"Exactly," I said. "Keir will send his vessels to London to find me. And if things go wrong…"

"I'll warn you." Keir nodded to the others. "Make sure they don't get into the guild."

At what point, and why, had he started considering the guild in his decisions? I didn't have time to question—there was too much at risk, and now the Soul Collector knew we were on his tail.

I tuned out the sounds of the others leaving and focused on my body once again. I didn't really expect it to work, but again, I felt a whisper of a connection, of Evelyn's presence—

And the smell of burning.

I opened my eyes. "Found a vessel yet?"

Keir's expression was distant, glazed. "Found one. There's a fire…"

"I smelled it." I swallowed hard. "I'm going into the forest, and if the Hemlocks have any shortcuts, I'm demanding they let me use them."

"I'll be waiting on the other side, Jas."

I paused, then faltered. If I reconnected then lost the connection, I might end up anywhere, adrift, without any way to get back home.

No. I wouldn't lose my connection. Keir was there, holding onto me, steadying me. As long as I wasn't alone in the spirit realm, I'd be able to find my way home.

I took a deep breath, and crossed into the Hemlocks' forest once more. Magic hummed in my fingertips, faint yet resonant, and I clung onto it. I didn't need to be in the forest to travel along the spirit line.

A faint whisper trailed along the back of my neck. "Keir?"

"Right here," he whispered. "You're on the spirit line. I can't follow you this way, because I can only track you through vessels. But if you keep going, you can reach London in seconds."

"And you know this because…"

"Because you're a master level necromancer. They can do the same."

"Er, only when they're *dead.*" I sincerely hoped I wouldn't run into any necromancer Guardians moving the other way, but Isabel had said the spirit line had already been attacked on at least one key point. The Soul Collector was after the forest.

Maybe with Evelyn Hemlock at his side.

"Keep moving along the line," Keir murmured, and he was gone.

The forest flickered in the corners of my vision, and I looked down at my feet. A thin grey line extended in each direction. Keeping an eye on the line, I floated on. Occasionally, Keir's presence brushed against mine, like he was trying to track me even as his own spirit sight reached its limits. The greyness under my feet turned to a blur, seconds merged together—and without warning, it all stopped.

I stopped moving, the spirit realm turning transparent again to show me the world underneath. The line came to an abrupt halt beside a park and a road filled with panicking humans. London, judging by the crowds and the tall buildings. *Evelyn. Where is she?*

The spirit line lay over a busy street, where several cars had caused a pile up—presumably when a flood of furies had spontaneously appeared in the air. Oh, hell. They were everywhere, huge winged beasts dive-bombing everyone in sight.

As a ghost, they didn't see me. I floated over the park and felt Keir's presence tug me downward. On the other side of the park was a building in flames. Several bodies lay around it, and one person stood alone in the ruins. Evelyn Hemlock.

20

I stared at the ruined building, the human bodies, the screaming and terrified bystanders running from the dark shapes of furies in the sky. Then I shot through the air like a bolt, planting myself in front of Evelyn. "You didn't."

"This isn't what it looks like," she said, lifting her—*my* —head to look through my ghostly form. "I missed him, again. Go home."

"Are you fucking kidding me?" I said. "You're in my body, and I'm not going home without it. Give it back."

"You're holding me back," she said. "I nearly caught the Soul Collector, Jacinda."

Now she's feigning innocence? "Nice try. Let me back in, Evelyn."

Through the spirit realm, Evelyn glowed with blue-white light. I grabbed for the Hemlock magic, calling it to my own hands. "I'm on the spirit line, Evelyn. Last chance to let me back in or I'll shut you permanently *out.*"

I focused, hard, on being back in my body. Evelyn's

hands glowed as she fought and I briefly glimpsed the world through my own eyes again, but before I could gain dominance, she pushed me out. Evelyn was stronger than before. Had she gained a boost from the spirit line, too?

"They're coming, you fool," she snarled. "They can see you."

Several cloaked figures approached the burning ruin. Necromancers? No—mages, some with blazing hands, some wielding lightning.

"You there!" one of them shouted.

"Now you've done it," I said to Evelyn.

A fury flew overhead, momentarily drawing their attention to the fracturing sky above the park. The spirit line had began to tear apart at the seams. Terrified-looking humans pointed at other transparent figures appearing above the line. Like in the faerie invasion, the dead were drawn back into the land of the living.

While Evelyn's attention was diverted, I shoved my way through, back into my body. Grabbing the spells on my wrist, I twisted the nearest one. Smoke poured out, masking me from view. Smokescreen spell. Pushing up my sleeve, I found an illusion spell and activated it.

My arm changed, and so did the rest of me, turning into a balding middle-aged man.

"What are you doing?" Evelyn hissed.

"Running away, since you won't." The alternative was giving myself up and letting the mages arrest both of us. *Thanks a lot, Evelyn.*

Shielded by the smokescreen spell, I broke into a run. Another man caught up with me at the road's edge, his guts hanging out. Keir's voice spoke through his mouth.

"Just thought I'd keep you company," said the zombie.

"Thanks. You might have picked a better vessel. That one's falling to bits."

"You can talk. You're absolutely hideous."

A zombie and a witch wearing an illusion. What a pair we made. I hid a smile and kept on moving. "Where've you been?"

"I looked inside the burning building," Keir said. "The Ley Hunters' Hub… the sign said. It's them, all right."

"I thought so." I kept running, breathlessly. Sprinting across busy London streets in the shape of a huge redheaded man while speaking with my high, panicked voice drew more eyes than I'd have liked, but at least nobody would remember my real face.

Furies circled above the road, diving down at the humans, while mages attacked them with fire and lightning.

"Keep going, turn right," said Keir. "Get in the park—it's faerie territory, the mages won't follow you."

"Yeah, not so sure I'll be that lucky." I changed directions and ran into the park, which was also filled with the shimmering forms of ghostly spirits. The spirit line was close—really close. If I could just get to the—

"Jacinda Hemlock," said a voice, and a man stepped onto the curving path in front of me. "It's an honour to meet you in person at last." Blue-grey eyes blinked at me with humour, and a smile curled his lip.

"Joke's on you," I said to the Soul Collector. "I know you don't have a real body."

"That will soon be rectified." His gaze went to the dead man Keir inhabited. "Would you like to volunteer to be next? The souls I take are never truly lost, after all."

You sick bastard. He could possess and kill anyone…

even vampires. If I left my body and tried to use necromancy on him, Evelyn would take the wheel and either fight on his side or disappear again. I couldn't afford either outcome. Not with so many innocent people around us who might turn into collateral damage—and a spirit line beneath our feet.

The Soul Collector's grin widened. "Do you feel that? We're on top of a node. A lot of people died here. A lot of *powerful* people."

The key point. He'd already shut it down, but magic still hummed beneath my feet, and if he had another soul-absorbing device… damn.

"Why are you taking in humans?" I asked, to keep his eyes on my face. "What's the point in killing them?"

"There's something about a human soul that's so… pure," he said. "And I've consumed enough of them."

The zombie Keir had been controlling toppled over, and I turned to him in alarm. "Keir?"

The Soul Collector laughed. "He knows how to avoid me. Unfortunately, I'm always one step ahead—of all of you."

The blue-white light vanished from the man's eyes. His body crumpled to the ground, his spirit gone.

I tapped into the spirit realm, but there was no sign of Keir, not the barest whisper of his presence.

"Shit!" I snapped back into my body, only belated realising that Evelyn had not elected to take the wheel. Keir must have let go of the vessel—because the Soul Collector had tried to possess him.

And now he was a target.

"If you want to save your friend, you'd better let me take charge," said Evelyn, hovering next to me.

"Like hell." I searched for the spirit line's fractured presence beneath me, then I crossed over into the forest.

Evelyn fought for dominance as I stumbled down the path. "Don't you even think about it," I growled, getting a grip on her magic. "I'll put you somewhere you'll never come back from."

"That won't work again," she hissed in my ear. "You can't bind me from here, not without locking yourself to this forest forever. Besides, the spirit line is too volatile. If he breaks it, he'll free me along with it, and I won't let you have your body back ever again next time."

I pushed on, my head pounding. "A little help would be nice, Cordelia. Take your deranged relative and talk some sense into her."

"Sense?" hissed Evelyn. "You're the one blundering around without a clue what's at stake."

"I can't imagine it has anything to do with the fact that everyone in this family has conspired to keep me in the dark?" My head pounded, and I wished I could knock her out cold so she'd leave me in peace for a bit. "I happen to like being alive. You're the one who chose to spend eternity as a ghost just because you couldn't bear to give up your magic."

"I deserve it," she said. "The magic. It's mine. It's only fair."

"Life isn't fair," I said to her. "Millions of people died the last time the spirit lines broke. My parents did. I never knew them. That doesn't give you licence to destroy innocent lives yourself."

She went silent for a moment. Had I actually got through to her? I didn't dare hope. After all, even if I couldn't bind her now, I would later. I had to.

"I never wished you ill, Jacinda," she said. "Nor your friends."

"That's funny, because you tried to strangle Morgan when you were at the wheel. And that's not counting how you forced me to drag my friends out of the guild so I could track you, when there's a madman on the loose trying to kill us all."

"I was trying to knock your friend out before he realised what I was," said Evelyn. "And I have no control over anything your companions do."

"They know the truth about you now." Where did this bloody forest end? "You sided with Leila Hemlock against me, and you *wanted* to open the spirit line."

"Only temporarily," she said. "I worked with Leila because I planned to claim her body, so I no longer had to share this vessel, and my magic would truly be mine. You would have survived."

I stopped walking. "Give it up. Just admit you want the Ancients back and it'll make things easier for all of us."

"Yes, it will." She appeared, hovering next to me. Her dark hair streamed behind her, and her grey-blue eyes shone in the forest's dimness. "If we draw them out first, we'll win. The Soul Collector is just the beginning. I would have caught him if you hadn't stopped me."

Damn. She sounded so reasonable... just like she'd sounded when she'd talked me into leaving her in control of my body behind a spirit barrier. "We'll revisit that one later."

The forest turned transparent, revealing Edinburgh's abandoned train station. About damn time.

"Here." I stepped out onto the bridge, feeling Evelyn push at me again. "Not happening. I'm in charge."

"He's here, you fool. He knows where we came from."

My head snapped up, and I spotted a figure on the other side of a wrecked car. "Keir?"

The man walked towards us, eyes glowing with greyish light. "Hello, Jas," said the Soul Collector. "So nice of you to join me. I couldn't find your friend, but maybe you'd like to tell me where he might be hiding?"

"Let go," I warned. "Face me as yourself, not hiding behind a human shield."

"Why not both?"

There was a flash, the light went out of the man's eyes, and he fell forwards, dead.

"Who should I target next?" whispered the Soul Collector's voice. Fog swirled around, and when I crossed into the spirit realm, I saw him. Blue-grey eyes, a crooked inhuman smile…

"I know what you are," I said. "You're nothing. You're not even alive."

"I'm nothing," he whispered. "And everything." He blinked out of existence, and the spirit realm faded.

A moment later, another human shambled into view. The Soul Collector watched me through the man's eyes, smiling, and he raised a hand. Shimmering encased his palm, solidifying into the form of a long, oval object made of—something silver-coloured, almost metallic. Though it was nowhere near me, an icy sensation burned through to my bones when I set eyes upon it. As though it drew on my soul from a distance, threatening to suck me in.

"Thank you for this, Jacinda," he said.

The shimmering silver device in his hand blinked once, and the man fell down, dead. As he did, the odd silver device disappeared, like it'd evaporated into smoke.

My throat went dry. "What in hell was that?" Unlike the other spirit devices, it sure as hell didn't look man-made. But it'd gone as quickly as it'd arrived.

Evelyn stirred. "Let me take over, Jas," she whispered. "Or he'll kill everyone he touches until he reaches your friends."

I shook my head, fiercely. "I won't."

"Don't let her take over," said a voice from behind me.

I spun on the spot. Lady Harper climbed to the bridge from the ruins, walking stick and all. Her face was set, her hair streaming loose. "Leave us, Evelyn Hemlock, or we'll seal away your soul where you stand."

"I'd like to see you try," said Evelyn.

21

"Let go of Jas," Lady Harper said firmly. "Now."

Surprisingly, Evelyn's presence faded a little, allowing me to break through. "What are you doing here?" I waved a hand at the dead bodies the Soul Collector had left behind. "There's a maniac possessing and murdering everyone in sight, if it wasn't obvious."

"Why do you think I came here?" Lady Harper said.

Isabel stepped up behind her, panting for breath. "Jas—sorry it took so long to find you. The forest isn't playing nice at the moment."

"Were you both in the forest? Why didn't I see you?" I shook my head. "Never mind. Isabel, you should be at the guild, out of harm's way. Lady Harper… unless you know where the Soul Collector actually is, you're best off staying in the forest."

"Certainly *not*," she said. "I came here to help you bind Evelyn."

"Excuse me?" I blinked at her. "Now is *not* the time. Where's Keir? Was he in the forest?"

"I didn't see him," said Isabel. "Why?"

"The Soul Collector is after him." Worry clawed up my throat. "What *is* that thing he's using to drain people's souls? I just saw it—he had this silver thing. It looked sort of like the devices we found, but it… vanished." I indicated the dead man a few feet away.

Lady Harper sucked in a breath. "What he has is the original weapon, the Ether Converter—a device capable of storing the energy of an infinite number of souls. He stole it… or someone gave it to him."

"What?" Evelyn tried to step in, but I shoved her aside. "*Where* did he get this… Ether Converter?"

"It was hidden deep within the Hemlocks' forest," said Lady Harper. "Not only is it a repository of souls, it contains enough spiritual energy to reset the spirit lines and destroy everything we've spent our lives trying to protect."

"Wait—" I broke off. "He keeps taking people's souls with a touch. You mean… those other devices he made were like… copies." But that wasn't the worst of it. "Did you say he stole it from the forest?"

"Someone stole it for him," said Lady Harper, looking right through me. At Evelyn. "Someone who already has access to the forest."

"Not me," Evelyn said, loudly, floating beside me. "He already had it when I followed him."

"Lies," said the old mage. "We have a traitor in our midst, and while they may be flawed, Cordelia and the other Hemlocks would never willingly betray their own. It is you who's stayed in the background, listening to every part of Jas's life, and plotting to help the enemy. Don't deny it."

"She's got you there, Evelyn." I turned to her, and saw her ghostly face whiten.

"I *did not steal the weapon,*" she said.

"You took my body right to the enemy," I said. "Who do you think I'm going to believe here?" Lady Harper might not like me much, but she knew treachery when she saw it.

"Jas." Isabel moved in close, her eyes bright with worry. "Lady Harper, that's irrelevant now. The Soul Collector must be stopped. The weapon isn't a physical one, Jas. It's not like anything I've ever seen before. He can move it between hosts, even, and it's invisible most of the time. We have to get it away from the crowds—and the guild."

This just got better and better. "He has a weapon he can even use as a ghost? How are we meant to compete with that?"

"We aren't," Lady Harper growled. "And you can start by binding that second soul of yours before she gives the enemy any further assistance."

"No," snarled Evelyn, speaking through my mouth. "You're accusing the wrong person."

"Nice try." I pushed my way back in. "Assuming I get my hands on the Ether Converter, how do I destroy it?"

"You can't," said Lady Harper. "The only way to contain it is to take it back to the Hemlocks—and away from any traitors."

Holy shit. "Why the bloody hell did the Hemlocks create it?"

"They didn't," she said. "They stole it from the

Ancients in order to prevent it from being used for precisely this. The Soul Collector might have no body of his own, but with that weapon, he can take out both you *and* Evelyn—and you can guess what he'll be capable of when he has someone with Hemlock magic on his side."

The seams of the world would fall apart. "He set Evelyn free so he could take her soul. Right? Yet she still helps him?"

"I'm not helping him!" Evelyn yelled in my ear, but I ignored her.

"He's a monster," said Isabel shakily. "I haven't seen him in person, but he's leaving bodies everywhere. The guild's sealed against outsiders, but he gets closer every time. This is a game to him."

My heart dropped. "Keir. Is Keir here? He had to leave his vessel because the Soul Collector nearly got him."

"I don't know," said Isabel. "We went into the forest, but the weapon was already gone. Lady Harper tells me you're likely the only person who can get your hands on it without having your own soul compromised, but you have to bind Evelyn, otherwise—"

"She'll push my soul into the Ether Converter." I pulled out my phone. No calls from Keir. Maybe he'd gone into the forest again—but even the forest wasn't safe. I did have another call from Ilsa. "Do the others know?"

"No. I planned to warn them, but Lady Harper insisted we need to find you."

I jumped when my phone rang. "Ilsa?"

"Jas!" Her voice sounded staticky. "Did you make it back?"

"Are you at the guild? Is Keir with you?"

"I'm here, but he's still out there," she said. "I saw him

—he came back to the guild when he was tracking you, but he said he had to stay outside to keep hold of his vessels. And something about the spirit lines, and the Ancients—"

My blood turned to ice. The Ancients. They'd taken his brother—but he wouldn't be foolish enough to go chasing the enemy alone now. Right?

Oh god, Keir. Please don't.

"Jas? You still there?"

I clenched my hand around my phone. "Yes. I… have to go. But you need to know. The Soul Collector has a weapon, like the devices we found, but worse. He's using it to collect souls, and can possess anyone at any time."

"I know," she said quickly. "Mackie warned us. As for that device, it sounds like… a talisman."

"Talisman?"

Ilsa spoke quickly. "They contain power that originally belonged to the Ancients. Just fragments, a fraction of their power, but they're that strong, even the tiniest amount of their power can be deadly."

"Fucking brilliant," snapped Morgan in the background. "Oi, Jas, get back here before he gets to you. Mackie and I are trying to track him from a distance."

"Don't," I warned. "Keir is either his prisoner or about to do something very reckless. I need to save him."

"Jas, I—" Ilsa broke off. "Jas. Run. He's behind you."

I spun around, and Isabel's hand clenched around my throat. "Hey… Isabel. Let go."

A smile traced her lips. "This one had *very* strong defences, but I do like a challenge. Go on. Ask your little friends where the vampire is hiding. I was interested in hearing the rest of your *fascinating* conversation."

"Let her go!" I choked, my vision blurring at the corners.

Isabel wasn't a necromancer. One trip over the veil would end her life.

Her grip tightened on my throat, and the blood roared in my ears. Evelyn's magic tingled in my palms, demanding to be unleashed. *No.* if she took the wheel, they'd fight to the death.

Lady Harper raised her walking stick, and Isabel's body lifted into the air. She let out a startled scream, limbs flailing, but the Soul Collector was screaming, too. I gasped out, massaging my throat, scrambling to get hold of my magic—

Lady Harper watched Isabel struggle with an almost calm expression, one hand holding her walking stick. I stared, unable to move, as Isabel—and the Soul Collector—fought for dominance.

This is how she killed two Sidhe. Lady Harper's ability, when fully unleashed, involved manipulating the minds and bodies of her targets. The Soul Collector and Isabel were both trapped, suspended in the air like birds caught in a net.

I dove into the spirit realm, and found him watching me through Isabel's eyes, blazing with anger. "You... cannot defeat a god. Your friend will die first."

"Lady Harper, let her go!" I shouted, panicked. "Please—"

Isabel dropped to the floor, and Lady Harper's stick clattered to the ground.

"Don't," I pleaded.

Cracks spread across the ground. A blast of air knocked me into Isabel, and we crashed onto the concrete. Stars winked before my eyes, and I lifted my head, blood trickling down my face, to see the former Mage Lord sink to her knees. Her gaze caught mine for an instant—whether her own or the Soul Collector's, I couldn't say—and she was gone.

22

Isabel moaned with pain, pushing herself to her knees. I managed to drag my gaze away from the fallen former Mage Lord. "Do you… do you need a healing spell?"

"I have one." Her tone was calm, but her hands were shaking. "Is—she—?"

I nodded. One sharp jerky motion, that was all.

I'd always felt Lady Harper would laugh in the face of death. Not die without a word, sucked into a place nobody could reach. As a necromancer, I knew when someone's soul had departed this world. My own heart beat too fast, and even Evelyn's presence had vanished, pushed aside by my own shock.

I clicked on a healing spell, though I barely felt the sting of my injuries, and checked into the spirit realm. But Lady Harper's soul wasn't headed to the afterlife. The Soul Collector had stolen it for himself.

"She's not gone," I said to Isabel. "I guarantee, she'll be the most stubborn ghost ever, once we get our hands on that talisman. She won't want to resist haunting the new mage trainees."

Isabel's mouth trembled. "She didn't have to do that. My witch defences—"

"He broke into your mind, Isabel. Even witch defences can't go against the gods. Where did he go?"

Nobody else was around. I looked down at Lady Harper's body, as though if I stared long enough, the truth would sink in. Isabel crouched down, too, her hands moving up her spell-covered sleeves. I checked mine, too, as though either of us could find a spell that might be able to save her. But it was too late, far too late.

I leaned over and hugged Isabel, tears stinging my eyes. "We'll find him," I whispered. "We'll make him pay for this."

"I'm right here," said the Soul Collector.

I jolted away from Isabel, whose hands glowed as her spells activated. Another man peered down at us, his eyes glowing blue-white.

"Touching," he murmured. "Were you close?"

To him, our horror was entertainment. Rage momentarily overcame my shock, and white-hot magic seared my palms.

"Actually, we hated one another," I told him. "But if you don't face me head-on instead of running away like a coward, I don't need a body to do you some serious damage."

"You and Evelyn will fare much better if you choose to take my side in this new order," he said.

Then with barely a ripple in the spirit realm, his host dropped down, dead. Another soul fed into the Ether

Converter. He must have more than enough to break the spirit line by now, even temporarily.

But what was holding him back?

"I do wish you'd put up more of a fight," said a woman, the companion of the man he'd just killed. "Then again, you *are* hopeless in this particular situation, aren't you, Jacinda?"

"I'm not the one running." I raised my hands, but the woman was still alive. If I attacked, she'd take the damage and not him. He wasn't just able to switch bodies, he could use anyone else to take the fall instead of himself. Nothing could hurt him.

The woman smiled. "Wouldn't you like to know where your vampire friend is?"

My throat went dry. "Keir. What did you do to him?"

"Not a thing, yet," he said. "I planned to have fun with him for quite some time. I've never taken a vampire with a shade's magic before."

"What do you—"

The woman dropped dead, in a flash of light. The Ether Converter, and the Soul Collector, were gone.

I tensed, spinning on the spot, but no other humans were close by. The instant we went into a crowded place, though, he'd find someone else, and leave a trail of bodies in his wake.

Isabel let out a choked noise. "They—what's the point in all this?"

"It's a game to him." My voice sounded distant as I looked down at Lady Harper's body. "Keir... what did he mean by that? *A vampire with a shade's magic?* Keir can't take in magic... only souls."

But feeding on my soul *had* affected him. Had I done permanent damage?

"Don't look at me," said Evelyn, piping up entirely too late. "The vampire never fed on me."

"Oh, *that's* good news," I snapped. "Where the hell is he, then?"

Keir!

He was either outside this realm, or drained and injured—or on the brink of death. The Soul Collector had found him after all, and had decided to lead me along for his own entertainment.

"He's alive," Evelyn said. "Like us, he's hard to kill."

I whirled on her. "And you'd know? You planned to offer us as bait."

"He can't take us." Her mouth lifted into a mocking smile. "Neither of us. Why do you think he's going to the trouble of attacking your friends? If you hadn't blown my cover, I'd have walked to his side and stolen that Ether Converter from his hands before he could use it to take any more lives."

"You can't blame me for this. You're full of shit, and besides, even if you're not on his side, you already betrayed me once."

"Jas…" Isabel looked from Evelyn to me with frightened eyes. "I think we should get off the spirit line. And— if you want to bind her, you can, but I think she's right. He can't take you—either of you. You're immune to the Ether Converter."

I shook my head, too numb to take in her words. "You —you should go. Ask the guild to let you in, before he catches you again. Please."

"I'm not letting you run off alone," she said firmly.

"He doesn't want me dead," I said. "He wants me—and Evelyn—on his side. Maybe he can't possess me and kill me because I have two souls, I don't know, but he'll go after you again and this time Lady Harper won't be around to die for us. I can't lose anyone else."

Not when Keir might already be dead for all I knew.

"I'll go," said Isabel shakily. "But if you die, the Hemlocks—"

"They'll die when he gets into the forest anyway," I said. "It doesn't matter."

"He's already there," Evelyn whispered. "I told you… we're too late."

My hands tingled with Hemlock magic. I didn't believe a word she said. She'd betrayed us—taken the Ether Converter from the forest and handed it over to the enemy. Leaving a path into the forest wide open.

"Go!" I said to Isabel, then turned on the spot, feeling my way through to the forest. Though I didn't sense Evelyn trying to take control, I wouldn't let her. Not this time.

"He's already here. I'm not the traitor, Jas."

Tangled trees appeared, surrounding me. Evelyn floated at my side, glowing in the dimness. There were no other witches in sight, but a furred body lay sprawled across a tree root. The half-faerie servant of the Hemlocks.

Evelyn made a low, disgusted noise. "He's here."

"Cordelia!" I snapped. "Get out here and tell me who the traitor is."

But—Evelyn had been at my side for every second I'd been in here before. Unless he'd already come into the forest, but Cordelia would have sensed him. The forest missed nothing.

Something is wrong.

Blood on the ground. Trees tight, quiet, free of the usual whispering magic. I focused on the spirit realm, seeking for a trace of Keir's presence, but I couldn't track people in a realm not bound by the usual rules of reality. My hands clenched, my throat constricting.

"Cordelia!" I shouted. "Answer me."

"She's been temporarily subdued," said a female voice.

Not Cordelia. "Leila," I whispered.

Leila Hemlock's ghostly form appeared, floating between the trees. *Oh, god. I should have known.* She must have passed into the forest and not over the veil when she'd died. Being a Hemlock witch, even a dead one, must have allowed her to hide even from the other witches. The forest could instantly track anyone who came in, but ghosts… I'd bet ghosts were an exception.

"It was you who stole the Ether Converter," I said. "You led the Soul Collector here, didn't you?"

"He still cannot pass within," she said. "The Hemlocks made sure of that."

Damn. That meant he was still in the waking world. I really, really hoped Isabel had made it to the guild in time.

"So you decided you hate your coven enough that you'd willingly side with one of their enemies?"

"Our goals aren't entirely in alignment, but close enough," she said. "He desires your two souls, and *I* desire to make you pay for what you did."

"Does that include Evelyn?" Despite myself, I couldn't help wondering… had Evelyn been right this time? Lady

Harper had believed she was the traitor, but it was Leila who'd lurked in the forest, surviving beyond death.

"I know of her desire to betray me," Leila answered. "I will not be destroyed."

Tangled tree roots rose and knotted around my legs, fixing me in place.

"How are you doing that?" I snarled, fighting against the bonds. I scrambled to get a grip on my power, but pain burned through my legs.

"It's not me," she said.

The dead faerie lifted its head. "Hello, Jacinda," a male voice rasped. "It's harder for me to possess a creature that isn't human, much less one with such a warped soul as the poor foolish inhabitants of this forest… but not impossible. She carries the Hemlocks' magic, and through her, so do I. But I would much prefer a stronger vessel."

Damn. He'd managed to use the Hemlock magic by taking temporary control over someone who wasn't even the heir. What would he be able to do if he took over me —over Evelyn?

He can't. He can't possess either of us. That's why he's doing this.

Small comfort. The forest was hostile territory now.

The tree roots twisted, revealing a gaping hole in the ground. A roaring wind whipped at my hair, and the knotting tree roots moved, dangling me over the edge of the crumbling path. Even my Hemlock magic wouldn't save me if I fell to my death.

"Is this what you wanted, Leila?" I said loudly. "Your own magic, turned against your fellow witches?"

Leila's ghostly form appeared, her face grim. "There is no punishment great enough for what you did to me," she said. "You took my rightful position, then you took my life."

"You tried to kill me." The wind snatched the words from my mouth as I spoke, but I raised my voice. "You tortured people. There's no reason to kill innocents over a grudge, just because the Hemlock magic passed you by."

"This is more than a grudge to me, Jacinda," said Leila. "Your family betrayed me, kicked me out of the bloodline, left me to ruin. As they did to you, Evelyn."

Evelyn's voice spoke through my mouth. "So you wish to destroy me along with Jacinda?"

"You cannot be separated," she said. "So yes… I think the Hemlock bloodline should end here. It's only right."

"Then join with me," croaked the fae, the Soul Collector's presence still possessing its half-dead form. "Join me, Leila. And we will be one."

Leila's mouth twisted, traces of fear rippling across her features. "No. I will not be caged—I won't be trapped again."

"Pity," said the Soul Collector.

There was a flash of white light—and Leila Hemlock vanished.

Another soul, sucked into the Ether Converter.

"I have a Hemlock soul," he said. "Unfortunately, she has no power of her own, so I still need your help, Jacinda."

"I'm not helping you. And I won't let Evelyn, either." Blood rushed to my head as the roots trapping my feet tipped me over the edge. Even my Hemlock magic… it couldn't turn against itself. *Dammit. I should be able to break this spell.*

"No, I suppose not," he said. "Evelyn's ingratitude for

my helping her escape your prison comes as no surprise, but I hoped for better from you, Jacinda."

"What are you talking about?" I didn't have a damn clue what was going through Evelyn's head at the moment, let alone whose side she was on, but his words made no sense. "You've done nothing but torture my friends and kill innocent people."

"You misunderstand, Jacinda," he said. "I can do so much for you… I can set you free from that curse that binds you. The curse your own ancestors cruelly used to capture your soul."

"Yeah fucking right." I struggled against the bonds, Evelyn's magic sparking to my hands. *Go on. Break its hold.*

"And in return, I need you," he said, "to get back the life the Hemlocks stole from me."

Magic burst from my hands, the tree roots released me, and I fell into blackness.

23

I tumbled into the dark, and kept falling. For a heart-stopping moment, I thought I'd fallen off the edge of the world—then I landed on my knees amongst leaves strewn at the roots of another mass of trees.

I was still in the forest.

"Hello?" The word burst from my mouth, in a high frightened voice that wasn't mine. "Hello. C… Cordelia?"

Evelyn?

Silence.

I scrambled to my knees, looking up at trees which suddenly seemed much taller than before. And the hands I held out in front of me weren't mine.

Oh, damn. I'd fallen into a memory. The forest read the thoughts and impressions from every person who entered its depths. And once it started, breaking out was another story entirely. Especially when I didn't know who I *was*. A child, I'd guess by the high-pitched voice and the tallness of the trees. A child who knew Cordelia.

The trees were thick enough to block out the sun as I

ran, as helpless as I'd been when the net had held me captive.

"You should leave, child," said Cordelia, her face appearing in the tree.

"The world is burning." My voice cracked. "They're dead. They're all dead. Please, please give me the magic and I'll save them."

"I cannot do that. This forest can only preserve time, not reverse it. And we cannot give our magic to another. You have none, and you never will."

Oh, god. Leila. I was Leila Hemlock.

And I *felt* it—her rage, her grief. She'd run into the forest to save her own skin, and lost her family, the same as me. And the Hemlocks had spurned her.

I looked Cordelia in the eyes. "I don't trust you." My voice sounded like mine again. "If you're on my side, help me find Keir and defeat that Soul Collector before he claims your souls, too."

Cordelia's face vanished. An illusion, nothing more.

I swore and kicked at the nearest tree. "Dammit, Evelyn. What does he need me for and not you? You're the one bound to me, and working for the villain."

"I'm on your side, Jas," she said. "They played both of us for fools. And you're the bigger fool if you go after your vampire friend instead of chasing down that bastard before he figures out how to take the Hemlocks' power."

"It's not like I fell into that illusion on purpose," I shot at her. "Besides, the Soul Collector can't possess the other Hemlocks. They're not really alive."

"Do you want to chance that?"

My heart sank. For all their power, the Hemlocks never did explain to me the exact nature of their curse.

For all I knew… their souls *could* be taken by the Ether Converter. They certainly weren't dead, even if they weren't alive in the usual sense.

"Oh, Jacinda…"

I spun around. The fae creature—or the Soul Collector—stood there looking at me, eyes aglow. And behind him was the door leading into the Hemlocks' cave.

My heart jumped into my throat. The cave was sealed—that much was obvious. New glyphs formed thick patterns covering the symbol on the door, wrapping around the trees. He needed a Hemlock to undo it… and Evelyn rose to the surface, magic glowing in my own palms.

Magic blazed from him, too, only recognisable because it was out of sync with the hum of the Hemlocks' magic in the forest. A vibration, like a ripple on a spirit line, the sound of a thousand voices crying out.

Souls. He carried the power of all the souls he'd stolen.

The talisman needed to be destroyed before he used it to tear the world apart.

He jerked his head at the cave's door. "They sealed themselves off, the crafty witches," he said. "But you can undo their magical boundaries, Jacinda."

"I don't think so." I clenched my fists, pushing Evelyn aside. "They can stay there for quite a long time, you know. Years, even. It must be driving you out of your mind, being stuck in here without a body and with that weapon of yours useless against me."

Anger flared in his eyes. "You know nothing of us, Hemlock."

"I know you've been hiding in Edinburgh terrorising vampires and psychics for years. I know you've been stuck without a body for so long that you're desperate enough to try to claim one that already belongs to two people."

"Your ancestors chose to save their own skins by pushing us out of reach," he said. "The walls between the worlds will come down one way or another, and I will be there to see it."

A shimmering stick-like shape appeared in his hands, glowing with pure blue-white energy. *The Ether Converter.*

"Give me your magic," he said. "Join me, and we will make these worlds anew."

Evelyn stepped in. "Yeah, I'm going to have to say no. Your move, Jas."

Whips of magic burst from my hands, lashing at him. The fae's body fell, cut in two. I shuddered, despite knowing she'd died long before I struck her—but the Soul Collector had gone.

To claim his next soul.

The Hemlock magic continued to buzz in my palms, and I clenched my hands tight, looking away from the glowing door. *Take me to the enemy,* I ordered the forest. *Now.*

The trees went transparent, to be replaced with damp grass. Not Edinburgh. I'd landed in the middle of a deserted field.

A tall man on the path ahead turned and smiled at me, his eyes glowing.

"Get *back* here!" I snarled, lashing him around the ankles with a whip of magical energy.

"Catch me if you can, Jas…" The Soul Collector's voice faded, the light went out of the man's eyes, and he fell into the dirt, dead.

In the distance, lights blazed. My blood ran cold. I knew where I was… close to where the forest actually existed in the real world. Near my former home.

He must have learned my past… hell, the forest itself would have shown him, if he'd looked hard enough. And the mind-link would have taken care of the rest. He was going after the mages, and Isabel's coven—everyone I'd grown up with. Drake. Wanda. They had no idea he was coming.

"Evelyn," I hissed. "Now would be a *really* good time to tell me you have a way to beat him."

"You know how," she said. "Let him in."

"I can't—what? You know he can't possess us. We're two people in one body. Right?"

"Not if one of us leaves," she said.

I stared at her, hovering on the spirit line on the muddy grass. "You have got to be kidding me. You're saying I have to leave you at the wheel so he can possess you?"

"No, you don't have to," she said calmly. "But if you do, I'll be able to wrest that weapon out of his hands and turn it on him."

"Then why can't I do the same?"

"He seems to think you're different to me." She looked directly at me, her blue-black eyes shimmering. "Him or me. Your choice."

Some choice. "Dammit, Evelyn." I cast a panicked glance at the distant town. I'd never reach it in time no matter how fast I ran. "He already killed dozens of people, and so help me, if I leave you to it, you'll be one of them."

Her presence vanished so abruptly, the sudden lightness in my head made me dizzy. "Evelyn?"

Silence. She'd gone. The pressure on the back of my mind, that had been there ever since she'd woken up... it'd disappeared.

Which meant I was open to being possessed by the god.

"Hey." I walked on, my head still swimming. "Hey. Soul Collector. Surprise. I'm here, alone. Nobody else needs to die."

"Well, well." My head pounded as he pushed against my skull, his thoughts dark and slippery and impossible to grasp. I swallowed down bile as violent images exploded before my eyes.

He was going to make *me* kill my family.

Hemlock magic seared my hands, whipcords of light zig-zagging across the ground. If I pulled the seams of the realms apart, that power would fracture cities and topple worlds. And now—thanks to me—he had that power.

The spirit realm formed a grey film over my vision. He'd been using that realm to get around between hosts, but he belonged to all the worlds at once. Nothing was off limits to him.

"Yes..." His voice purred in my ear, so close. My hands glowed as the Ether Converter appeared in my hands, silver-white, its magic sparking against the lingering remnants of Hemlock power. "Tear the worlds apart."

I directed my magic into the device, gripping tight, willing it to break open like the other one had. But nothing happened.

"Nice try," he whispered. "It won't break. But *you* will."

Burning magic seared my palms. Beneath my hands, the air tore in two, a rift opening, and a fury flew out, slamming me to the ground. With a wrenching scream, it took flight, talons out. *Dammit.*

"Was that your plan!" I yelled at him, still gripping the Ether Converter. "Damn, those things don't even have souls, do they?"

The rift I'd torn open lay wide, a gaping slash in the air with seemingly nothing on the other side. A ferocious wind current tore at me, threatening to pull both of us into the void.

"Don't," he warned. "Jacinda Hemlock, I command you to close that hole."

I remained still. He didn't have complete control. The wind tore at me, at the weapon in my hands.

"No!" He screamed, wildly, and I smiled.

"Evelyn," I said. "Wipe him out."

The Ether Converter left my hands at the same time as Evelyn slid into the back of my mind again. The Soul Collector screamed, momentarily floating free of my body, his hands reaching out desperately for his weapon—

Magic flared from my palms, pulling the rift's edges closed as the Ether Convertor disappeared from sight. With a last desperate motion, the Soul Collector reached out a hand—and Evelyn took it, pushing him through the rift. With a final tug, I closed the rift, and the void disappeared, taking the Soul Collector along with it.

A scream resounded, and the fury dove at me. I called my magic once more, its whip-like shape yanking the beast out of the sky. Twisting the whip, I severed the beast's head.

Breathless, I turned to the side, seeing Evelyn Hemlock watching the spot where the rift had vanished with an unreadable expression on her face. Then in a blink, she was gone. I felt her presence settle back into place and closed my eyes, too relieved to care.

I opened my eyes again to see trees all around me. The forest… I was back in the forest.

"Cordelia," said Evelyn, through my mouth. "We won."

We won… we're alive. Except…

"Keir," I said, alarmed. "Where is he?"

My whole body ached, but I broke into a sprint through the trees, the forest's magic in my control once again.

"You live." Cordelia's voice croaked. "Where is that abomination?"

"Gone. I threw him into the place where the furies live." I gasped, my breath coming in short pants. "Is Keir still alive?"

"He lives," said Cordelia. "The Ancient was unable to finish the job, for the same reason he couldn't take possession of your soul, so he abandoned the vampire here to finish off later."

"What do you mean, for the same reason he couldn't take over me? I'm not a vampire."

"No," said Cordelia. "You're a shade."

I kept moving through the tangled trees, my heart thundering in my chest. I couldn't be a shade. Shades were evil spirits bound to living people. I'd still been alive when Evelyn had been bound to me. *She* was the shade.

"A shade is a spirit that survived death, bound to a mortal body," whispered Evelyn. "You did."

"Er, so did you," I said. "By way of being bound to me. The nine lives thing Lloyd talked about was a *joke.*"

"All human sayings have their roots in truth," Cordelia commented.

"You're the one who told me *she* was the shade," I said

to her. "Or you're saying you lied to me all along and Lady Harper had it right?"

"Lady Harper was human. She had her limitations."

"What does that mean? The Ancients aren't human, and you have more in common with them than you do with us."

"You're mistaken, Jas," growled Cordelia. "Both of you are shades, according to your limited definitions. But you're stronger than both."

"I don't want to be stronger. I want the Ancients to stop trying to kill my friends. Tell me I didn't make things worse with what I did."

"I cannot say that," said Cordelia. "But you did succeed in sending the Soul Collector to a fate worse than death."

Yeah. I did. "There are a lot of fates worse than death." And the Ancients… if they were all so dangerous, and all-powerful, and cruel, they could never be allowed to return to the world.

Abruptly, the forest warped before my eyes, trees turning into mud-caked walls, ceilings closing in as it turned into a mirror image of the tunnels beneath the vampire king's house.

Fury cries ripped through the air, and one of them lunged over my head. I ducked, a cold breeze buffeting my head. Whoa. My surroundings looked exactly like the underground tunnels, without a tree in sight. The forest must have thrown Keir into an illusion of the place where the furies had stalked his fellow vampires to death.

"Keir!" I shouted, running forwards.

The tunnel opened up, to a cave ending at a steep cliff. Keir stood at the very edge, over the abyss, and didn't turn around when I approached.

"He's here somewhere," he murmured. "He's close—"

My heart gave a sickening dive. His brother—he thought he was chasing his brother.

"This isn't real," I said, catching his arm. "Keir. Look at me. I killed the Soul Collector. He's gone."

He turned on me, his gaze wild and distant. "Then why can I sense him here?"

"Because—we're close to the Ancients' realm. I'm sorry, Keir, but we can't—we can't follow him. This is an illusion. A cruel trick. Cordelia, this is low, even for you."

"The forest merely reflects the thoughts of those who enter, Jacinda," said Cordelia's voice. "He created this trap himself."

"*You* did." I tightened my grip on Keir's arm.. "Keir, he's not here. The witches' forest is just screwing with you. Come with me."

Hemlock magic buzzed within me, through my body. *I can control this, too.*

I concentrated on the image of trees crowding overhead, and the cliff disappeared. We were in the forest once more.

"Uh. Keir. Talk to me."

The distant look faded from Keir's eyes, and he stared at me, his face pale. "Jas."

"Keir." I wrapped my arms tight around him. His skin was icy cold and he was shivering, and so was I. I pressed my lips to his cheek. "I'm so glad you're okay."

Light swarmed from me to him as he gripped my shoulders, taking my spirit—my life force, or one of them —into him. As he glowed, I saw the truth.

It wasn't Evelyn who'd damaged him, but me.

I had to fix this.

24

"**G**o beyond the veil," Mackie spoke in triumphant tones, waving a hand over her first summoning circle. The ghost within vanished in a spark of white light, disappearing from the spirit realm.

The four of us—Ilsa, Morgan, Lloyd and me—watched her check the circle for any gaps. Technically we could check ourselves, but as we'd learned the hard way, it was best to let Mackie do it herself. Mackie had made real progress with her guild training in the last few weeks, which was a relief to the rest of us. For some reason, the holiday season brought out all the ghosts, and it was only a couple of weeks until Christmas. Not that any of us were in a particularly festive frame of mind.

At least Evelyn hadn't graced me with her presence lately. She'd been nice enough to withdraw to give me space to get over the shock—of Lady Harper's death, of the Soul Collector's attack, even the fact that I still hadn't told Keir what I'd inadvertently done to both of us when I'd let him feed on me. Nor had I found a way to undo it. We'd seen each other only briefly since the battle. He needed to feed on me every couple of days, but he could do that through the spirit realm as easily as the waking world, and didn't often stick around to chat.

Mackie picked up the candles, smiling to herself. While she hadn't completely managed to get her psychic powers under control, not having the Soul Collector anywhere near her thoughts helped a lot.

"Nice one," Lloyd said. "See, you're a natural at this."

She shrugged. "I could have screamed the ghost out of the spirit realm and saved a lot of time and energy, but sure."

"Not on my watch, you won't," said Morgan.

"You have to admit I did a better job than you did," Mackie said.

"Yeah, if I was blindfolded."

"Morgan," Ilsa warned, poking him in the shoulder.

"What? She knows if I shout meaningless encouragement, it's bullshit, right?"

"Obviously," said Mackie, passing the last of the candles to Lloyd. "So does the boss."

Lady Montgomery also knew that my old mentor had died—I'd told her that much—but not the exact circumstances. She could forgive me for being spaced out, up to a point, but avoiding the subject hadn't entirely banished her suspicions about what'd really gone down in the battle with the Soul Collector. Helping Mackie with lessons got me out of my own head, and weirdly, knowing she'd been *in* my head kind of helped. I didn't have to explain I wanted to avoid certain subjects, like I did with other well-meaning people—even Lloyd. She just knew.

Morgan sidled up to me. "Hey, Jas," he said, in a low voice. "Thanks for the spell. It worked."

I turned to him. "Which... oh. The unlocking charm." I'd put my plans to steal from the boss's office on hold, not wanting to rock the boat when I'd come so close to losing my freedom, but I'd figured the guild's resident troublemaker might have time to try.

He nodded, passing me a stack of papers. "Ilsa and I photocopied the book. Reckoned you'd be less likely to get caught that way."

"Reluctantly," Ilsa said dryly. "I'm not sure how much help it'll be, but I dug out all the info on shades."

My gaze flicked to the pages. I skipped over the details of the rituals required to attach a shade to a person. The Hemlocks had as good as said they'd used their own magic in the ritual and that was why Evelyn and I were so much stronger... but it didn't mean I needed to know all the gruesome details. Yet.

I kept reading. To summon a shade and bind it required a blood sacrifice... one body died, and the spirit was immediately transferred to the other body during the binding. And to undo the spell... the only way to undo it was for both spirits to perish at the same time.

"No," I muttered. "Come on. That's not fair."

"What is it?" asked Lloyd.

I looked up from the pages. "There's got to be a way to detach two bound souls without *killing* them both."

"Ah, crap, really?" said Morgan. "I didn't know... I mean, shades aren't my strong point, but I thought they were like fetches. They can hop between bodies."

"Nope, that's more a vampire thing," I said. "And the Soul Collector, to some degree."

"Sorry," Ilsa said, her mouth pulling into a frown. "I thought it would help. The other spirit… is she likely to take control?"

"I haven't heard from her lately," I said. "But right now I'd say we're at an impasse."

Cordelia had said *I* was a shade, and the page did list the definition of a shade as someone who'd thwarted death by means of a ritual… but not someone who'd survived death because they *already* had another person sharing their body. Maybe even the writers of the top-secret annals of the necromancer guild had never encountered anything like that before.

I skipped over the page, wondering if I was more likely to find the solution in the 'vampires' section or the 'shades' one. Most shades, the author insisted, did not survive for long in their host. Smothering a sigh, I flicked to the vampire section instead.

Mackie leaned over my shoulder. "Vampires?" she said. "Thought you were looking up shades. Unless you're still letting that vampire walk around with your essence?"

"Your what?" asked Lloyd, Morgan and Ilsa simultaneously.

"Is there anything you didn't swipe out of my thoughts?" I asked. "What do you mean, essence?"

"Is that the word?" Mackie pointed at the page. "Vampires feed on spirit essence. You're worried because that Keir has some of yours…"

My face heated. "He's fed on a lot of people."

Mackie jabbed her finger at the page again, and I read the section more carefully. Shades were named as spirits who'd survived death. That made them stronger. And if a vampire fed on them…

"Holy shit," I breathed.

"What?" said Lloyd, staring at me. "What the bloody hell did you do?"

I looked at the page, at Mackie, and then at Lloyd. "You had it right. I did have nine lives. And I think I accidentally gave one of them to Keir."

Lloyd's jaw unhinged. Mackie burst out laughing, while the Lynn siblings both looked bewildered.

"It's not funny." I lowered the page. "When my soul was bound to Evelyn's, it made both of us twice as strong. I can die, and then come back unharmed. When Keir fed on me, I think it passed on the same ability to him. I'm not sure if that means we're the same…"

"It does," said Mackie, still snickering. "If anything, it's good news. Don't people keep trying to kill both of you?"

Jesus. She might well be right. But as long as he had my spirit essence inside him, he'd be forced to feed on me. How was I even supposed to tell him that?

"I'll get back to this later," I said. "Come on, let's report in before the boss comes to check up on us again."

I didn't blame Lady Montgomery for being a little paranoid. The guild had remained safe throughout the Soul Collector's rampage, but the humans were rightly terrified. While Keir had told me that his fellow vampires had begun to return to the city, it'd take a long while for everyone to recover.

Lines of cloaked guards moved aside at the guild's entrance, allowing us to pass through. The boss, to nobody's surprise, stood in the lobby alongside her son,

River. She'd insisted that I add her to the rota, and came on as many patrols as the rest of us these days.

River smiled at Ilsa. "No issues?"

"None," she confirmed. "Mackie did all the work."

"Good," said Lady Montgomery. "Jas, a word, please. Alone."

Crap. What had I done now? She hadn't found out about my little spirit-related trouble, right? If anything, I'd been on my best behaviour lately, considering the circumstances.

As we moved away from the others, I said, "She did do it all on her own."

"I don't doubt that, Jas," said Lady Montgomery. "Your guardian contacted me before her death to explain that she suspected she'd be forced to sacrifice her life to destroy the Soul Collector and his weapon, and that you were his captive."

My mouth dropped open. "I—she did? How?" I'd thought Lady Harper had acted in the moment. I also hadn't known she had the guild's phone number, but in hindsight, it was obvious. And... she'd covered for me. The story I'd told the boss had been filled with holes, and I'd been so sure the council would see through it. Grief could only be used as an excuse for so long. I'd mentioned that I'd gone after the Soul Collector alone to find Keir, but as for the forest, the weapon, Evelyn Hemlock... she hadn't asked the details. Now I knew why.

"She explained to me that the weapon he had was not of this world," said the boss. "And that she intended to give you the means of destroying it and him."

She knows? I supposed it was too risky to keep the Ether Converter's existence a secret when it was such a dangerous weapon. So Lady Harper had tipped her off that it was a talisman, and now… it was out of my hands.

Someday I'd blow that geas wide open, but with the Hemlocks close to being wiped out at the hands of Leila and the Soul Collector, now was not the time to start trying to expose their secrets. Especially with the Mage Lords closely watching the guild.

"You'll have to write a report on what exactly you experienced, which I can give to both the necromancer council and the Mage Lords," she said. "I won't deny that you were put in a precarious position and that it's unfair for us to pressure you when you so recently lost your guardian, but we need to ensure it never happens again."

Oh, damn. The mages *and* the necromancers? And—I'd forgotten that Lady Harper hadn't just been a former mage council member. She'd also once been the Hemlocks' ambassador to the former Council of Twelve.

Without her, if they chose to elect another ambassador… I was the only remaining candidate. *Assuming they don't arrest me first.*

I looked away. "Talk to Mage Lord Colton. I don't know how much he knows about Lady Harper's final wishes, but—she never told them to me."

"And it's not the guild's business, naturally, if she wished to keep it to herself," said Lady Montgomery. "I'll call him. Take care, Jas."

Lady Harper would have been outraged that so many people showed up for her funeral when she'd made it her life's mission to make scores of enemies. A large number of supernaturals filled the town hall, including every mage who'd ever served on the council with her during both her stints as head mage. Most witch covens sent a representative, even the ones she'd argued with, and the local necromancers also made a showing.

The only people *not* here were the Hemlocks, for obvious reasons. Cordelia hadn't even talked to me on my brief trip through the forest. Maybe she was mad at me *and* Lady Harper for thinking the worst about Evelyn. I didn't trust any of them, not at all, but Evelyn maintained her silence. Lady Harper's death left me with no living allies who'd known the Hemlocks before the invasion. She'd literally taken her secrets to the other side of the grave, never to be retrieved. The idea of her death being final refused to hit home, and part of me kept expecting her to hobble into the hall at any moment, waving her stick at us and demanding to know why we were all being so morbid. My eyes stung unexpectedly, and I dug my hands into the cold metal bench.

As Lady Harper's only surviving close relative who'd shown up to the funeral, it was on Wanda to greet everyone who entered the town hall. While she looked a little nervous in the spotlight, Vance joined her on the stage, and the two of them summarised Lady Harper's life and accomplishments. It was a long list, and not for the first time, I felt like I'd never known the woman at all. Granted, she'd lost nearly her entire family in the faerie invasion and I'd been told she'd never been the same person since, but still...

I jumped when Vance said my name. Ah, crap. They didn't expect me to speak, did they? I guess we *were* related, distantly, but I could probably claim a connection with half the mages here.

Evelyn's presence whispered in my ear, urging me to my feet. "Go on."

"Look, I'm done fighting with you," I whispered, too low for anyone to hear. "Just leave me be."

"I knew her, too," said Evelyn. "I'd like to say my piece."

I don't think so. Even if she was on her best behaviour, everyone would get suspicious if she said things I wasn't supposed to know.

"I'm not a fool," said Evelyn, as I reluctantly began to walk to the stage. "Trust me."

I took the stage, preparing to push Evelyn aside if she tried anything, but she simply listed several more of the former Mage Lord's accomplishments as a council member, finishing with, "Lady Alice Harper was brave in the face of adversity and terrible loss."

I hadn't known she and Lady Harper were remotely close. But it wasn't like I'd asked.

When I checked back into my body and sat down, I touched my hands to my face and found dampness on my cheeks. Why was I crying over my former mentor who'd utterly failed at any kind of mentoring and had insulted me almost every time we'd spoken in the last thirteen years? Maybe because I'd been to countless funerals, wakes, and other death-related events as a necromancer, but never—never for anyone I'd been close to. I'd been lucky, or unlucky, in that I'd lost my entire family in the invasion. That was the only explanation I could think of for how weirdly it'd affected me. That, or Evelyn had control over my tear ducts now.

I rubbed my eyes. Okay, I regretted our argument, and

the fact that Lady Harper and the Hemlocks had fundamentally disagreed made me worry that there was more she might have known about the nature of my bond with Evelyn. But a force greater than death separated us now.

After the main event drew to a close, several mages converged on me before I could make my escape.

"Hey, Jas," said Drake, waving at me. "I'm impressed. I didn't know you had so much to say. You didn't even mention her 'encouraging' magical lessons."

"Eh," I said. "I'm not sure she'd have appreciated it. You know what she's like, she'd have wanted to feel like she left an impression. Even a negative one."

Drake moved out of the way of several people leaving the hall. "Vance, you should have brought up the time she gave us a bollocking for teleporting ourselves onto the manor's roof."

"If I related all the times you got us both into trouble with her as apprentices, we'd be here all day," Vance said mildly, walking over with Ivy at his side.

"Not always me," Drake said. "You were just sneakier about it."

"Are you okay, Jas?" asked Ivy, handing me a tissue.

I nodded, conscious that I had Evelyn's tears smeared all over my face. "Sure."

"I know you were close," said Vance sympathetically.

"No, we weren't." I blew my nose. "We spent every moment we were in the same room as one another arguing like hell."

"Likewise," said Ivy. "I'm kind of sad she's missing our wedding, but I think she'd have wanted us to leave her off the list so she had an excuse not to speak to me for a while."

"She'd have come up with an urgent appointment at the last minute like she normally does at societal functions," Vance said.

"Probably." She took his hand and squeezed it. "I know she was a total grump, but I think she'd be pretty flattered at your singing her praises. You did great."

Vance gave her a smile tinged with a hint of sadness. I guess I wasn't the only one here with mixed feelings. If the Mage Lord suspected any gaps in my story about how she'd died, he hadn't mentioned it. I appreciated that, at least.

"She killed two Sidhe, I heard," I said.

"Oh, probably more," Vance said. "She refused to discuss much of her history."

"You're telling me," said Wanda. "Even I got a tongue-lashing if I asked her the wrong question."

"She was private, and liked her secrets," I said. "Er, I don't know if you've had a call from my boss yet, Vance, but—"

"I have, actually. I wanted to talk to you about it."

"Oh. All right." I should have known. I took in a deep breath, hoping that the cover story Lady Harper had left behind wasn't about to come crashing down.

Ivy walked with us out of the town hall. "Don't look so freaked, Jas. It's good news."

"It is?" I said warily. "I never thought my boss and Lady Harper being mentioned in the same sentence would ever be good news."

"Your boss asked Lady Harper had left anything to you," Vance explained.

Oh. Of course. For all her endless complaints, the old

mage had amassed a huge fortune in her lifetime… mostly through outliving everyone else in her family.

"I don't want it," I said quickly. "Whatever it is." God knew money could solve almost none of my problems.

"She left most of her possessions to the mage council," Vance said. "And the Council of Twelve. She was a founding member. But she left you some cash, and some of her possessions from the house. We're planning to clean the place over the holidays, if you'd like to join us."

I'd quite honestly rather join Lady Harper in the ground than go through her things, but it was a genuine, kind offer and there was no need to tick off the Mage Lord on top of everything else.

"Vance, Jas doesn't want to go through Lady Harper's junk any more than the rest of us do." Ivy rolled her eyes. "You're welcome to join us over the holidays, though. Drake pretty much insisted on it."

I nodded. "I'll see what I'm doing." Who knew… maybe Lady Harper had left me something useful in her old house.

"Also," said Ivy, dropping her voice, "Vance and I know about the weapon. It's gone?"

Vance's intent grey eyes pinned me to the spot. Oh, boy. I really shouldn't have assumed the Mage Lord would brush off the circumstances of his former mentor's death without asking questions.

"We've both met the Hemlocks," Ivy explained. "Isabel told us the item the Soul Collector used was likely a talisman. It's definitely gone?"

Right… they're immune to the geas. To some degree. So that meant Vance must know the Ancients existed, even if

Lady Harper had been as reluctant to share information with him as anyone else.

I cleared my throat. "Yes. Positive. He and the Ether Converter both fell into the rift." No need to let on that *I* was the one who'd opened the rift. I was still liable to be punished for the Hemlocks' crimes, after all, and now one of the few people still walking this earth who might have had the clout to defend me was dead and gone.

"Good," said Ivy. "Trust me, we're better off without it."

"Couldn't agree more," I murmured. "Is Isabel around?"

"Over there." Ivy pointed.

I made my way through the crowd to Isabel, and this time, nobody stopped me.

"You did great," said Isabel. "Considering you didn't prepare a speech. I was ready to intervene."

"Er... you know that wasn't actually me, don't you?" I muttered. "Evelyn felt she needed to say her piece on her old mentor."

"I think Lady Harper would appreciate it," said Isabel. "She did like to feel important."

"Yeah" I said. "I suppose at least she can say an Ancient was responsible for her death. That's kind of a badass way to go. Sorry, I'm a necromancer. We do funerals like they're going out of style."

"I bet," said Isabel. "Are you heading back?"

"I'd better. Before anyone else works out I wasn't quite myself back there."

Now I knew for sure there was no getting rid of Evelyn... I still didn't trust her. Maybe I should have bound her again, but for now, I left her be, and she left me alone. For the most part.

My phone buzzed. I checked the number, then answered. "Hey, Lloyd."

"Hey," said Lloyd. "How'd it go?"

"It was okay," I said. "As far as funerals go. She'd have found something to complain about, I don't doubt. It's just so damned weird her being gone."

"Yeah, I bet. Are you on your way back?"

"I'll leave in five. Might take a detour on the way to the guild, okay?"

"Sure. Take care of yourself."

I hung up, shivering a little in the cool night air. Tilting my head back, I looked up at the clear night sky and the crescent moon. My eyes stung again. I never thought I'd regret never seeing Lady Harper again, and yet…

"Hey," whispered Keir's voice through the spirit realm. "You holding up okay?"

"Yeah," I said. "Want me to come and see you when I come back?"

"I'd like that. I'll be waiting on the other side."

———

Keir met me on the bridge, his cheeks pink with cold. "Hey, Jas."

"Hey." Guilt washed over me. I still hadn't told him I was a shade, and the funeral had hammered home how quickly life was over. Even in a place where nothing ever really died.

He frowned. "Was it that bad?"

"No, just… funerals. I should be used to them, considering my job, but we usually leave after we hand over the bodies."

He took my hand and squeezed it. "I can walk you back to the guild if you'd rather go home?"

"Actually…" I paused. "There's something I have to tell you. And I want you to know that it's okay if you don't want to see me anymore, after."

He blinked, looking a little startled. "Sure. Fire away."

"It's—about your vampire abilities. And shades. I have no idea how it happened, but it's the only explanation." I quickly ran through what I'd read in the book, and the conclusions I'd drawn from that.

His brows shot up, but he kept listening. "That makes sense. I think," he said. "How… how many lives do you have left?"

"I have no idea. Might be a limited number, might not." It worried me a little, but not as much as the shade situation being irreversible. "So, your choice. Is the idea of seeing me every couple of days worse than death?"

"In the spirit realm, what's the difference, really?" He smiled, and took a step closer to me, resting his hands on my shoulders.

"Not going to run off?" I queried.

"I shouldn't have run the first time."

His mouth parted beneath mine, and by the time we broke apart, I'd forgotten the cold, inside and outside.

"I have to say," he said. "I prefer knowing you did it, not Evelyn."

"Sure you don't want to pin the blame on her?" I grinned and rested my forehead against his. "Don't worry. She's behaving. Can't say she's all there, but who am I to talk?"

"So you're reserving judgement?" he queried.

"For now."

After all, the Soul Collector was dead and gone. Losing the weapon along with him was less disastrous than the thing ending up in anyone's hands. And Evelyn? I'd leave her be if she did the same to me. Tomorrow was another day.

I turned away from the spirit line, towards the guild, and home.

ABOUT THE AUTHOR

Emma is the New York Times and USA Today Bestselling author of the Changeling Chronicles urban fantasy series.

Emma spent her childhood creating imaginary worlds to compensate for a disappointingly average reality, so it was probably inevitable that she ended up writing fantasy novels. When she's not immersed in her own fictional universes, Emma can be found with her head in a book or wandering around the world in search of adventure.

Find out more about Emma's books at
www.emmaladams.com.

www.ingramcontent.com/pod-product-compliance
Lightning Source LLC
Chambersburg PA
CBHW020745190726
48285CB00006B/1885